MID RIFT

A novel

Rebecca Rosenblat

Manor House

Mid Rift / Rebecca Rosenblat

Library and Archives Canada
Cataloguing in Publication

Title: Mid rift : a novel / Rebecca Rosenblat.

Names: Rosenblat, Rebecca, author.

Identifiers: Canadiana 20190234059 |
ISBN 9781988058535 (hardcover) |
ISBN 9781988058528 (softcover)

Classification: LCC PS8635.O6499 M53 2019 |
DDC C813/.6—dc23

Cover art: Oneinchpunch / Shutterstock

First Edition
Cover Design-layout / Interior- layout: Michael Davie
272 pages / 78,560 words.   All rights reserved.
Published Nov. 21, 2019 / Copyright 2019
Manor House Publishing Inc.
452 Cottingham Crescent, Ancaster, ON, L9G 3V6
www.manor-house-publishing.com   (905) 648-4797

This project has been made possible [in part] by the Government of Canada. *« Ce projet a été rendu possible [en partie] grâce au gouvernement du Canada.*

Funded by the Government of Canada
Financé par le gouvernement du Canada | Canada

***

*Dedicated to Sonja and Leah
for filling my life with laughter
and inspiring me to pay it forward!*
***

Foreword

Join Jillian Briggs and her crazy, almost "forty-ish" friends – Cyn the sex therapist, Darla the lesbian lawyer, Alison the gorgeous glossy-haired accountant who has sworn off sex, and Randy the gay fashionista – as they try to reinvent themselves before hitting middle age. Their fun-filled journey will have you laughing at life, while drawing you deep into their juicy secrets.

For anyone who has ever feared going through a mid-life crises, this hilarious story will walk them through any situation, with more fun, wit and understanding than their best friend or therapist! Despite their quirks and neuroses, this bunch has arrived where we all want to be, 'cause they know how to handle life with finesse – how else do you make your own millions, buy yourself a Porsche, get covered in Tiffany diamonds, and have quality men line up to tempt you every which way, while all you want to do is focus on reviving your stale marriage?

Between the group of them, they've conquered everything from getting men to getting laid, saving a sagging marriage to getting along with a nagging ex, making money to spending it guilt-free, hot flashes to knock-your-socks-off hot sex, eliminating wrinkles to rekindling passion, losing weight to gaining fame and fortune, dating the second time 'round to finding first class men – all the while enjoying life to the fullest. Find out their delish secrets to what it takes to be happy, while validating every real – possibly heinous – emotion that you've ever felt. You'll never look at your own life the same way again!

Prologue

I, Jillian Briggs, am fast approaching mid-life, with a brand new Porsche in the garage, mega-bucks in the bank – thanks to my successful catering company – and a tall doctor by my side, who also just happens to be the father of my two great kids, Jack and Amber.

Now before you go green with envy, let me tell you that it wasn't always like this. I grew up in a household where we were too poor to waste money on low-cal food, yet rich enough to afford junk food – most of which went straight to my thighs. And kind as my mom tried to be, blaming genetics, the only fat genes I could think of were the fat jeans straining across my behind. Needless to say, every time my best friend Alison Fletcher tried to drag me out to parties with her, I faked socio-phobia – not that it was much of a stretch. Like any self-loathing girl my age, I truly didn't see the need to become someone's fat chick.

So exactly what did I do on all those lonely nights? After paying my dues, watching the mandatory *Colombo* and *Ironside* with my dysfunctional family, I got to spend time with any and every celebrity of my choosing. I went from dancing with Liza, to singing with Bette, to singing and dancing with Tina – nice prep for the disco era. And then it happened – my body began to transform from a disco ball to a sleek ABBA lookalike. All I needed was a bottle of peroxide for my brown hair, and my socio-phobia could be cured for good! But in as much as I was the dancing queen in my fantasy world, my "fat shadow" kept me as far away from publicly dancing as it could.

How was my crush, Randy Chan, ever going to notice me, if I kept hiding like that? Of course my friend Darla Haines never had to worry about those things. With her clear mocha skin, full lips, and mile-long legs poking out of the shortest skirts possible, she was a walking billboard for her cheerleading team – a lot of good that did! Even with all the eyes peeled on her, Mademoiselle Gorgeous wasn't interested in *any*body, not even the captain of the football team – a total waste of good looks, if you ask me. Then again, nobody asked me ... about much of anything ... except maybe Cynthia Kennedy – our clique's wannabe therapist. "Hang in there, Jilly," she'd say, "Your day will come," a forbidden cigarette dangling from her red lips.

That was then, this is now. My day *has* come. And it's only gonna get better and better! How do I know this? I didn't get this far without a healthy dose of persistence – from getting into shape, to doing odd jobs to pay my way through college. It's amazing what a difference a college education can make, not to mention twenty pounds, especially when you're five foot zip. Gave me enough confidence to catch Jeremy's eye. It was a match made in heaven. I loved his hot bod, he loved my lust for life – together we enjoyed both lust and life ... way back when.

My goals: Spice up my marriage and get it back on track, before it's too late. Live life as fully and gloriously as I'd want it stated in my obituary!

And what an exciting journey it's gonna be, thanks to my am-a-a-a-zing nucleus – my family and my four best friends, Alison, Randy, Darla, and Cyn. Now I know what you're thinking – who has time for friends at this stage in our lives? Well, *we* do, since we make it a priority. Working in the same building also helps. You see, the five of us own a gorgeous property together, a waterfront brownstone ... actually, the four of us, with Randy as an honorary member – we're all the family he's got, since his parents disowned him.

It all started when my lease was coming up for renewal and I couldn't bear the thought of yet another rent increase, for a small and sterile space that didn't excite me all that much to begin with. So I started to look for a place that I could buy and fix up to suit my needs. But everything I liked – particularly my favorite, the brownstone – was too huge; the possibility of renting out some of it, too daunting. When I shared my predicament with my friends over our longstanding traditional TGIF martini date, Darla and Alison jumped all over the possibility of going in on it with me. As for Cyn, it was just the push she needed to leave her charming-but-small office, to set up a full blown clinic of her dreams.

Once we acquired the brownstone, we renovated it to create cozy offices for ourselves. Coziness is so important to us that we've dedicated an entire floor to "The Cocoon" – our chill zone. Now while the occasional client is allowed in this place to sample my goodies, everyone else can expect to get grilled if they invade our space – we're very protective of each other and our hangout.

So exactly how do we fit into each other's lives? ... Wait, I'm getting a little ahead of myself here. Allow me first to introduce you to my friends. We have Cyn, a fiery natural redhead dyed blonde, with a hot, five foot six bod to match. She's a big-mouthed sex therapist, with more grit and attitude than teenage sons Jonathan and Michael and she manages to embarrass them every chance she gets. Rich divorcee from Justin, her somewhat older ex, she's put her money where her mouth is, in opening up her own sex clinic, thanks to her mammoth divorce settlement.

In as much as she loves us all, the way Cyn goes at Randy, one would think he was her nemesis ... or at least her husband, since they can't live with or without each other. But that would be an impossibility, the hubby part that is, since Randy is as gay as they come. If there were degrees of gayness, he'd be beyond flaming red – right down to his

Asian hair, concave stomach, tight dernier, and wild clothes. Being our resident fashionista, we all turn to Randy for wardrobe advice, goshe as some of his own choices appear to us.

At the opposite end of the continuum lies Alison – actually more like sits than lies, since she's given up on sex altogether, treating it like a complication she'd sooner do without. But looking at her, you'd think she was a sex goddess, with her tall and lanky bod, upholding the perfect pair of C cups, and glossy hair cascading over her business suits. A successful accountant, she must dress the part – though her expensive, designer threads make me wonder where she gets her money. Why, she's even better dressed than the loaded lawyer amongst us – Darla. But uptight as her wardrobe makes her appear, Darla is anything but. Her closet is full of lesbian secrets just dying to come out. And not a moment too soon, since her divorce from Daniel – ex-hubby, current best-bud and colleague – is practically a done deal. He let her take the quick and painless route, since he intends on keeping their business relationship intact, while remaining the best of friends. Tall, well-dressed and handsome, with beautiful chocolate skin, he's a sight to behold, with that expensive scent about him.

Want more details? Why don't I let them speak for themselves? Here they are:

Alison Fletcher: "I've always been accused of thinking like a guy, doing math and sports like a guy, and handling business like a guy. Yet, I'm not remotely interested in what guys seem to obsess over the most – sex!

It wasn't always like that. In fact, if anything, I was known as the ultimate party girl in my high school days – a lusty one at that! My philosophy: show me a hunk and I'm there, willing to put up with all sorts of B.S. if he's gorgeous enough, even at the risk of demolishing my self-esteem and grades. Then, one day, after repeating the I'm pissed at you ... what was I thinking, please take me back ... did last night not mean anything to you cycle for about the bazillionth time, I decided to go for something more reliable – good grades and ice cream. After all, outside of Cyn and Jill, they were the only things faithfully waiting for me after each and every breakup. Who needed to mount the make-sick roller-coaster of sexual highs and lows, when one could actually accomplish a lot more being steadily grounded! My mother, in her infinite wisdom, couldn't agree more, being quite anti-sex herself.

Now, I'm a successful, corporate accountant, with my own company, content to channel my energy and passionate juices into my business. After landing a big account, I'm so satiated that I can't be bothered to even *think* about sex – not even *mange a moi* style. And who has the energy anyway? But in as much as I don't crave the crazy, messy part of sex, I'm the biggest cuddler amongst us. To me, "good in bed" means "fits like a glove, in the spoon position". Now if I could only find a way to nail a like-minded man – what a task that's gonna be! My goals: Negotiate the bedroom as successfully as the boardroom – non-sexually of course. Become a self-made millionaire ... applying myself fully to *whatever* it takes.

Darla Haines: Growing up as the only African American kid in my neighborhood was hard enough. Growing up as the only cheerleader who couldn't feel a thing for boys, harder still. Perhaps that's what gave me the drive to excel at everything – becoming and marrying a lawyer being a case in point. The downside: faking everything from desiring boys to the orgasms they never gave me. Thank goodness my gaydar didn't defy me entirely! Unbeknownst to me, I was picking up and sending off just the right vibe to grab Danielle's attention. She ended up inviting me to her thirtieth birthday party, at "The Pussy Palace", no less. As far as "no boys allowed" clubs go, it's the chicest, right down to its vulva shaped entrance. I felt like a swan who'd found her own, instead of the ugly duckling who never seemed to quite fit in. There was no turning back now. The lawyer in me stopped yelling "Order in the crotch" and made a case for me coming out. ... So far, I've only spilled the beans on Danielle and I to my best friends – Jillian, Alison, Cyn, Randy, and my barely-ex, Dan. But in as much as Cyn and Randy are applauding me and Jillian is supporting me, Alison just doesn't seem to get it ... and Dan is rooting for getting in on some lesbian action. I wonder how my uber-rich, prim-proper, ultra-religious parents will take it? My mom's a church choir leader for heaven's sake! I can still remember the look on her face when she intercepted Cyn's note, declaring how bored she was, so she was going to head out to the adult store and was wondering if she could pick anything up for me? If Mom only knew that I'd wanted to ask for something pink and non-phallic. My goals: Come out.   Live my life for myself, for a change.   Build a successful practice.

Cynthia Kennedy: Okay, so I always wanted what I couldn't have, including other girls' boyfriends. But they never seemed to catch on, or perhaps they just let me get away with it, since I was the only one they could turn to with their sob stories.   The only one who listened incessantly, binged with them excessively, and then put them back together, armed and dangerous with better mating skills.

Naturally, getting my degree as a sex therapist seemed to be the obvious thing to do.   Marrying someone totally dysfunctional and loaded, even more so. Going in, I knew that my marriage to a much older husband wasn't going to last, because of my fast approaching "expiry date". But I did it in any case, since I myself didn't have a much longer attention span than Justin – and who could resist the lifestyle he offered?

The way I looked at it, my predicament was a small price to pay for someone who paid for everything else. Anyhow, when it came time to divorce, I wasn't surprised. Like I told you, I half expected it, since my "best before" date had already come and gone a few years back with my thirtieth birthday – right around the time when we both started to outgrow our starter marriage.

The irony? My divorce from Justin ended up being the best thing that ever happened to me – I'm in a much better place now than I ever was. And here's the punch line: after the divorce, Justin was left with a lot less cash than he'd planned on, to successfully woo my much younger replacement like he once wooed me. Sure hope she loves him for the overactive bulge in his pants, not the underactive bulge in his wallet – most of which is now securely nestled in *my* wallet.

But unlike Justin, I'm no flake with my money. My wealth is safely invested in my sex therapy clinic. My goals: Make a huge success of my practice. Get important *original Cyn* points across to improve sexuality the world over. Learn discipline – not the whip kind, more like finish-writing-your-sexuality-book-already after putting it off for lord-knows-how long.

Randy Chan: Growing up, I remember Jillian having similar tastes as myself – she had to, since she always managed to show up to the same events as myself, football games being a case in point. Now don't get me wrong, I don't think that either one of us actually wanted to *play* the sport, more like gawk at the football players. How could we? I was too delicate; her, too out-of-shape.

Beyond football, there was also our similar taste in strange-wear – though I think I pulled off mine far better than her ... at least back then.

And now, while I aspire to be a red, hot Diva Glam – move over Viva Glam – Jillian is the one who can afford better bling. And lots of it.

All *I* can afford is, refurbishing goodies from second hand stores – bet you can see a mah-velous TV show in there somewhere! Believe it or not, I've wanted to do a TV make-over show long before there was such a thing as make-over shows, but I've run into every obstacle imaginable.

And now, time is running out. The idea is growing old faster than moi, almost like dog years. But I haven't given up yet, not as long as Steven my fiancée continues to double as my financier. My goals: Adopt a kid with Steven. Have my own TV make-over show, or at least launch my own fashion line, with a little help from Steven.

As you can see, we're one eclectic bunch. But we still hope to go into business together someday ... somehow.

With my ability to throw the best darn parties, Randy doing the most amazing ego-boosting make-overs, Cyn's insights into relationships and hot sex, Darla's legal advice, and Alison's financial genius, I'm sure we could combine our talents to come up with a winning formula!

Chapter 1 - *False Pretenses*

Of all the things that we've ever agreed upon – and trust me there aren't that many – setting up "The Cocoon" was by far and away the very best! Loft-style that it is, it's still the coziest place around, with gorgeous brick walls, mahogany hardwood floors, and warm track lighting. Two large picture windows overlook a never-ending expanse of water; the space between them houses a chic martini/late/juice bar. Directly opposite is the main wall – a perfect backdrop for boasting all the art and memorabilia that we've accumulated over the years, between the five of us. And then, there's the mammoth stone fireplace with bookcases nestled on either side, a matching stone island with a mahogany counter-top, and wall mounted ovens. Doesn't get any better than this, especially when you consider the added creature comforts – soft leather couches and state-of-the-art stereo and exercise equipment.

I look out the window, to catch millions of diamonds sparkling off the surface of the water. Soon, they'll be consumed by a bright orange fire and stilled for the night. ... I've been mesmerized by the glorious site a hundred times before and will be again, since it always manages to take me back to my Grammy's house by the ocean. We'd sit on the porch and rock side-by-side in rocking chairs, listening to the seagulls, while she'd share how different things were in her day. I can practically smell her Ponds cream and hear her shaky voice. *"When I was a young lady, marriages weren't about romance and happiness – you did what you had to and didn't really think much about it. Today, everybody expects so much more out of them."* But I wonder if we're truly happier than Grammy was? Didn't take much to put a smile on her sepia face. Then again, did anyone *really* know how she felt inside, the way she'd trivialize everything.   If someone complimented her, she'd slip into her 'Oh this old thing?' mode. Ditto for when she was hurting. Like the time when she burned her arm, supposedly on the stove. She told everyone it was nothing, but I knew better. I'd seen the blisters and the horrible scarring they led to, even though she did her best to hide them under long-sleeved blouses. Still wonder how she *really* burned herself in the first place? She'd have to be doing some serious gymnastics near the stove to hit *that* part of her arm. Stray tears start to tumble down my cheeks. I don't have time for this – too much to do.

I wipe my face with my hands, walk back to the island, and rearrange the lilies in the vase for about the millionth time, making sure the counter looks just so before I start laying out the food on it. It's a nervous habit I have – fussing, fidgeting, trying to make things look perfect, especially when nothing could be farther from the truth. But I've done such a damn good job creating the right impression all these years, that absolutely *no* one has a clue how I'm dying inside. To an outsider, I have the perfect home, job, car, kids and marriage; to me, our marriage is no more than a sham. Both hearth and hubby are so cold that there isn't even a pilot light left on any longer, to reignite things. But determined as I am, I plan to get us back on track if at all possible – aching for each other like we once did, when the mere thought of Jeremy would leave me breathless. Told you I'm going to make sure that everything only gets better and better from here on – for real. ... But this is not the time or the place – tonight's all about Darla ... and Jeremy couldn't be farther away – Grammy would understand!

With the lilies coaxed into perfection, all I have to do now is let the salmon bake, while I change out of my filthy tank top and cut-off shorts. One sniff of my pits and I appreciate the urgency – nobody needs a dash of B.O. in their soup. With the fireplace and the ovens blazing at once, "The Cocoon" turns into a sauna bath.

"Shoot, is that footsteps racing up the stairs already? Please, don't let it be the girls. I'm sooo not ready yet."

Of course they come barging in, early as always, ready to pick at my hors d'oeuvres even before I've had a chance to lay them out properly. And if that isn't bad enough, Cyn and Randy are already going at each other. Honestly, the way the two of them act, they should just get married, bring home some fine-looking specimens, and share them for their extra-curriculars. After all, they *do* have the same philosophy – get 'em young and well-hung, then use 'em and lose 'em.

"Randy, how the hell am I supposed to fit my ass into this thing you call a skirt?" Cyn barks, helping herself to one of my coconut shrimp. Personally, I think she looks pretty damn hot in her tight little Louis Vuitton denim number, blonde curls picking up her coral accessories.

Of course Randy doesn't appear to think so. Never one for flattery that could ruin your bod, he dishes back, "For starters, by avoiding stuffing your face like that!" slapping her hand ever-so-gently, before it makes it to her mouth.

"Oh F Off. Not everyone has an anorexic metabolism like you." Tracing the new boob-job that's trying to break out of her halter neckline, she continues, "Besides, I'll have you know that I happen to *like* my curves."

"Does that include the food baby that you're always complaining about?" he emphasizes, left brow raised high to make his point, right hand stroking her belly as if she were an expectant mother.

Silly me, instead of leaving bad enough alone, I decide to break it up. "Girls ... girls ... cha-ill. We have more important things to worry about tonight."

"Do *you* think my ass is getting bigger?" she asks me point blank, turning her rump toward me for a better look.

"When will I learn? There's nooo way I'm *butting* in ... uh-uh ... not touching that one with a ten foot pole."

Randy pinches Cyn's butt-shelf and lisps, "And neither will anyone else, Girlfriend, if you keep scarfing like that," his tongue salivating at the duck pate he's now licking off his right index finger, showing off his never-gain-an-ounce tendencies. Just look at his concave stomach, nestled in his fishnet T, tight jeans showing off a butt that has less inches to spare than even Cyn's well-toned ass.

Now it's my turn to slap *his* hand. "Hasn't anyone taught you the use of utensils?"

"He eats like Hannibal the Cannibal," laughs Cyn, jiggling her tongue at him.

"And you could certainly use a muzzle like him, before you bite someone's head off," he retorts.

As they plunk themselves into the comfy, white leather couches, I fire them both a dirty look. Point taken. The two of them blow Hollywood kisses at each other and mouth their "I love you's to show me that they're calling it a truce. And not a moment too soon. Sounds like Darla is coming up the stairs – I'd recognize that clip-clop of her stilettoes anywhere. ... Wait, there's two sets of footsteps – shit, I'd so wanted Alison to get here early for once. Betchya she's ruined the surprise.

The door opens, the three of us yell "Surprise", only to find out that we're the ones in for a big surprise! The second set of footsteps belong to Danielle, Darla's girlfriend. Tonight was supposed to be our private little party for Darla's fortieth, even though she thought she was just coming over to sample some eats for her "official" party. Had she known that the rest of the gang was going to be here also, I bet she would've left Danielle behind, putting off her debut and inquisition a while longer. Too late now. But lucky for her, the spotlight will have to be shared with two other newcomers joining the gang for the very first time – the twins, a.k.a. Cyn's new lady-lumps. And if that isn't enough, guess what else just walked in – a string of mega-diamonds that could trump the Donald's best, dipping shamelessly into Alison's natural-born cleave. Looking at everyone's reactions, I think the evening promises to be juicier than ever.

Following the introductions, we all gather around the island as I pour everyone a glass of Dom and propose a toast. "To good friends – old and new".

Randy chimes in, "To groovy accessories, old and new," only to get kicked discreetly under the island by both Cyn and Alison, from either side of him.

Now, I'm the one feeling left out. Cyn has her new boobs, Darla has her new love, Alison has a new something or the other, and I Jillian am just the shabbily dressed, chef extra-ordinaire, with my head stuck in the oven yet again – sounds too much like old times. *Don't go there, Jill, you've come way too far for one of your neurotic attacks*, I tell myself, feverishly cleaning the counter.

Darla notices and asks if I'm okay. Lie, Jill, lie, I urge myself, managing the perfect smile to go with my perfect hostess persona. But she's not buying it. She sashays over in her turquoise blue mini, to get close enough to grill me. And here I thought that Danielle, Cyn and Alison were supposed to have that honor. Stall, Jilly, stall, just long enough for Randy to create a diversion, with one of his smart-ass comments about someone else.

But Cyn beats Randy to the punch, putting Alison on the spot with, "So what's that on your chest – synthetic or real?"

"Not that it's any of your business, but the Tiffany's are as real as they come. What about what's on *your* chest?"

Cyn shows off, "Hundred percent synthetic, made to order perfection!" and walks over to Alison, to take a better look at her latest acquisition. As she examines the gems closely, her tell-tale facial expression says that she's impressed indeed. ... "So, dare I ask who bought you those?"

I too am wondering that, seeing that Alison couldn't possibly afford something like that on her accountant's salary – nor is her job one where she could be on the take. But I guess we'll never find out, since Alison points to Cyn's new boobies and snaps back with, "Why, who bought you *those*?"

Cyn knows when to back off, "Touché!"

We all head back to the couches and plunk down, me hiding my midriff beneath a camel colored suede cushion that I happen to be hugging for dear life. Not that it matters, since all the eyes are glued on gorgeous Danielle, barely contained in spray-painted tight jeans and a crop top, straining apart to show off her belly jewel. Trying hard not to get distracted by a waistline that's thinner than one of my ankles, I ask, "So, how did the two of you meet?" – a fairly innocuous question ... or so I thought.

Darla strokes Danielle's flaxen hair, as she shares that they'd been chatting back and forth online for quite a while, until they felt that it was time they met. Originally, it was just business, which Danielle felt was turning into a flirtation – but she just wasn't sure until the night of her thirtieth birthday party. She figured that if any place could settle the dispute of whether or not Darla was interested in her, *that* way, "The Pussy Palace" – her favorite, hard-core lesbian bar – ought to do it.

"You were taking quite the risk, Sweetie, were you not?" chortles Randy. "For all you knew, she could've been a serial killer."

"Yeah, Randy, that was my first thought exactly – I was just hooking up with her to ask her how much she'd charge to kill *you,* for being the most paranoid, shit-disturbing, drama queen of the century."

Wiping some goopy makeup off Randy's neck, Cyn chimes in, "At least he's coffin ready."

Always a good sport, not to mention a queen who just loves attention, Randy jumps up and takes a little bow, while the rest go back to sampling the treats on the coffee table – tucked conveniently in the middle of three couches that form a U shape around the fireplace.

I take that as my cue to slip downstairs, to change into something less stinky, more slinky. While the rest gutted out everything to make their offices larger, I kept my on-suite bath, because of it's deep, brass-clawed tub and hand held shower. It was my best reno decision, precisely for moments like these, when I have to switch over from being an overheated cook to a polished hostess. Too bad I still haven't managed to get Jeremy in the tub with me – but I'm not giving up yet.

After a quick-clean of my bod, I barely poke my head through my sienna slip-dress, when I hear some major pounding at the front door. Not expecting anyone else, I'd locked it on my way down – who the hell could that be?

Darla sprints down the stairs with her mile-long legs and meets me near the front door, informing me that it's more than likely Dan. Since she thought that we were finalizing the menu tonight, she wanted him in on it. After all, he is the one hosting her big 4-0 party, footing the entire bill as his birthday present to her.

Dan walks in, poured into tight Levis and a white T, cradling two bottles of Chardonnay, to liven up the evening a bit. Always a lech, he wraps his muscly arms around our waists and says, "Can't wait to spend an evening alone with my two favorite gals!" Little does he know that it isn't going to be just us, but the whole clique, including the new gal he was dumped for.

Dan helps me lay out the salmon and shares that he feels sorry for his ex's new love, remembering the first time the whole lot of us grilled him. "Now it's Danielle's turn, while I just get to watch – oooh, has a nice ring to it, especially when it involves my gorgeous Darla and her stunning new girlfriend."

I try to biff Dan's head for going there. He ducks out of the way and sticks his ass out for penance. Looking at it's perfect shape, I'm sure he's just showing off. But I digress – back to the party.

The heat is on – Danielle just has to pay her dues. But Cyn seems nosier than ever. "So tell me Darla, is the sex better with Dan or Danielle?" You gotta hand it to the girl – she sure is direct.

Passing around a tray of chicken skewers, Dan saves the moment with, "Don't answer that – I know if *I* had the choice, I'd pick Danielle any day."

"But you don't have that choice, do you Dan, as much as you'd like to?" laughs Cyn, teasingly ripping the meat off one of the skewers with her sharp teeth.

"Hey, haven't given up yet!" replies Dan, lasciviously licking the sauce off another.

Never being one to be left out, Randy decides to start round two. "So Danielle, have you ever slept with a guy before? You know, to do the comparison thing?"

"Been there, done that, not interested," she says, winking at Dan, the only straight guy in the room.

Alison just shakes her head. "I don't know what the big deal is anyway? Sex just messes up the whole relationship thing."

With a youthful rebelliousness, Danielle challenges her. "Oh Yeah? How the *hell* did you come up with that?"

"Think about it. Love is so mushy and selfless. Throw in sex and it suddenly goes crazy, with all that possessive, painful, vulnerable bullshit – not a good gauge for picking the right mate, evolutionary speaking. ... And there isn't a damn thing you can do about it either – 'cause e-e-e-very time you fuck, you release this dangerous hormone, that has you hooked and coming back for more ... even when you're hurting."

Cyn jumps in, "The hormone's called oxytocin – it's in my book. And yup, you get pretty damn addicted to whoever is giving you the rush – that's why it's often called the *stay versus stray* hormone in the industry. Funny thing of it is, since it's the same hormone which mellows you out so you cuddle, most people fall asleep right after the rush – so *of course* you're going to stay ... it's not like you have a fucking choice or anything."

Feels like a good enough reason to keep doing it in my book, especially when things are a bit rocky and you may not feel like it. Like Grammy said, "You do what you have to do ... and wifely duties sure beat doing the laundry".

Cheekily, Danielle snaps, "And the problem with getting a rush and feeling connected is ...?"

Alison rolls up her eyes and says, "With the right person, no problem; with the wrong person ... oh never mind, you probably won't get it anyway."

Now Danielle is really mad. "And why wouldn't I? 'Cause *I've* never fallen for a wrong person?" Seeing that she's gay, I'm sure Grammy would think that *everyone* she falls for is the wrong person.

Alison becomes detached. "I was thinking more along the lines of – 'cause you probably don't have enough experience under your belt ... the *emotional* kind."

To keep the evening from deteriorating, I jump in before Danielle has a chance to rebut. "Let's not be so melodramatic tonight. Besides, messy sex can be good – dirty, filthy sex, even better," I wink!

For once, we all seem to agree, if only to save the day – all except Alison, who still manages enough grace to clink her glass with the rest of us and drink to that.

Once we're lubed up with enough libations, we decide to move the couches and teach the "inexperienced" spring chicken – sorry, couldn't resist – our "Disco Divas" routines from way back when, to prepare her for the big night. Thank goodness we no longer look anything like we used to back then, even though Darla is insisting we dress the part, the night of her big 4-0 party. Just this once, we'll let her call the shots, if she promises to wear a huge 'fro wig.   With everything out of the way, we start off with the *bus-stop*, go into the *hustle*, and then just freeform, Travolta style. The way we're slutting it up, we're a mere disco-ball away from an 80's skanko-rama.

As the evening winds down, everyone rushes out to make their way home – everyone but Dan, who graciously offers to help me clean up. We share a few laughs over a sink full of dishes ... later, a few glasses of wine and some smooth jazz, as we plop on the couch to unwind. ... And then, it happens, totally out of the blue – Dan leans over and plants a big kiss on my mouth.

I'm shocked ... and flushed from being taken like that. It's been a long time since even Jeremy overwhelmed me with that kind of unexpected urgency and passion; a kiss so full of hunger, promise and excitement – like the beginning of a dangerous journey. I hear blood rushing in my ears. ... After what feels like an eternity, I finally manage to catch my breath and say, "What the hell was that all about? Did you forget that I'm a married woman?" Hope Grammy didn't catch that – ever since she passed away, I keep worrying that she can see me. It's the worst during sex.

Not looking terribly upset, Dan winks at me and says, "You're even sexier when you're mad. ... Didn't you know that I've always had a thing for you? ... If you and Jeremy ever decide to go your separate ways, remember I'm pining away over here."

"I'm not buying that, Dan," I say sternly. If he thinks that I look sexy when I'm mad, I must be looking damn-near-irresistible right about now. Calm down, Jillian, don't want to encourage the guy too much.

Dan's expression changes to a bemused look. "In that case, how's this – I'm sorry, I haven't been myself lately. Really missing Darla and all that ... plus I'm kinda worried about her."

"Worried? Why?"

"Just some stuff with Danielle that doesn't seem to sit right with me."

"Like what?"

"Don't have any proof yet, but I'm working on it."

"I thought you just met her."

"Don't tell anyone, but there's some history there."

"What kind of history?"

"I'd rather not say."

"Do you actually expect me to believe that she's had something with you ... possibly at the same time as Darla?"

Assuming a Maxwell Smart tone, he giggles, "Would you believe me if I said 'yes'?" After a long pregnant pause, he continues a bit more seriously, "Maybe it's just my penis talking, but there's definitely something that just doesn't seem to fit – especially since she claims to be a dyed-in-the-muff dyke."

"Are you implying that she's up to something?"

"It wouldn't be the first time."

"What do you mean?"

"Oh, just something that Darla confided in me about, a suspicious thingy on her computer – don't think

Danielle ever intended for Darla to find out. ... And then there was something else – a very intense e-mail that was intended for someone else, but Danielle accidentally sent it to Darla by mistake."

"That settles it then, I don't want to hear any more about it. If Darla knows but doesn't want me to know, this is where it stops."

*   *   *

The next time I see Dan is at Darla's big 4-0, looking as tempting and dangerous as the devil himself, in his white, Saturday Night Fever suit, contrasting beautifully against his dark skin. As cool as the decor is, with lava lamps, purple linens, black walls, and disco balls creating the perfect ambiance, nothing looks quite as delish as him, not even the yummy Chicken Parmesan I've gone to great lengths preparing. I guess I owe Dan some gratitude – I liked the way he made me feel about myself. In his own twisted way, he helped me realize that I'm not completely dead inside, like I'd feared all this time – just the push I needed to convince myself that I *can* revive my relationship with Jeremy after all.

I look around me and take in the ambiance. Everything looks all set, as per Darla's request. She wanted the evening to be a throwback to our "Disco Divas" days. Brings back memories. ... Why the hell did I waste all that time on Randy back then, when I should've known better – he *did* do Boy George better than Boy George himself. Hope he can lip-sync tonight as well as he used to. Even if not, the music is the last of my worries. Yup, the D.J. is to die for ... that is until he invites the birthday girl to the dance floor, for her first dance.

Shoot, what's Darla gonna do? Her mom and dad expect her to dance with Dan, as do the majority of the people in the ballroom. Her divorce status isn't public just yet, since Dan is the host who sent out the invites and mom and dad are still out of the loop, on *both* counts. But if she goes out there with him, Danielle will be pissed off beyond belief. From what Darla's shared, being kept as her dirty little secret for much longer will definitely become a deal-breaker. But leave it to the queen bee – she's got it all covered. She doesn't look to her left or her right – where the two competitors are seated – she just marches on toward Daddy and asks him for the first dance. What sheer genius – wish I'd thought of it myself, since I *am* the queen of proper impressions.

The two of them glide across the dance floor like they've done it a million times before – definitely smooth sailing. Now if I could only believe that for real. Of course Danielle also has her own idea of how things are going down. And if Darla is to ever have her go down on her again, she'd better make a move, fast. Darla catches Danielle's eye and glides over to the head table. Without a moment of hesitation, she gives Danielle a tender little kiss, right on her mouth. Darla's mom looks confused. Thank goodness Dan planned the shindig for when his own parents were traveling through the Caribbean.

Even with the safe distance that I'm assuming, I can tell that Mrs. Haines isn't looking all-too-pleased. "Would someone mind telling me what's going on?" I hear her say.

All those years of suppressed propriety somehow end up forming into, "Mom, Dad, it's over for Dan and me. Danielle is my partner now," grabbing a hold of Danielle's hand. Gotta hand it to Darla – she sure is brave. I'd never have the courage to come out with *my* relationship woes, conventional as they might appear by comparison.

Mrs. Haines throws her purple napkin onto the table and starts to walk away, not wishing to dignify that with a response, or for that matter, create a scene in her prim-proper world. Mr. Haines follows close behind. I try to run after them, hoping to get them to stay. But all Mrs. Haines has to say to me is, "I'll talk to her when she's done with this crazy phase of hers and *apologizes* to me." She then turns to her husband and continues, "After everything we did for that girl, *this* is how she pays us back? Doesn't she realize that we're proper, religious people? How embarrassing! I never imagined that I'd see the day..."

I hear myself saying, "She's not trying to do anything to *you*. Don't you get it; it's not about *you* at all. For the very first time in her life, it's just about *her*." Funny how courageous I can be defending someone else, when you won't hear a peep out of me in my own defense. Boldly, I continue, "She's waited all this time precisely because she didn't want to hurt *you*!" But it's no use – the Haines have already hightailed out of here. ... I can feel Darla's pain – disapproval is disapproval. Worse – I know only too well what it's like to have your mother turn her back on you, when you need her the most. If Grammy only knew! ... Funny how we can be most cruel to the ones we love the most.

I go back inside, grab the microphone and announce that Mrs. Haines wasn't feeling too well and apologizes that she had to leave. ... But since there's still tons more food coming, everyone should continue to eat, drink and make merry. ... Our disco routine would have been a nice save at this point, but I think the mood's definitely ruined, the disco fever finally broken – my slinky, off-the-shoulder, purple dress notwithstanding.

To my relief, not everyone from the Haines clan has left Darla high and dry – Granny Haines is having an intimate conversation with her. Dare I butt in, or do I let them be? Against my better judgment, I decide to butt in, just in case she's giving Darla a hard time – damn it, I promised her the best 4-0 party, so I'd better do whatever it takes to at least salvage some of it.

With my hand across Darla's shoulder, I overhear a voice with a bit of vocal tremor say, "In my day, we didn't have a choice. Why do you think I never remarried after Gramps died? ... If pussy's what you're after, Hun, go for it!" Well that's one I would've never expected from *my* Grammy.

Even Darla's shocked. *"Grandma!"*

"Well you had to get it from *some*where," she cackles, hand jiggling her cane, pointed at Darla.

"Of all the people, I was most terrified of coming out to you – and here you are," she says, hugging the poor old lady tighter than her frail body can handle.

Seeing that I'm not needed here any longer, I go back to check on other things, like Cyn and Randy for instance. Cyn's got her tired footsies in Randy's lap. He's giving her a foot rub as they eye every hot waiter-slash-actor's spandexed ass, trying to guess which camp each belongs to.

Randy claims "They're all gay; they just don't know it yet." To which, Cyn responds, "How about I take everyone under 30 and you take everyone over 30, to find out for sure."

"Waist size or age? ... Not that it matters – you can have them all, Sweetie. I'm sooo totally in love with Steven and can't wait to start a family with him. Too bad he couldn't make it tonight. I miss him so much. His business trips are driving me crazy – but better now than when he becomes a papa, right?"

All's well that ends well, I suppose. If only I could keep Dan from groping Alison so blatantly. Not that I'm jealous or anything, but I was under the impression that he was saving himself for me. It's probably all an act anyway, to throw off my Jeremy – a very *believable* act, if I should say so myself, even though Jeremy is as involved in his surrounds as a tree stump. Not that it's *his* fault, he just has a very small social window – one drink to loosen up, two drinks to switch over to the nasty side of his split personality. Damn it, Jill, do not even go there. You're supposed to be getting things back on track with Jeremy, remember? 'Cause you *love* him. And even though the earth may not move, at least there's a bed tremor every now and then that you can work with. ... "Speaking of Jeremy, when do you plan on telling him about what Dan did?" I hear Grammy's voice ask in my head. ... Never – don't want to shift focus away from *our* relationship. Besides, what's a little kiss amongst friends? But *what* a kiss – now if I could only get the orchestra to stop playing every time I think about that night. I guess we all like to be reminded that we still got it, especially when we feel invisible ... and Mother Nature starts playing its dirty tricks.

I reach into my pocket, to look for my glasses – the light's too damn soft for me to read the bar tab, even though I've moved the paper as far away from my face as I can possibly manage. Isn't it funny that the day I was able to afford expensive, dimly lit restaurants is the day that I stopped being able to read their menus, sans spectacles. The good thing of it is, Jeremy's also in soft focus – unable to see my little flaws.

Chapter 2: *Egg-sis-tential Crisis*

I feel like I'm two-hundred years old, by the way my feet hurt from my shop-until-drop expedition – couldn't be helped though, since I love taking my time at the farmers' market every Tuesday afternoon, for their fresh jellies and chutneys. I know, I should probably wear sensible shoes, but my high heels are worth the torture, for how fab they make my legs look.

No sooner do I get home, when I truly want to take off my stilettoes and drop into my couch; but if I let my feet out for even a few seconds, they'll taste freedom, swell up, and refuse to fit back into my shoes again. And then, Prince Charming will never be able to find me. Speaking of Prince Charming, where's Jeremy? I've been looking forward to this evening all day long; and so will he, once he finds out what I've planned for us later. I can barely contain myself as I squeeze the key in my pocket – it's still there, real as ever – the key to our exciting new future! But if we don't leave right now, we'll never make our dinner reservation.

"Honey, are you home?" I call out to him, dropping my shopping bags onto the floor, my bod onto our buttery suede couch. It exhales with me, to share in that comfortable, home-sweet-home feeling. I guess that'll have to do for now, since there's no sign of Jeremy. The kids are at sleep-overs tonight, hoping that our special evening out will turn into a very special night in – little do they know!

Sunken into my favorite spot, I put my feet on our marble coffee table and find a note on it. "Sorry, Hun, had to go back into work. Looks like Mrs. Johnson's baby has decided to come early. Catch you later. Big kisses, Jeremy."

I'm truly disappointed! But I should've known better than to get my hopes up. Pretty sure that Grammy never ran into stuff like this – she didn't have any expectations to begin with. ... The thing of it is, work or play, anything involving Jeremy *truly* involves Jeremy – except for maybe his marriage. ... While all *his* hobbies require skill, commitment, equipment, considerable time and expense, with nothing to show at the end of the day, *my* favorite hobby just requires a slim credit card, with lots to show for it. At times, I feel guilty about how much I've accumulated – dresses I've never worn, even though I *had* to have them. But as far as retail therapy and hobbies go, they've served their purpose. My latest purchase of course is a different story. It's bound to change our lives forever!

I go into the kitchen, rummage through my pantry, and find myself a non-perishable food item – never know when you're going to need them ... like right now, for instance. As the barely edible dish heats up in the microwave, I kick off my shoes, since it doesn't look like I'll be going out to dinner anytime soon. Two minutes and three beeps later, soup's on.

I take my chalky, non-recognizable concoction to the family room, and turn on the TV for company. First sip and I burn my tongue. I wanna soak it in a cold drink, but before I have a chance to do that, the phone starts ringing. Thick tongued and lispy, I answer, "Hewwo."

I hear Randy say "Wrong number" and promptly hang up on me.

I call him right back and explain my gourmet crisis. More hyper than usual, he squeals back, "Never mind your soup, join us at The Lizard Lounge ... pronto! I'll even spring for your favorite nachos."

"What's going on?"

"If you e-e-e-ver get here, I'll tell you. And oh ... I

almost forgot, I've asked everybody to bring their baggage – so let Jeremy tag along."

"Jeremy's busy delivering a baby – that's how the whole soup crisis started."

"In that case, screw Jeremy, you're ours tonight. Just hu-r-r-r-y!"

I do a faster changeover into my casuals than David Copperfield and run out the door – in my comfy *Rockport's* of course. Damn Prince Charming for making me fly solo yet again. It's not like his resident and midwife couldn't have handled it without him. Wish he'd jump to *my* plumbing needs for a change, with the same urgency as his patients'.

*   *   *

The Lizard Lounge is as eclectic as ever, with its teal walls, billowy white curtains juxtaposed against pool tables, has-been rock star posters, and the occasional roman sculpture holding a pool cue. It used to be a high-end Italian restaurant, but just couldn't cut it in the neighborhood. This 'hood is more about shooting pool, downing a few bears and burping up hot chili and nachos, damn good nachos at that – hence our favorite spot to chill, outside "The Cocoon" of course.

I see the gang across the room and notice that the girls are already here, all except Alison – what else is new? ... And Randy and Steven appear really chummy with the double Ds – a.k.a. Darla and Danielle. I blow kisses to everyone and park myself next to Cyn. "So what's going on? What's this urgent meeting all about?" I ask, scooping a mammoth amount of melted cheese sauce onto my nacho.

Unable to contain himself, Randy says, "Steven and I were rejected yet again, by the adoption agency."

We all say "Aw" in unison, even though he appears to be smiling like a Cheshire cat.

"Wait, hear me out first. ... Anyway, like I was saying, since Steven and I have been turned down yet again, I came up with a great idea." Looking straight at Darla, he continues, "This is where you come in. ... Now I know you claim that biological clock thing doesn't *scare* you, even though you might want kids some day; but Sweetie, let's be honest – this might be your last chance before hitting an egg-sis-tential crises, with no turning back. ... 'Cause believe you me, your eggs are getting more and more compromised even as we speak ... and their 'best by' date is about to become a distant memory."

Danielle snaps, "Hey, not that this has anything to do with you, but hello, she's got *me* ... and last time I checked, my eggs weren't *close* to expiring ... or being compromised ... just primo and robust, that's all."

"I'm sooo glad you said that," continues Randy, "since this has *every*thing to do with the *both* of you – you're also an important part of our plan."

The double Ds give him a faux smile, as if to say "Go on".

"Anyhow, now that the cat is out of the bag and you two are planning on taking the next step, I know that sooner or later – hopefully sooner – you're going to find yourselves in the exact same spot as Steven and I." Steven grabs his forehead and squishes it together, deepening the frown lines below his curly black hair, conveying his discomfort. "So, how about we come up with an arrangement that will work for all four of us?"

"And exactly what might that be?" asks Danielle,
"How about we make babies together? One for each couple? Of course we don't have to do it the old

fashioned way – who does that these days anyway – just our sperm, your eggs, fertilized and implanted into you guys ... well, you know the drill."

The double Ds' jaws drop open in disbelief, as does mine. I motion for the waiter – I need a drink, badly. ... Somebody, say something please, before I feel compelled to fill in the silence with one of my stupid comments! Why is it that I always have the perfect thing to say when I re-run conversations in my head after the fact, rarely when it actually matters? If Grammy were here, she'd get right to the point, "What's wrong with the old fashioned way?" and give everyone a piece of her mind, even though Randy's right – hardly anybody seems to do it that way anymore, certainly not in our age group.

The uncertain faux smiles have now transformed into definite sneers with the double Ds. Danielle finally says, "Is *that* all?" and grabs her purse to leave, with Darla in tow.

Awkward! Really awkward! Really, really awkward! Leave it to Cyn to finally break the ice with "I guess that means that I'll be returning the turkey-baster I bought you guys. Though I must admit I thought I'd finally found the perfect gift, with no chance of re-gifting."

Steven finally speaks up, "The way I'm feeling right now, I wish I could re-gift you, Randy."

Never one for confrontation, Randy bats his lashes at him and says, "You don't mean that. Remember I'm your dangerously gorgeous boyfriend – the one that 'any number of girls would line up for, only to have their hearts broken', 'cause I belong to you?"

Steven just shakes his head, throws a twenty on the table, and leaves, with not even as much as a "Nice save", or "Not this time" – just deafeningly loud silence!

The twenty finally gets the waiter's attention. Just as I order myself a martini, Alison walks in, late as always, "What's with Steven? He nearly ran me over on his way out. ... And where's everybody else? Don't tell me that I actually beat them here this time?"

Cyn chuckles shamelessly, "No, Hun, they've already come and gone – you've missed out on all the fun."

"Beep, beep, beep, back up – what did I miss?"

"Don't ask," I say, hoping to diffuse her inquest.

But Cyn's only too happy to fill in the blanks for Alison. "As it turns out, our sweetie pie over here is just like *any* other man – obsessed with parking his seed in women. After all this time, we're nothing more than walking vaginas in high heels to him," she chuckles. "Of course Steven Dah-ling isn't too happy about it."

"Another coming out party, where our 'mo is really straight, and I missed it? Damn! ... But seriously, what's going on?"

I want to spare Randy's feelings, so I try my best to deliver the punch-line, sans the juicy details, but it's no good – never was any good at telling jokes either.

Logical Alison – bless her heart – tries to reassure him next. "This is what I've been trying to tell you guys all along. There's love, and then there's sex – different kinds of sex at that." Counting on her fingers, she continues, "We have procreational sex, recreational sex, kinky sex, and don't-wanna-go-there sex. When are people going to learn that if you try to mix them all together, you're likelier to end up with a situation that's shaken, not stirred? I've seen too many people fuck up perfectly good marriages when sex turns into a baby-making experience, or for that matter, when the handcuffs come out."

Cyn sighs, "Unfortunately I have to agree with Alison on the different kinds of sex part – seen it many times in my practice. ... Ehm, definitely something that should go in my book – if I *ever* get around to finishing it. ... But as far as the mixing love with lust part goes, I wanna go on record saying, mix 'em up if you want, leave 'em separate if you'd rather – both ways can work."

Always wanting to stand by her word, Alison adds, "I still think you're better off keeping them separate, at least when it comes to your important relationships – both with friends and lovers. Randy, why don't you just do a proper business transaction with a surrogate?"

"Maybe you're right, Sweetie. I'd just hate to mess up with Steven or the girls on this, as much as I want a kid."

"You're such a girl, Randy. And here I thought, only *we* were supposed to feel the tic tocs. Just promise me that you won't start having PMS also," says Cyn, hoping to get him to smile.

"I think I'm about to start right now!" he smiles back. Only Cyn could make fun of him in a loving way and still let him know that she cares.

The waiter rests my martini in front of me. As I try to kick it back all at once, Alison asks him for a dessert menu. "What? Isn't that how you take care of *your* PMS?"

"And heartbreaks," chimes in Randy.

"That's a bit premature, isn't it?" I say.

"See, I do have some man left in me," he laughs.

Alison shocks us all by giving him a big hug and saying, "We love you either way, don't we, girls?"

Never saw that coming out of the most logical, non-emotional one of us. Then again, this is all about love and friendship, sans the sex "screwing everything up" part. I suppose it *could* make relationships a lot easier if we didn't have sexual expectations – can't get disappointed that way. ... Nah, I'm still not buying that, I love sex w-a-a-a-y too much – the recreational kind, since my life is free of any egg-sis-tential crises. Grammy adds in my head, "Or any other major crisis, if you really think about it." ... I look at the plethora of relationship screw-ups and mishaps around me, and realize that my own relationship is indeed pretty decent by comparison – definitely worth saving. I'm not about to give up just 'cause our plans fell through earlier this evening. If anything, the more I think about Jeremy, the more I find myself wanting him. Perhaps absence does make the heart grow fonder, even though Cyn swears that it only makes it wander. ... I decide to call my love on his cell phone to see how much longer he'll be? I could really use a bed tremor right about now – and some post-oxytocin cuddling – even though my big surprise will just have to wait for another night. ... As luck would have it, it seems like Mrs. Johnson was readier than anyone thought, 'cause Jeremy's already done and headed home.

Eager to join him, I grab my purse, settle my bill, and stand up. "Not meaning to ditch you all at a time like this, but I've had a long day and I'm dying to get into bed – so will you please excuse me?" I give Randy a kiss on his forehead, "You know where to find me if you need me, my little breeder. And don't forget, this was just the initial meeting – at least you planted the seed." Oops, wrong choice of words, but kinda funny all the same – maybe I should try my luck at telling jokes one more time. Better yet, skip the jokes and just have a tryst with Jeremy – guaranteed to be a lot more fun! We have to start somewhere, right? Grammy would be proud, though I still hope that she can't actually see us doing it.

Our night together ends up being a whole lot of fun

indeed – more than expected – thanks to me being so psyched about it. Jeremy too seemed more adventurous than usual, trying out new things. Where did he learn to do that? ... I wonder how my surprise will fit in with his bravado and my commitment to push the boundaries just a wee bit? The very thought makes me go weak in the knees, as I prepare to fall asleep in his arms, reliving the *fierce* passion.

It's now morning and I'm barely coming out of my oxytocin induced coma. Bleary-eyed, I look at my alarm clock. "Shit, I'm gonna be late for my 9 a.m. meeting." I'd so wanted to get in before the Japanese. From what I've heard, they're supposed to be really punctual. Just this once, I wish they'd work on Alison-standard-time, or at least get stuck in the same predictable traffic jam as me and my Porsche will, soon enough.

*   *   *

Flabbergasted, I step into my waiting area, only to find Martha, my secretary, wiping coffee off of one of my client's trousers. Shit, shit, shit – not a good start at all. Just look at his angry face! With Martha's shaky hands, I've told her a million times to let people get their own coffee – but I guess she's just too old-fashioned for that ... and so are they from the looks of it ... not budging an inch to give the blue-haired gal a hand. ... I'll just have to take them into my office and wow them with all the glossy pictures of how the food will be presented at their banquet. Like the menus and the window displays for the restaurants in the old country, they want the final product to match the picture exactly – right down to the last sprig of parsley. They insisted on making it a part of our contract.

Not wishing to waste another moment of their time, I usher them inside my office and seat them on my burgundy couch, easels set at eye level, ready for their perusal.

Following the initial pleasantries, I begin, "As you can see, I've respected your colour schemes, while still offering a variety of dishes to please a myriad of palates at your gathering."

They look impressed. Is that a smile I see on the coffee dude's face? No, that would be pushing it a bit. But they do appear to be quite happy with what I can do, judging by the animated discussion they seem to be having amongst themselves, in Japanese of course, since the big boss doesn't speak any English. Low to the ground, he's a man of small stature, but quite flamboyantly dressed in a saffron silk shirt and black trousers.

After about five minutes, I muster up enough courage to ask, "What's Mr. Takahashi saying?"

"He loves it," is all I get.

Hoping for a bit more, since they did have a much longer discussion amongst themselves, I say, "Please let me know if there's anything else you'd like."

Coffee dude shuffles in his seat, and says, "No, nothing else, let's just sign the papers," as he reaches for something behind his back. Looks like he's pulling something out from underneath my beaded, Indian cushion. Yikes, it's a cod piece – a.k.a. a studded leather G-string. Oh, the shame of it!

Don't know what moved faster – the questionable object flinging across the room like an out-of-control slingshot, or my ex-clients racing out the door? There goes the account that was to pay the balance on my big surprise.

"Damn it, Randy! If you're going to crash on my couch, do you think you could at least have the decency to drop some change in the cracks, instead of what graces your own crack!" I'm furious with him, even though I should be feeling sorry for him – things must be pretty bad for him to crash here. Either way, we must talk. Betchya I'll find him in "The Cocoon".

I race up the stairs, only to hear Sade's silky crooning. Uh-uh, that's Randy's pre-breakup music. Next stop is usually Annie Lennox. To my surprise, I open up the door to Randy *and* Alison, with a million letters littering up our humongous coffee table. I fling Randy's butt jewelry at him and hiss, "Missing something?"

"Oh Gawd, Jilly, where did I leave that thing? I hope I didn't embarrass you in any way."

"You left it in my couch, to puncture Mr. Burned Thigh's unhappy ass, costing me a *major* account!"

"I'm sooo sorry, Sweetie. As I fell asleep on the couch last night I felt uncomfortable and remembered that I had it on. So, snip, snip, I undid the snaps and pulled it off," the latter he does by holding the offending object against his crotch, making a snip snip motion with his hands. Mile a minute, he continues, "Then this morning I cleared out so fast that I totally forgot all about it."

No response – a rare moment for me, since I'm usually the one who fills in those awkward pauses. This time, I'm going to let him sweat it out a bit more. I'm thinking, why me, why my couch? Maybe having an en-suite bath wasn't such a good idea after all.

It's amazing what remaining quiet will do – makes people nervous – I should try it out more often. "Please, Sweetie, don't be mad at me. I'm hurting enough already," says Randy, with a downcast mouth doing that pooh bear thing that always gets me.

"So this is all about you yet again, is it?"

Alison cuts in, sorting through the letters, "Stop it

you two, it's not about you – this time it's about *me*."

I'm really curious, since Miss Private rarely lets us in. And she looks quite excited to boot. Her hair is neatly pulled back into a French twist; her taupe Armani jacket is making her look more exquisite than ever.

"Randy, the whole idea *was*, if you help me out with my issues, hopefully you won't think about your own."

"Would someone puh-leaze mind telling me what's going on over here?"

"Grab a seat," instructs Alison. I plunk down on the couch beside her. Never one to mince words, she gets right to the point with, "In a nutshell, these are the responses I got to a 'personals' ad that I took out for myself."

"A personals ad? Pray do tell, just what did you promise them to get such an overwhelming response?" I ask.

"You'll be shocked when I tell ya. Suffice it to say that I'm thrilled to no end, that there are so many men out there who are smart enough to see eye to eye with me."

"Now you've lost me – men who *don't* want sex?"

"Bingo!"

I grab the ad out of her hands. "Gimme that!" The title says it all – Wanted, Impotent Men!

"Never in a million years did I suspect that there are plenty of rich and successful CEO-types out there who'd also kill to be in this kind of an arrangement, just so they don't have to let the cat out of the bag ... or out of the panties, for that matter," she brags.

"Particularly with all those women out there wishing to address their own egg-sis-tential crises. I mean, can you just imagine one of those high society girls landing the perfect guy, only to find out that his pee pee doesn't work? It would make the rounds faster than any Hollywood gossip," I laugh.

"I'd *kill* myself if *my* pee pee stopped working. One would think that the Viagra-genarians today don't have to worry like the octogenarians any longer. But from the looks of it, I guess they do ... meaning, more dates than ever for you, Girlfriend!" squeals Randy, high-fiving Alison. "And here we thought that dating in your thirties is significantly more challenging than dating in your teens or twenties!"

As Alison looks through the letters, her "Yes" pile continues to grow rapidly. I'm surprised that she has so many recruits, considering the shocked faces she's making.

"What?" I pry, moving myself to the armrest right beside her, trying to sneak a peek over her shoulder.

"I must say that I'd never counted on the alternate ways some of these guys get their thrills. ... Spank me ... hog-tie me ... bungee-jump with me ... hope you're not opposed to me cross-dressing ... how about playing mommy ... etc, etc, etc. ... Perverts I tell you."

Randy chimes in, "They don't sound perverted to me. Do you even know the difference between kinky sex and perverted sex?"

I jump in with, "Kinky sex is whatever you're doing and perverted sex is what everybody else is doing," hoping to convince myself that my little secret plan is A-Okay!

"That, and ... whereas kinky sex involves feathers, perverted sex involves the whole chicken," adds Randy. "And I don't see any requests for chickens in here. ... So see, not perverted."

"Think I should make an appointment with Cyn to find out what's most fun ... perhaps decode their psychoses?" asks Alison.

"Maybe then she'll stop buying you vibrators for your birthdays, trying to remind you of the 'omnipotent nature of orgasms'," I chuckle.

"Doesn't she get it that that's precisely the reason I'm not going there? I don't want that kind of power over me ... and all the addictive hormonal bullshit that goes with it. It just messes with your brain, breaks your heart, and has you making irrational decisions from your crotch. I think the female praying mantises have it right – biting the males' heads off immediately after sex, to eliminate the risk of any of that happening. ... As a sex therapist, one would think that Cyn would get where I'm coming from."

Randy puts in his two-cents, "Honey-child, you know with Cyn it's always been about pushing the limits on pleasure."

"Maybe there's some business potential in that," Alison smiles, holding a seemingly interesting letter close to her heart, where I can't read it.

"What?" I ask again. But she's not letting me in on this one. All I can say is that the last time she looked this happy was when she landed her first six-figure account. Didn't know that men could excite her as much as money.

Personally, I love both men and money ... and I'm about to add a third "M" to the list – mischief. But before I give anything away, I take my filthy little smirk to the window and watch the moon bathe the dark water with a milky streak.

Across the bay is a private island, twinkling in tempting ways, beckoning me to come over and play.

My key is still in my pocket, teasing me with promises of things to come – now more than ever, after last night's games.

Chapter 3 - *That Was Then ... This Is Now*

Cyn's son, Jonathan, is having his eighteenth birthday party – and guess who gets to cater it?

Normally, I'm all over everything until the party itself – my very capable staff take over at that point. Tonight, Cyn expects me to be there the whole time, so she'll have some company. Jonathan agrees, hoping that I'll keep her in line. The sex therapist that she is, she has a very different way of looking at things.

Now while all her kids' friends think it must be pretty cool to have her for a mom, Jonathan and Michael consider it brutal, from all the embarrassing situations they've found themselves in – not that Cyn deliberately intends it, she just doesn't seem to get it.

The streamers are up, leading to a piñata in the middle of the party room. It looks a little juvenile if you ask me, but Cyn insists, "Wait until it pops open – the kids will just love it! I have a special surprise planned for them." I'm afraid to even ask and Jonathan just looks up at it and says, "Whatever! At least it's not a crazy sex toy or something like that, just a harmless goat – how bad can it be?" Like me, I'm sure he's assuming that it's there because he was born in the year of the goat, according to the Chinese calendar.

Cyn and I place finger foods on the banquet tables laid out at the periphery of the room, making sure there's enough napkins and whatnots. Surround sound is already blaring out hip hop tunes, with music videos dancing across the two plasma screens on either end of the room. My gosh, the girls are practically naked in there, contorting in provocative ways. "If *I* tried to do that, I'd throw my back out in a second."

Cyn laughs and says, "But you have to admit that they do have some cool threads."

"Maybe as bedroom-wear for some, but certainly not for me."

"Oh come on, don't tell me that Jeremy won't get a kick out of watching you dressed like that? Maybe just what you need – a little CPR to revive your relationship."

I'm thinking, you have nooo idea what my version of CPR involves – clothes don't even factor in. As they say, desperate times call for desperate measures. But I play along, since beating myself up has never been a challenge for me. "Yeah right – maybe if I had the booty and the moves to go with it."

"Wish *we* learned to move like that, back in our 'Disco Divas' days!" she says, trying to mimic the Beyoncé booty shake that's rapidly heating up the screen.

I just shake my head, "I was definitely born in the wrong era. I should have been a teen right now, when belly flashing is cool, no matter what the belly size." Assuming a British accent, I add, "Better yet, a young lady in the mediaeval times, when fat thighs were vogue and an inspiration to artists."

Cyn snaps back, "Not me, I'm very happy right where I am. Would hate to be a teen – who needs all that angst? ... And what's with you – quit being so hard on yourself. You're Salma Hayak gorgeous, remember? Short and sweet, with proportions to die for."

Cyn always did know how to cheer me up ... and I, how to make her laugh, even through the crabbiest of times. Had she not picked me as her roommate in college, I would've never felt comfortable hanging out with the cool kids.

Speaking of cool kids, Jonathan looks more excited than I've ever seen him. Normally he's as quiet as a church mouse; tonight, he's talking faster than the speed of light. I totally get it, since I too do that when I'm nervous. But what does he have to be nervous about? He's a handsome, five foot ten young man, with his mother's green eyes and his father's jet black hair, unlike the carrot top that his brother inherited. Then again, this *is* the first co-ed party he's ever hosted.

Clusters of guys and gals arrive, in their own little cliques, distinguished by their uniforms – a.k.a. distinct fashion statements. We have the preppie *Old Navy* types, with the odd goatee or chin-strap; the nondescript wall flowers in their khakis; the grunge meets Goth contingent with scary tats and piercings; and diaper-loading, cool hommies with their pants hanging just beneath their butts, flashing their double underwear. One girl in particular, Marsha, catches my eye. Looking at her, I swear she could be a poster child for up-to-no-good punks, with her chewed up fingernails, thick black liner, and ripped fishnet stockings. Who let her out of the house looking like that? Shit – I catch myself – I'm beginning to sound just like my mother. Still, I can't help but stare at her – only to get busted. Peering through her long, black bangs, she stares right back at me and grunts, "Take a picture, it'll last longer."

Cyn is pissed. "Just who the hell does the little skank think she is? A party crasher, I'm sure. Can't imagine Jonathan ever inviting the likes of *her*."

"Stop it, Cyn; we don't wanna let her ruin Jonathan's party."

"I suppose," she huffs, quite disappointedly.

"Besides, do you really wanna go down in a cat fight on your son's eighteenth birthday – all that body jewelry will scratch the hell out of your Prada. ... Let's just lay low, okay?"

Cyn promises me that we'll discreetly do our thing, like we're not even here – as discreet as is possible with Cyn. D'ya think we succeeded? Not a chance!

A senior from the preppie brigade walks over to Cyn and says, "Yo! Weren't you on cable last night, talking about blow-jobs?"

Being recognized is always a high point with Cyn. She smiles back and says, "Yes, guilty as charged."

"Sw-e-e-e-t!"

"Shouldn't you be in bed at that time?" she says coyly.

"I'd rather watch you." Not being one to leave bad enough alone, he flirtatiously adds, "In bed or otherwise – you really know your stuff, man."

Ohmigosh, there's Jonathan, standing right there, furious at where the conversation is headed. I grab Cyn by her elbow and steer her away from Mr. Jail-bait. Jonathan follows us and gives his mom a dirty look. Cyn says, "Why are you looking at *me* like that? *He's* the one who started it."

"I thought we had a deal, Mom. I could have gone my entire life without needing to hear that conversation. Next time someone recognizes you in front of me, could you just say, 'No, not me, though everyone seems to make that mistake all the time' – end of discussion?"

Cyn knows when she's fighting a losing battle. She

grabs her purse and says, "Later. I know when I'm not wanted. I'll catch you at home."

Jonathan looks upset at having hurt her feelings. Poor guy. Talk about being caught between a rock and a hard place. I say, "She'll be fine. You know her, quick to heat up and just as quick to simmer down. ... Go on, have some fun."

"Are you sure she isn't mad at me, Mrs. B.?"

"Nonsense! You and I both know that it'll take a hellova lot more than that to get her mad. Her bark has always been worse than her bite."

My comment must have satisfied Jonathan, since everything's back to normal. The party seems to be moving along without a hitch, with everyone grinding to rap meets house meets hip hop tunes. Small clusters of kids keep sneaking out, probably to grab a smoke, or possibly make out – standard teen stuff, nothing terribly eventful. ... But wait, did I speak too soon? Just as I'm ready to head out, Marsha races my way, looking all pissed – like I need this. "Yo, you gotta help us out in the parking lot, like right now," she gasps.

"What's going on?"

"These guys brought some shit they weren't supposed to? And I'm like r-e-e-e-ally scared that we're all gonna get busted?"

I did not see that coming. I make a mad dash for the parking lot, convinced that it's Marsha's little clique that's causing all the commotion. To my shock, it's the preppie gang, smoking up. Yup, I recognize that all too familiar smell of pot – brings back a lot of memories. What am I going to do? I guess there really is only one thing to do. I reach into my pocket to pull out my cell. But before I can dial, Jonathan lunges for it and begs, "Please, Mrs. B, don't do that. I promise you that I'll take care of it."

My heart wants to listen to him, give him a chance to be an adult, but my head says, maybe it's my responsibility. Sucker that I am, I let Jonathan do his thing. After all, it is his entry into the world as a man.

Jonathan issues an ultimatum, laced with threats of parents finding out all kinds of stuff, if they don't stop right now and hand over the goods – pronto. I put out my hand. Pissed as they are, they give me their baggie of joints and take off, screeching tires marking their dramatic exit.

Jonathan asks, "Will you tell mom?"

"I'm not sure yet." Looking at his disheartened expression, I add, "Do you have any idea how proud I am of you? ... Why don't you go inside and enjoy being a kid while you still can. I believe there's a piñata waiting for you?"

Marsha points to her Hummer and says, "Want me to get a baseball bat from my ride? Like, only if you need it for the piñata or something?"

I say, "Sure," and watch her take off with a smile. Memo-to-self: never judge a book by its cover.

We go back inside and try to discharge our pent up, nervous energy on the fringy, colorful goat. One by one, the teens take a go at it. Finally, the baseball champion amongst us gives it a hard enough hammering to make it explode. ... Time stands still as condoms and cherry flavored lubes descend onto the floor in place of little treats. Jonathan's jaw drops down in disbelief. Equally shocked, I cover my mouth with my hand. Marsha saves the day yet again, by turning to Jonathan and saying, "Like how kewl is that Dude, your mom making sure that we play safe and everything?"

Everybody laughs – the *with* kind, not the *at* kind. Nonetheless, redder than ever, Jonathan starts to leave the room. My very capable staff picks that precise moment to come out with the birthday cake. Everybody joins in to sing *Happy Birthday*. Jonathan finally manages to crack a smile. "So have you decided what you gonna do yet?" he asks me again.

"If it were my son Jack, hanging out with those kids, I'd wanna know." Watching his pleading eyes, I continue, "Unless I was certain that he could handle it as well as you." Of course the last part is just to make him feel better. "Jonathan, can I be sure that I have nothing to worry about with you personally?"

Marsha jumps to his defense, "Like he's only the kewlest kid in the school ... as far as that whole don't mess with drugs thing goes. Please Mrs. B, like he doesn't need to pay for what other kids did, does he?"

I'm amazed at how her interior doesn't quite match up with her tough exterior, not unlike the preppie gang, or for that matter Cyn. Betchya Marsha's a straight A student also, grammar notwithstanding. My old English lit professors would have a field day with her. ... I give them both a reassuring smile. She takes Jonathan's hand and marks her territory. Is that a kiss she just gave him? Boy oh boy, what Cyn would give to be here right now! For her son's sake, I'm glad that she isn't. In any case, since everyone looks happy and settled, I guess that's my cue to leave.

*   *   *

As I drive home, purse full of pot and condoms and lube, I pray that I don't get pulled over – would hate to get locked up in some filthy facility, only to become someone's bitch. ... And what would the kids think? Grammy on the

49

other hand, would hopefully understand. Conventional as she was, she'd sneak in a hidden cigarette or a shot of whiskey the odd time, to "put the life back" in her, so she could keep on going.

*   *   *

I park my Porsche in the garage and head upstairs to soak in a desperately needed hot bath. I'm not looking forward to calling Cyn about the pot. Maybe I'll break it to her in person. Since she's bound to be home – having cleared her evening for Jon's party – and it's still early; I'll call her up and invite her to share a bottle of wine by the pool. She's game and asks if we should invite the others also. "Why not? Though Randy is away for a sexcapade weekend with Steven, and you can bet that Darla and Danielle are having some sexcapades of their own. ... But sure, we can invite everybody – as long as you can call 'em up, 'cause I really need to have a long soak. ... And tell everyone to just come around to the backyard. It's such a lovely night and the pool is as warm as bath water – we have to heat it at this time of the year."

I go upstairs for my long-awaited bath, only to be intercepted by Jeremy. Without as much as a hello, he grabs my boobs and says, "Glad you're home early – I could really go for some Saturday night dirty."

How romantic does that sound! Normally, I'd give anything for him to desire me ... initiate sex – but fuck, I'm sooo not in the mood for this, not this way. But Mr. Horndog has other plans. He takes my hand and places it on his erect penis, figuring, alas he's found the secret to turning a woman on. As an Ob-Gyn, you'd think he'd know better. But poor guy, he doesn't even understand that the F word really means foreplay. ... I guess I'm too tired to argue, 'cause I find myself giving in like Grammy would've expected me to – not that it's a huge undertaking – but the jury's still out on whether or not it beats doing laundry. ... Despite the unimaginative start, I'm still hoping that things might take a turn for the better, like last time.

Alas, a couple of pokes here, a couple of tweaks there, he heads south, hammers away, and it's all over before it even began for me, sans as much as a slight tremor. See, no point in fussing and arguing when the alternative is sooo much easier – you lay still long enough until he races the clock to beat his own record and rolls off, mercifully quick. Still, as I feel Jeremy shrink inside me, part of me wants to go down and take his soft penis into my mouth, to revive it again – sure could use a little tremor, pissed off as I am – but then I think better of it. I mean, why bother – other than that one isolated night, it's been quite a while since he's taken the time to leave me breathless, or feeling remotely connected to him. I can almost overlook him not doing things for me, as long as he's doing things *to* me. But the way things stand right now, it's nothing doing, period – either way. I'm disappointed that our animalistic night never repeated itself again – wonder why? There's got to be more to life than career, kids and clichéd copulation!

I twist away from Jeremy's heavy grip, roll off the clammy spot, and decide to take things into my own hands – less complicated to get off that way, since there are no hurt feelings or bizarre agendas that can ruin it for you. As I slide my hands between my legs in the bath, the man I imagine touching me isn't Jeremy – it's someone tall, dark and handsome, a man bound to treat sex with me as a privilege, not something to be taken for granted, placed at the very bottom of the list of exciting things he'd rather make time for.

Pretty discouraging, ain't it, after everything I've

done to cherish what we have, and revive what once was. Thank goodness Grammy can't read my mind!

By the time I come out of the bath, I find Jeremy in a deep snore. I sneak downstairs quietly and set up the patio table for the girls – a bottle of Merlot, wineglasses, a small plate of sandwiches, some fruit; it's all there, as is the baggie of joints, nestled safely in my sienna coverall pocket. No sooner do I finish the setup, Cyn and Alison come bouncing over. Hugs and kisses ensue, wine is poured, we plop into the chaises and get right into small talk about each other's swim-wear. But my mind is miles away, trying to figure out a way of breaking the news to Cyn, gently.

Cyn interrupts my revere with, "So, how did things go after I left?"

"What?"

"Jon's party – was it all smooth sailing after I left?

"Oh that? Pretty much, except for a little glitch that I was meaning to talk to you about."

After a long, pregnant pause, she says, "And?"

"Jonathan didn't do anything wrong himself, but some of his buddies brought pot to the party. Have no worries though, everything's taken care of, thanks to your son. ... Ehm, just thought you'd wanna know anyway – you know, what his friends are up to, just in case ...."

"If that's the worst thing that happens to him, some pot-head buddies, I should consider myself lucky."

"That's it, you're not concerned?"

"Nah, it's not like *he* was doing anything. Even if, don't you remember what we were up to when we were his age?" Boy do I ever. "Besides, a little experimentation never hurt anybody," she adds nonchalantly.

I reach into my pocket and pull out the baggie with a handful of joints still in it. "Well, here it is, in any case."

Without a moment of hesitation, Cyn lunges for it, says, "*Now* we're talking party," and lights one up, using my barbeque lighter. Next thing you know, she's passing it back and forth to Alison, who's also really getting into it, like old times. The way her face lights up reminds me of her party girl days, when she'd be the first one to jump up on top of the bar and start dancing. ... My resistance lasts only so long before I say "What the hell" and take a drag, feeling like a bad cop for doing it – after busting the teens for the same. It brings back memories of my own youth – shy and insecure as I was, the gang always included me in everything – giving me a hit of courage when I needed it the most.

Cyn winks at me, "Way to go kiddo – I was worried that Ms. Responsible Mom had forgotten how to have a good time. ... Honestly, Jill, I can't believe that you're the same person who flashed Grammy, when she yelled at you for going to church braless."

I wonder whatever happened to that girl, and ask, "I'm not *that* bad, am I?" Watching them nod in affirmation, I take a long drag. "You know what they say – 'If you don't keep an eye on your kids, they turn to drugs; if you do, *you* turn to drugs'. I'm just making sure, better *me* than them." ... Feeling quite brave now, I sarcastically add, "By the way, nice touch with the condoms."

Before Cyn can comment, Alison says, "What did you do now – try to talk somebody besides me into having sex?"

"Nah, they don't need to be talked into it – they'll hump anything that holds still long enough. But I figure, if they're gonna do it anyway, I'm going to make damn sure that they're at least safe about it. ... Do you have any idea how many teens screw up, just because they're too embarrassed to go out and buy condoms? ... Don't tell me they complained?"

"When are you going to learn that you can't keep embarrassing your boys like that?" I say.

Alison finally catches on that it has something to do with Cyn's kids. Her face goes from confusion to an eye roll, "Always pushing sex, aren't ya?"

"I wasn't pushing sex, just trying to be a cool, responsible mom."

"It's never cool when *your* mom is doing shit like that – maybe to the other kids, but not your own. You're lucky you're still alive. If I pulled a stunt like that with my Jack or Amber, they'd *kill* me – or at the very least never speak to me again." I take another drag and practically choke on it, laughing, "Not that they speak with me all that much anyway."

Cyn joins in the laughing fit. "We *have* to give them reasons to be pissed at us. It's good for them – provides them with an excuse to go into therapy and sort through their shit. ... Think about it – if someone can't blame their mother, why bother going into therapy – it's no fun?"

We keep laughing and passing the joint around, getting sillier by the minute, as Alison and I try to remind Cyn of what it was like to be a teen in *her* household, with *her* parents.

Alison starts with, "Cyn, do you remember how your dad would try to act all cool whenever we'd practice our "Disco Divas" routines in your living room?" Chuckles all around. "He'd pretend he was John Travolta and shake his belly, attempting Mr. Saturday Night Fever moves?" More chuckles. "Then your mom would yell at him, 'Stop acting like a child!' ... and he'd grab her and say, 'If I'm a child, I guess that makes *you* a child-molester,' and then laugh at his own joke, even though the rest of us were going ewww."

Cyn gives us a faux frown and says, "Don't remind me. There was *that* and all the other crazy stuff that mom did through her topless phase. ... I always wanted the earth to open up and swallow me, whenever I'd realize that they were a little different from other parents – and you *know* I don't embarrass too easily."

Assuming a high-pitched Cyn voice, Alison and I do the thing she used to do with her fingers, as a teen – snapping them in a vertical sign wave – and say, "Tell me she didn't just say that?" in her trademark singsong way.

"Okay, okay, point taken. As a teen you think that you invented sex, and the mere thought of your parents having anything to do with it is just plain disgusting."

We break into hysterics. I'm having w-a-a-a-y too much fun. Looks like tonight's going to be one of those nights that I'll regret later – gosh how I miss those nights! The last time me did anything crazy was, mooning the crowd at *The Rocky Horror Picture Show* and getting arrested for indecent exposure.

I'm now sooo stoned ... and feeling happy. But Cyn and Alison are even gigglier than me. Louder still is Alison's cell phone with its annoying tune. "Who the hell keeps calling you at this hour? I thought most guys just expect you to sit by the phone for a call that never comes. ... Could it be one of your non-protocol, impotent guys?"

Cyn bolts straight up in her chaise, "What impotent guys? Am I missing something here? You wouldn't be holding out on me, would ya?"

Always to the point, Alison says, "Relax ... I just took out an ad for an impotent guy, okay? I figured, this way I can have the romance, the cuddling, and all the mushy things people say to each other, without having someone stick his dick inside me ... or inside someone else, for that matter."

Cyn totally gets it and educates me with, "The official term for that is 'affectionate bonding' – a love attachment with all its warmth, affection, tenderness and nurturing, without the pressure of sex – you can read about it in my book." The last bit she says with the confidence of someone who might actually be working on finishing it up.

I laugh, "Read and weep?"

Obviously Alison disagrees, with the weep part. "You have nooo idea how great it feels to be able to fall asleep in each other's arms, without someone reaching between your legs and whining for sex, and then making you sleep on his weenie phlegm. ... And, do I really want a relationship with someone who's driven by his dick?"

I'm thinking, I wouldn't mind a dick every now and then, the kind that's *attached* to a guy, not the kind where the guy *himself* is the dick – a sentiment I'm all too familiar with, from what went on earlier. I raise my wineglass and say, "Like Jeremy!"

Alison tries to change the topic with, "So what's going on with you two anyway? Trouble in paradise?"

"I don't know – I guess we all go through that depressing stage, where nothing seems to work out the right way. But I've had Jeremy for so long that I can't even *think* of taking him back for a refund, even though he's been malfunctioning quite a bit lately ... usually makes love like he's the only one in the room."

Cyn interjects, "That's just him recapturing his youth – a throwback to the days when he *was* the only one in the room. ... Have you tried having a 'vagina monologue' with him – as in, if my vagina could talk, it would say..."

"You gotta be kidding," I laugh, "Did you forget that he makes a living talking to vaginas all day long? Maybe that's why he's completely detached ... and in and out as quickly and efficiently as possible. ... Probably too sick of looking at them to be *charmed* by them."

"How about spicing it up a bit then, with some slap and tickle ... for variety? I'll just bet that he'll *love* that ... and at least start to function properly in the bedroom," suggests Alison.

"And what would *you* know about that?" I ask, recalling our rough play from the other night.

"More than you think," she winks.

Cyn butts in with, "Now *this* I gotta hear."

Always one to swallow her tongue instead of needing to pull her foot out of her mouth, our very mysterious Alison unwraps her orange sarong and jumps into the pool – a stunning kidney shape, with discreetly lit waterfalls pouring into it, from a raised hot-tub in the garden above. ... Of course Cyn isn't far behind.

I thank my lucky stars for being spared yet another lecture from the girls – a lot more brutal than anything practical that Grammy would ever say. ... Watching them splash each other and squeal like little kids, I say, "What the hey?" and start to take off my coverall. But just before I jump in, Alison's phone goes off again – this time it's a text message. Not that it's any of my business, but since I'm feeling pretty giddy and brave, I decide to read it, to see what her secret admirer has to say for himself. It'll make for some endless teasing. The message reads: need huk up now - ansr damit! Suddenly I don't feel so good anymore. Is she a dealer of some sort? Alison sees me with her cell phone in my hand and yells, "What the hell are you doing?" She looks mad, real mad, as she comes out of the pool.

But Cyn's new flotation devices are still keeping her afloat. Just as well, 'cause I'd hate for the party to be over so soon. Caringly, I ask Alison, "Are you into something that you shouldn't be into?"

Alison tries to make light of it. "Don't let your overactive imagination run away with you, Hun." She then smiles at me – dare I say almost apologetically – holds out her cell phone, and continues, "But I do have to get this." Two seconds later, she's wiped, towel-wrapped, and walking a safe distance away from us, toward our twinkly light-studded cedars – cell phone in hand.

As Cyn dries herself, she asks, "What's with her?"

I shrug my shoulders and pour myself a fresh glass of wine. Cyn lights up another joint and passes it to me. I take a deep drag and find myself in yet another coughing fit. Then, just as I stop, I overhear Alison say, "Gorgeous and playful, I promise," louder than she'd intended – kinda like music stopping suddenly and catching you in a loud voice. Now I'm *really* confused. None of it makes any sense to me – Cyn's too high to care.

Alison walks back to us and says, "Sorry girls, but I have to head out."

Cyn assumes it's something delish and waves her goodbye, without as much as a second thought. I, of course, go into my own little world, imagining the worst case scenarios. After Alison leaves, Cyn walks over and gives me a strange look – betchya she can tell that I'm worrying about something, quite unnecessarily, 'cause she says, "Don't believe everything you hear in your head," and pushes me into the pool.

I let out a little scream and splash around like I'm drowning. "Help," I say, jokingly. The hand which offers to pull me out isn't Cyn's – it's strong, muscular ... and velvety chocolate. Shocked, I say, "It's you?"

Dan looks at me hungrily – like I look at a cheeseburger – and smiles, "Yeah, I can definitely confirm that it's truly me."

"I mean, what are *you* doing here?" I fumble, trying not to give away his cheeseburger appeal, or for that matter the thoughts I was having about him earlier in the evening. I am so aware of his presence, his scent ... unable to breathe, lest I give something away. What can I say? I like the way he makes me feel, even though I shouldn't – but there's no escaping those thoughts when I'm around him ... especially not right after being treated like a comfortable old shoe yet again, by dear old Jeremy.

"I was fixing Darla's computer when the girls came home and got your message. Looked like they wanted to get rid of me, 'cause they asked me to come over here in their place. ... And you know me, never one to turn down a party." The last bit he utters over a wink drenched with double entendre and expectant possibilities.

Oh boy – tonight just keeps getting better and better, just when I thought I had it under control. I was so hoping to hit Cyn for some advice on sparking things up with Jeremy – not that I'm a sex maniac or anything like that. ... But here we are, with devil in a blue *Speedo*, causing a major distraction. And we're taking seriously ma-a-a-jor – if I showed you a picture, you'd think it was photoshopped ... I calm my heart – just as fickle as a man's penis – and do the only thing I can. I say, "I'm beat. I have to hit the sack, you guys ... but don't stop on my account. There's all kinds of drinks and munchies in the cabana – just help yourselves."

And here I thought that telling Cyn about the pot was going to be my biggest challenge tonight!

Chapter 4 - *Queer Cheer*

"The Cocoon" is a pigsty. Annie Lennox is blaring "No more I love you". "Raccoon eyes" doesn't begin to describe the state of Randy's face – his makeup's stained with enough tears to make him look as blotchy and distorted as a child's drawing. The only thing that looks worse is the day-old Chinese take-out boxes that are causing a major stench. I can't for the life of me understand why it doesn't dawn on anyone else to clean up a bit, give the boy a cold towel ... and possibly nurse his hangover, since they did supposedly come over to "support" him. Yes, even the baggage, as Randy would put it – Danielle and my Jeremy – making for a bonafide, five-star emergency.

As Jeremy and I try to tidy up, Danielle does her bit, wiggling across the room with a coffee for Randy, commando tight jeans teaching people how to lip-read. "Here, have some. And if it'll make you feel any better, we're actually considering your baby idea – no promises though."

Jeremy stops dead in his tracks and says, "She's so nice!"

I hiss back, "You forgot to complete your sentence."

"Whadya mean?"

"She's so nice ... *looking*." Why is it that men always assume that nice-looking means nice? They'll say that after a two-second look, or at most a two-minute conversation. And it doesn't stop there. If you show a hint of disagreement, they'll stop at nothing to try and change your mind, convinced that it's just *your* insecurity talking. Never mind that you've known this person your entire life, not to mention been victimized by their not-so-nice, psycho-bitch tendencies. ... Not that Danielle is a psycho-bitch or anything like that.

Jeremy interrupts my mental drivel with, "Did you hear anything I said?"

"No, sorry, what were you saying?"

"I just said that I hadn't noticed. Besides, doesn't she hit for the other team?"

"Would it matter if she hit for the right team?" Can't believe I actually said that out loud. Memo-to-self: we're here to cheer up Randy, *not* make ourselves miserable.

Jeremy also knows when to shut up – I think that's been the secret to our marriage, though every now and again I wish he'd piss and moan a bit and give me a jealous fuck, or at the very least moan when we fuck – like the other night. The silence is intolerable... Enough already – I remove myself from my situation, stand behind Randy's couch and lean over to rub his temples.

He leans back into me and sobs, "It's over, Jilly."

"How do you know that – just 'cause he hasn't called for a couple of days?"

"That ... and the fact that Charlie saw him dining with someone else last night. ... I'm pretty sure he's double-dipping."

"Double-dipping? ... How do you go from dining together to double-dipping? Isn't that a huge leap of un-faith?"

"I know Steven's M.O. – he invented cock smooching ... and he wrote the book on wine, dine and sixty-nine."

"At least you haven't lost your sense of humor," adds Alison.

Randy flips out, "I'm NOT kidding – this is serious stuff! One minute we're living together, planning babies, next minute he's ditched me and our dreams, for partying it up with a new piece of ass. Hope his new boy-toy is a homicidal maniac."

Leave it to Cyn to yell, "Snap out of it! Aren't you over-reacting just a bit? ... And for the record, if he's dumped you for someone else, it's technically not double-dipping."

Randy sniffles back, "I'm NOT over-reacting – you're under-reacting! And it's sooo double-dipping, until he makes the breakup official."

"Calm down, you two," I butt in, yet again.

Sucking tear-snot up his nose, Randy protests, "I'm not going to calm down! Maybe uncalm up, but never calm down!"

"Uncalm is not even a real word. And since you're not listening to real words anyway, let's at least get you cleaned up," says Cyn, wiping up his tears with a stray dishcloth that she found on the coffee table – ouch.

"For the record, I don't want to clean up either," protests Randy, pulling away from everybody, into his favorite corner on the couch.

Darla walks over and gives him a big hug. "You're right, this is *your* breakup. You've earned the right to run it any way you like. I'm just glad I didn't rush out to swell up like a whale, only to turn you into a single parent."

"Maybe that's exactly what I need – who needs a guy to raise a child anyway?"

I butt in, "You do, Sweetie. It's not as easy and charming as it looks, particularly for someone ...."

"Go on, finish it ... someone as helpless as moi? Well all that is about to change, so *I* can start calling the shots for a change. I'm sick of playing 'always a dumpee, never a dumper'."

"Next thing you know, you'll be someone's bride," grunts Danielle.

Before he can snap back, Randy's cell-phone starts to vibrate like mad. Cyn grabs it and holds it against her crotch. Randy lunges for it. "It's a text message from h-i-m," he barely whispers, eyes widening with hope. ... Few seconds later, all hope is gone – his face is sadder than ever. "I can't believe that he broke up with me in a text message," he sobs into his emaciated hands, "after all the plans we made together."

I grab the phone out of his hand, "Gimme that." I read out loud: bb thing freaking me – need sm time apart. ... "'Need some time apart' doesn't mean he's breaking up for sure, Silly."

"How much time? If he thinks I'm going to wait around forever, he's got another think coming, that Beeach," says Randy, blowing his nose into the Kleenex that Danielle just brought over for him.

Cyn raises her martini-glass, unashamed of drinking so early in the day, "Hallelujah ... *now* you're talking. What you need to do is, make plans for hitting a bar or two with us ... to test-drive the goods. Nothing strokes my ego better than that. ... And sometimes I get more than just my ego stroked," she chuckles devilishly.

Randy looks revived by the idea. He downs a glass of water at the sink and asks, "Can we hit a gay bar? If I'm going to be cheered up, I need some queer cheer."

"Gay bar it is," adds Alison. "And in that case, I think I might just bring someone along."

"You're not already trying to fix me up, are you, Sweetie? I can't stand the thought of doing another relationship thingy so soon after ...."

"Nah, wouldn't dream of it. You just need to go out there and get laid, *without* all the relationship drama! Gotta keep the two separate." The last bit she says with the conviction of a never-mix-business-with-pleasure oath.

This should be interesting, I think, running all the possible scenarios in my head that we could find ourselves in at a gay bar; with one – possibly two – gay guys, two dykes, a straight cougar, an asexual accountant, and a sex-starved mom. Grammy's voice nudges me with, "Don't even go there, Jill." ... I've gotta stop this before it drives me insane. Just wish that for once Jeremy would join me. But if doesn't involve chasing a ball on some court, with star struck co-eds in short skirts that him and his buds can gawk at, chat about, and possibly chat up, he's not likely to participate – they call it their escape from the wives. Watching us plan our night out, he's already gone glassy eyed, imagining his own night out. Just as well that I too escape by myself, since I'm just as capable of having loads of fun, sans his huge, post-two-drink embarrassment factor. This time, I don't even bother with the key.

*   *   *

Woody's is a sight to behold! Black, tufted leather walls connect the black floor to an equally black ceiling, creating a dungeon effect. The only thing lighting the place is the odd barb-wired wall sconce, highlighting a drink ledge, and some neon hugging the underside of the long bar at the far end, right beside the steel doors which lead to a communal bathroom. ... Hope Grammy can't see this – she'd be truly horrified at the thought of a co-ed bathroom. She used to tell me, "Always leave some mystery – no man needs to see you take a dump, shave your pits, or bend over to wipe yourself after a shower. Dress nice and he'll look twice – let it hang out and he'll take another route." ... Mystery or not, the guys in here have no interest in leaving much to the imagination ... and they seem to be doing alright.

It truly is raining men, just like the song vibrating out of the mega speakers is promising. Soon, as if on cue, "I will survive" starts to blare out just as efficiently. Randy jumps up and races to the middle of the dance floor, ready to have his ego stroked – and whatever else might manage to get in the way. Our gorgeous homo-sapien can certainly have his pick, judging by how everyone is trying to brush up against him. "Take a number, guys!" There is Mr. Fishnet T, Mr. Leather Chaps, Mr. Who-Needs-A-Shirt-When-You-Got-Abs-Like-This, Mr. Tight Jeans, and Mr. Average Guy, whose smouldering look screams bound-to-make-up-in-blow-job-skill-what-I-lack-in-eye-candy-way. Haven't seen Randy look this happy since the last time we went out to dinner with him and Steven.

Cyn and I are parked on aluminum bar stools, scattered around one of those high tables. She's dressed to the nines, dare I say looking like a drag queen – I'm sure there's a transvestite somewhere who wants her dress back. I, on the other hand, am barely stuffed into a tight pair of jeans and a daring halter; my brown hair ironed flat to give me the Salma Hayak look that my friends constantly tease me about. ... Still think I should've gone with my comfy, elasticized waist, buffet pants.

Cyn takes it all in and shakes her head, "I think I'm

suffering from a serious case of penis envy. ... If I only ... never mind. Just look at them. What a waste!"

"Randy doesn't seem to think so. At least he's getting into it. That *was* the purpose of this whole exercise, wasn't it?" No response. I shake my head as an afterthought, "Penis envy? Well that's one I haven't had before. The only kind of envy I get is food envy, where what's on everybody else's plate always looks better than what's on my plate."

"Tonight, I think everyone wants the same thing on their plates – a little Chinese," jokes Cyn. "So why is he headed our way?"

Randy traipses to our table and plunks down on one of the empty stools. He wipes his forehead with a napkin and says, "Phew, didn't know I still had it in me. It's been too long – Steven just can't be bothered to take me."

"Know what you mean – isn't Jeremy's scene either. ... A-n-y-way, if you were having such a good time, why did you split up the mellow yellow Randy sandwich back there? We were actually being quite entertained by it."

"Sorry to ruin your fun, girls, but the free show is over. Just don't wanna give them the wrong idea."

"And what might that be?" asks Cyn.

"You even have to ask? For someone who was watching so intently, you sure didn't pay attention. ... Didn't you *see* the way they were dry-humping me – I've practically developed a callus on my ass from it," he says, pointing to his little but, encased in silver lame pants.

"Wasn't *that* the whole idea? To get *over* someone, you have to get *under* someone else?" Cyn winks.

"No, Sweetie. I believe we only negotiated ego stroking. The last thing I wanna do is act like a slut.

Besides, I'm sooo not over Steven yet."

Late as always, in walks Alison, tightly bandaged in black lace – all six feet of her – with a petite East Indian companion by her side. "Hey everybody, this is Rajiv Gupta."

After the customary handshakes and let's-not-ruin-our-lipsticks-Hollywood kisses, Randy offers his seat to Alison and goes back to the dance floor, while Rajiv goes to the bar to buy us a fresh round of drinks. I ask Alison, "So what's the scoop with Rajiv? One of your impotent beaus?"

"Heavens no!"

"Dish it out already then," says Cyn, impatiently.

With hands up in the air, like an I-give-up gesture, Alison says, "Okay, okay! ... Ever since he turned twenty-four last month, his mom's been pushing him to get hitched. But from what he's told me, he's not interested in getting hitched the old-fashioned way. So when I heard that we were coming here, I thought I'd ask him to join us, to help initiate him into the gay scene."

Rajiv is all teeth as he approaches our table. Alison says, "Just look at him, he looks so happy. Betchya he can't believe his good fortune, being surrounded by sooo many prospects."

Once he's up close and personal, she asks, "So, are you gonna dance or what?"

"Sure!" he says, grabbing her hand, trying to pull her up.

After awkwardly bip-bopping with him for a bit, close to our table, I overhear Alison say, "Don't you wanna dance with someone else?" more than likely hoping that he'd take leave and mingle with the guys.

Rajiv responds, "Okay, if you want me to," then points Cyn to the dance floor, and asks, "Shall we?" She agrees and they take off.

I look at them across the dance floor and comment, "They sure seem to be having at least as much fun as Randy and le boyz. Are you *sure* he's gay?"

"He's been bitching about not wanting a traditional relationship, so I just assumed."

"Traditional as in an arranged marriage, or a straight relationship?"

"Ohmigosh, the thought never even crossed my mind."

"So here he is, possibly thinking that he's on a date with you, and you're lining him up for a threesome with Cyn?"

"Fuck, fuck, fuck! How could I be so stupid?"

I tease back, "Well you could always ... you know ... since a relationship isn't really a prerequisite in your books ... or Cyn's for that matter."

"Stop it, you little shit!" she squeals nervously. "So what are we gonna do?"

"Don't look at *me*. ... Speaking of looking, he seems to be getting a lot of attention from that chubby guy over there," I say, pointing to a heavyset, olive-skinned man, with a thick, curled up mustache.

Alison races over to cut in and clarify things, before anything terribly embarrassing happens. But it's too late, the guy has already beat her to the punch and honed in on his territory, as Cyn walks back to us for a breather.

Rajiv looks a little confused, but then recovers rather quickly by breaking into a *Bollywood* style dance routine, seemingly unaware that the guy wants him in another way.

Cyn pulls up a stool and asks, "What's the deal with Rajiv? Is he a bonafide 'mo or does he swing both ways?"

Alison replies, "If the truth be known, I haven't a clue – but I have a feeling that we're going to find out soon enough."

Chubby guy is all over Rajiv now, thanks to his hippy, hippy moves – I wonder if he realizes that in the animal kingdom a bum wiggle is a definite sign of being in heat.. Oops, there he goes, right for an ass grab. Rajiv jumps up in shock and grabs the first babe he sees, for a dance, to end the awkwardness once and for all.

A few dances later, as the two of them appear to be really getting into it, I tease Cyn, "I guess you had your chance, with *had* being the operational word."

Rajiv finally returns to the table and starts to introduce everybody. He then turns to said babe and says, "Sorry, I don't even know your name."

With a deep voice, she answers, "Chuck – but tonight I'm Chiquita."

Rajiv shocks us all with, "No way! As in a cock in a frock?"

"Why, what did you think? I've only been rubbing it against you for the last three songs!"

Rajiv's face drops – he's crushed. Cyn drags him back out to the dance floor, while Alison and I split our sides chuckling. Grammy, I'm sure, is turning in her grave.

I try to brag, "I knew it all along. Anyone with hot, cellulite-free legs like that couldn't possibly be a chick." No sooner do I say that when I see the double Ds marching toward us, with their ultra-long, sans-cellulite legs. "On the second thought, I take that back."

Alison and I gaze at all the pairings. I giggle, "Cyn and Rajiv certainly seem to have what it takes ... on the chemistry front."

"Yeah – young male, experienced female."

"Oh stop being so cynical. They look like they're really getting into each other – dancing close, gazing into each other's eyes."

"A lot of good it's doing. Poor Rajiv looks way too nervous to initiate the first kiss. I feel so bad for dragging him into all of this."

Once they head back to our table, Cyn finally takes charge. She pulls his head close to hers and says, "You gonna kiss me or what?"

Rajiv looks like he's hit the jackpot and is quite happy to oblige. But no sooner do they get into it when Randy decides to have some fun with it, sandwiching Rajiv between himself and Cyn. Cyn mouths a "Fuck off" to Randy and drags Rajiv back to the dance floor, to make out in "private".

Speaking of making out, the double Ds are also going at it ... and look like they're *really* into each other.

Don't know what Dan was worried about, 'cause from what I can see, they appear to have it bad for each other ... totally in love and all that.

How I miss that new love feeling ... and groping.

But I'd even be willing to settle for as little as Jeremy respecting my sexual peak every now and again, falling in sync with me the odd night. ...

After our wild and wacky night, I thought we were onto something, but it fizzled away just as quickly as it came.

I wonder what Grammy did with her sexual peak, if she even had one ... or an orgasm for that matter. On the second thought, I don't think I wanna go there.

The music switches to sexy Latino beats. I look around and realize that the only people who aren't intertwined in one way or another are, Randy, Alison and myself. I say, "Is anyone else hungry?"

Without a moment of hesitation, Alison jumps up, ready to leave, "I could really go for an ice-cream or a crepe."

Randy squeals, "Me too. I'm st-a-a-a-rving."

I tease, "Does this mean that you'll actually swallow something, instead of just moving things around on your plate?"

"Of course, Sweetie. And I'll have you know that lately I've been eating all the time – you know, dating the refrigerator to drown my sorrows?" Grabbing his non-existent fat where love-handles should be, he continues, "Gawd, if I don't go on a diet soon, I'll be no good to anybody."

I reassure him, "Trust me Honey, your market value is still very much intact – way up there to match your high-maintenance needs ... per chance you have to put yourself out there again."

"High maintenance? I'm hurt!" he pouts.

"I just mean that you have exquisite taste. Naturally, there's always too much month left after the money," I laugh.

Alison hands me my purse and says, "Are you guys coming or what? You *do* still want the dish on my not-so-*up*right citizens?"

I grab my purse and we head out. Randy says to Alison, "Please be as '*up* front' as you can."

*   *   *

It's a lovely spring night – warm air, full moon, roads just washed from a light spraying of rain.

We find an ice-cream vendor and grab ourselves a cone each. Randy licks his cone in an obscene way and asks Alison, "Have you tried doing this, to resuscitate the dead organs?"

"That's assuming I want to, and I don't. Although one guy would have given anything to get me to try," she laughs. "He assumed that my request had to do with me never coming across a good enough lover. So of course him and his grandiose cock were going to cure me. ... What a pain in the ass he turned out to be."

I laugh, "Then he must've been sticking it in the wrong hole. ... Any sincere prospects?"

"A few. One in particular. But don't ask me any questions, 'cause there's no way I'm going to tell you anything at this stage. He's a big shot – a household name of sorts – and Randy's big mouth could create problems I'd sooner do without."

Randy looks offended and says, "Who cares who he is – all I wanna know is whether or not he's a good kisser? 'Cause you know what they say about good kissers and their overall oral skills!"

"Is that even legal within your 'no sex' arrangement?" I ask.

Alison smiles, "Depends upon who you ask? A certain president might say that that's not really sex."

Randy jumps in, "Personally, I think that if a genital makes an appearance, it's sex! ... But can you imagine being so *huge* that anyone who spends a bit of quality time with your naughty bits becomes famous for doing just that?"

I ask: "As in president huge or porn star huge?"

"Either way, what a pick up line that would make," Alison chuckles.

Speaking of pick-up lines, there appears to be a hunky pick up artist with black curly hair headed our way, complete with a bouquet of white orchids – Randy's favorite.

Randy's face lights up as he races across the street, seemingly in slow motion, arms open wide for a hug. The soundtrack from *Chariots of Fire* kicks in my head.

"I wonder how the hell did Steven know where to find him?" I ask.

Alison says, "Look," pointing to *my* hot blonde pickup artist, standing right behind him. "I guess he must've let the cat out of the bag." ...

Jeremy walks over and hands me white lilies – my favorite. I hear a scratchy sound as my head switches tracks to Barry White. Maybe there's hope for us after all!

It's amazing what a girls night out will do – sure beats the alternative, where *I'm* the one sitting at home waiting for *him*.

Wonder if I'll get a jealous fuck out of it – I just love it when he gets all animalistic and marks his territory forcefully? And the good behavior which follows.

As we walk back to the parking lot, Jeremy places his jacket over my shoulders, to shield me from the cool breeze that's rising off the water.

Looming across the harbor is Paradise Island, with its private resort and club, "The Pleasure Palace", winking at me.

Too bad I left the key at home, convinced that I wouldn't need it. If I had it on me, we'd be boarding a water taxi right now, to spend the night in the cabin I've rented us for the summer.

Although I was only brave enough to ask for the prude side, where bikinis and water sports are par for the course, we're still allowed to visit the nude side – a decadent sexual oasis with more sin than the Garden of Eden itself...

But don't worry, I'm not planning on venturing out beyond some voyeuristic play, maybe participate in a fantasy theme night or two – I think it'll do wonders for reviving the carnal beast within, when we realize how the other half lives. ...

As for Grammy, she's been willed out of my mind for this one – she'd never approve of forbidden fruits ... or would she? Betchya Darla didn't think that *her* Granny would either!

Chapter 5 – *Man-O-Pause*

Is it that hot flashes that are causing me to sweat, or is it being faced with the most important decision of the decade? The success stories from my catering company have got a major broadcaster salivating for a saucy TV show, with me hosting it.

So what seems to be the problem, you ask?

If the truth be known, it's not as easy as it sounds. Beyond the early call times and long days of slaving over a hot stove – thought my days of doing that were long over – we're talking loads of travel.

Dare I leave at a time like this, when I'm trying my best to get things back on track with Jeremy? Or dare I turn down an opportunity of a lifetime, with more fame, fortune and excitement than I ever imagined? I think of my desperate need to shake things up a bit and find myself saying "Yes" right at the meeting. ... Now if I could only break it to the fam just as easily. The kids will be fine, I'm sure – make that more than fine, not having their overbearing mom breathe down their necks. Okay, so I'm exaggerating just a wee bit here, but you get the picture.

As for Jeremy, that's a whole different story – he always was and always will be the baby of the family, unable to fend for himself, let alone take care of the kids in a barely-there, rudimentary fashion. But passive aggressive that he is, he won't complain directly. Just this once, I wish we could have it out in the open ... followed by some great make up sex.

Momentous as the occasion feels, I decide to throw a little dinner party for my near and dear ones, to break it to all of them at once. I know, I know, I should've told Jeremy first, privately – but at least this way I'm guaranteed that there will be enough merry-making to offset his sulking ... oops, there I go again. I should probably cut him some slack, since I am trying to improve things between us, maybe even get real sex on tap like I used to, instead of mind-fucking myself to death. Then again, can you really blame me after what happened the last time? When Jeremy showed up with flowers, here I'm thinking that it's finally time for my big surprise, but all he did was pout about me abandoning him, by going out with the girls ... didn't even get laid that night. Maybe I should just return the key to marital bliss and lose my first half of the deposit ... *if* they'll let me.

On my way home, I call everyone up and ask them over to dinner. Looks like there will be eight of us – me, Jeremy, Jack, Amber, Cyn, Alison, Randy and Darla – yup, my entire nucleus. I pick up eight Cornish game hens, a jar of uncooked wild rice, a ton of veggies, some brie, a French stick, a green tea cheesecake, and the ingredients for my famous caprese salad.

When Jeremy and I bought this house, it was the dining room that clenched the deal – an oversized entertaining haven, complete with a glass wall overlooking the pool and garden. And what a lovely garden it is, with twinkling lights showing off the shrubbery and floods spotting the Japanese maples oh-so-exquisitely – of course you already know about the amazing pool and waterfalls. Jeremy used to be big into entertaining back then, inviting over fellow docs and clinicians, just to impress them with our *Architectural Digest*-perfect home and my *Good Housekeeping*-perfect cooking. We still have our twelve foot glass table and six foot side table, shining beneath a matching, one-of-a-kind pewter chandelier. ... I can clearly remember every single meal that I've ever served on it – it was my full time job in those days, sans any paychecks of course. ... At times I'd get really frustrated and ask Jeremy to put up my diploma for sale, since it was still in it's never-been-used mint condition. But he would just laugh it off and neglect it like his trophies ... including his trophy wife. I stop myself, before I get carried away by resentment. Tonight's a million miles away from all that – can't ask for better recognition!

The candles are lit, champagne is chilling, and fresh flowers adorn every table. One look and Jeremy will be certain how important this evening is to me – at least as important as all those nights I supported him through his medical internship, Ob-Gyn residency and clinical fellowship. But just in case there's any doubt, I pour myself into a black dress – a long slit baring my left thigh. One false move and Jeremy will be able to see my bikini wax. You could say that I've practically guaranteed it, with my come-fuck-me stilettoes – at five foot zip, a girl can use all the help she can get. I know they hurt a bit – originally I'd only bought them assuming that they'd be pointing up and I wouldn't actually have to *walk* in them – but here I am, forever grounded in them nonetheless.

I wiggle over to our streamlined B&O stereo in the living room and pop in a *Moby* disc. The dreamy tune is eaten up by the cathedral ceiling, overstuffed sofas and Persian rugs. I crank it up a notch and find myself dancing to it, as I make my way into the kitchen – haven't felt this elated since I recaptured my youth during our recent, impromptu, pot party ... maybe longer.

But all that's about to change now. From what I've been told, I'll be traveling across the country to all major cities, doing live demonstrations at celebrated gourmet facilities, camera crew and a handsome co-host in tow. ... Odd that they should pick James Richardson for the job, considering that he's never as much as boiled water. But he *is* the latest greatest, daytime heartthrob, spicing it up in other, more interesting ways. Personally, he doesn't do a damn thing for me, with his delicate Brad Pitt features – I'm more into the masculine George Clooney types, or the witty Steve Martin types. Just as well – don't need anything else to complicate my life right now, though the director is expecting great chemistry for our new *Spice of Life* series. She feels that between James and I, we'll capture the perfect romantic evening, with helpful hints embracing both the kitchen as well as the bedroom. Stepford Wives as it sounds, I'm there, since I myself lust for both great food and gourmet sex. Besides, who is to say that it won't be Stepford Husbands cooking for their career-driven wives?

I hear the garage door open. I pour bubbly into a Waterford crystal flute and greet Jeremy at the door – Stepford Wife style. "What's going on?" he asks, walking into the kitchen, sniffing his favorite meal roasting in the oven.

"Just have a drink, change into something nice and I'll tell you."

Tired and distracted as he looks, he humors me with, "Are the kids busy tonight?"

"No, it's not that kind of an evening," I say flirtatiously, almost wishing that it was.

Jeremy says, "Exc-u-s-e me, for having a one track mind." He then bends over the kitchen counter, offering me his ass, and continues, "You may punish me for that, if you like."

What's with men wanting their asses whacked? My

mind goes back to what Alison had suggested the other night. Dare I take a go at it with my spatula? Before I can decide either way, Amber walks into the kitchen and says, "Ewww – gross!" With my dark hair and her Daddy's amber eyes, she's a sight to behold, ripped jeans and attitude notwithstanding.

I compose myself and ask her, "Honey, could you please change into something nice – we're expecting company."

"Do I h-a-a-a-ve to?" she whines.

"Yes – don't want to hear another word about it!" I reply, in no uncertain terms.

She rolls her eyes, says, "Whatever" and heads upstairs.

My gosh that's the longest conversation we've had in a while. Jack of course is quite different. Not only is he the exact opposite of her in looks – he inherited my blue eyes and his Daddy's blonde hair – he's also very polite, not necessarily more talkative though. He overhears the conversation and says, "What are we celebratin'?"

"Just get cleaned up and you'll find out soon enough," I instruct.

"Sure, Mom," he says and heads upstairs himself – always a man of his word.

I hear the doorbell ring. It's the gang, everyone except Cyn. She's still in the cab, having an animated discussion with the hot cabbie. I let them in, asking, "What's going on with Cyn?"

Randy laughs and says, "Oh she's exchanging digits with some guy she just shared a cab with."

Normally I'd biff his head for that, but I'm so

excited that I just give everybody big hugs. Jeremy makes his way down the stairs and joins in, as do the kids, with Jack's hellos and Amber's grunts.

I walk everyone into the dining room and ask them to take their places – I'm too excited to do the hors d'oeuvres thing ... and it is a week night after all. Normally, someone else should be proposing the toast, but since no one knows what this is all about, I pour some bubbly for everyone, yes, even a sip for each of my teens, and raise my glass. "I have some amazing news to share with you all – hope you can be happy for me."

Everyone is looking at me, as if to say, go on. I take a deep breath and continue, "I've been asked to host a TV show as a gourmet chef, and I've accepted."

Glasses clink, "Here, here," ... Randy jokes, "I'm jealous."

Next thing you know, a flurry of giddy excitement takes over the room – doubly so when I share who my co-host is going to be. With sun-kissed skin and hair, and a pretty face and hard bod to match, the man could be anywhere from late twenties to early forties; his orientation equally dubious. Small wonder he has such mass appeal, even with the likes of Amber – told you the kids will be a cinch. Jeremy of course looks really put off. "I had no idea that you were even working on something like *that*. When do you start filming?"

"I wasn't, it just landed in my lap – like how often does that happen? And I'll be leaving next week for some preliminary stuff."

"*Leaving?*" Jeremy asks.

"Yes, there's a bit of travel involved," I say sheepishly.

As predicted, Mr. Passive Aggressive turns mute. Wish he'd say something. Then again, I expected as much from him. No matter, it doesn't keep the rest of the gang from being happy for me. Amber is particularly beside herself. "They're not going to fucking believe this at school!" she gasps.

"Young lady, watch your language," I say.

Jeremy finally decides to open up his mouth, to hiss, "It's only gonna get worse if her mother isn't around." All that without me even buying him a second drink? Maybe Grammy's ghost is speaking with *him* now – sure sounds like something she'd say.

Cyn barks, "What's wrong with her *father* taking charge for a change?"

I sooo don't need this tonight – this was supposed to be a celebration.

Amber is now furious. She throws her napkin on the table, jumps out of her seat, and starts to leave the room, but not before telling her father how she feels. "Was that *really* necessary? ... I just got carried away by my enthusiasm, what's your excuse?" Silence. "Honestly Dad, you should pay more attention to what comes out of your *own* mouth for a change ... the odd time you decide to grace us with a few words."

Awkward – make that really, really awkward.

Jack whips out the little headphones from the pod in his pocket, and plugs his ears like a stethoscope. It's not in his makeup to walk away in a huff, but he'll do the next best thing – block you out whenever he feels like it. Hope he's not a passive-aggressive in the making.

We finish the rest of our meal in pantomime mode – dead silence and lively expressions.

As I shove a dirty dish into the dishwasher, Alison reaches into her purse and pulls out a tampon. "Do you think Jeremy needs this?"

"Define need," I say, rinsing another dish, before popping it in.

"As in, is he on his period or something?"

Cyn says, "I think he's already got something stuck up his ass – this will only wedge it deeper. ... Don't let him take this moment away from you, Jill."

Easier said than done!

The awkward silence with Jeremy lasts ... oh about a week, bringing us to the morning of my departure. When he goes into a funk like this, unable to show his love, I often wonder if he actually loves me or just *thinks* he does – a love hypochondriasis of sorts. I would've so liked to patch things up, sealed with a bed tremor or two, but not a chance! Jeremy's into letting things brew, even as he tries to convince me that nothing's wrong and *I'm* the one who is making a big deal for no reason. Huh! Does he think that I'm an idiot or something? As a spokesperson for my species, I take pride in saying that women have mastered reading feelings down to an art form. ... At least he didn't assassinate my character this time, through his "helpful" comments – a.k.a. barbs that sink you lower than anything you ever imagined. Wish I was limber enough to sink that low with my limbo skills. Speaking of limbo, I find myself there yet again, with Jeremy's cold goodbye kiss. But the kids more than make up for it, giving me bigger hugs and kisses than all Christmases past – yes, even Amber.

The limo is waiting, so I leave – mixed feelings

taking away from what should be the happiest day of the decade for me. Damn you Jeremy! ... At least I managed to get myself out of the "The Pleasure Palace" deal – though it's a real shame that I had to lose my deposit ... and any chance at grabbing some pleasure with Jeremy.

*   *   *

My preliminary trip is a whirlwind tour of the first four locations that have been scouted out for the initial shoots, not that I have any say in those matters. Personally, I think it's just an excuse to allow James and I a chance to get to know each other. And let me tell you, James is making damn sure of that; not that I mind – the man is unbelievably charming, even off camera. Our PR gal, Lucinda, is practically wetting herself in his presence, promising to make our project her number one priority. But James is more focused on me. ... I catch him eye fucking me and point to my wedding ring. He chortles, "Honey, if I paid attention to symbols, I would never find a parking spot." The man's incorrigible ... and shamelessly flirtatious – probably his way of generating enough chemistry to light the screen on fire. Looking at our promo shots, one would agree that we do. Now if I could only revive my chemistry at home!

We wrap up our preliminary three-day trip in two days and head back. I'm thrilled to be able to surprise Jeremy and hopefully work on patching things up ... maybe even finagle some make-up sex out of the whole thing.

*   *   *

As my limo pulls up to our house, I see a zippy, baby blue Z4 parked in the driveway. I assume that Jeremy has a visitor. Well, he'll just have to get rid of him, 'cause I've got major plans for my husband – more delish than anything I've ever cooked on a stove. I grab my luggage and start to head to the main door. Just then, a cab pulls up beside me. Staring down at my bags, the cabbie asks, "Lady, you order a cab?"

I'm a little confused, so I say, "Not me, but maybe someone inside – let me go check on it for you." I suppose it's a bigger party than I thought.

As I go to open the front door, I'm nearly run over by a tarty, middle-aged woman, Goth makeup making her look like an older version of Jonathan's friend, Marsha. I can't quite imagine her in the Z4, particularly since her carry-on is nothing more than a cheap PVC concoction; but hey, I've been wrong before. Confused, my eyes follow her into the cab, which takes off almost as quickly as she darted out the front door. "Who the hell *was* that?"

I step inside and find Jeremy standing in the main hallway, looking whiter than the marble on the floor. I break the ice with, "You look like you've just seen a ghost – didn't mean to scare you." Awkward silence continues, stiffer than ever! "We wrapped up early, so I raced home, to be with my wonderful husband." God, please let him prove that he truly is wonderful, and remind me of all the reasons I married him in the first place, beyond the lust that's fading fast as of late. Fat chance! Now I'm in my fill-the-silence mode, speaking a mile a minute. "Who was that who just left? ... And who else is here?"

Aha, I seem to have hit jackpot, 'cause this he can answer. "Nobody, just us two," he says, giving me a tighter hug than I've felt in a long time. I guess he *is* happy to see me after all.

"So whose car is that?"

"What?"

"The Z4 – whose is it?"

"Oh that? ... It's mine."

"*Yours*? Exactly when were you planning on telling me about it?" I say, trying my best not to show him the full extent of my irritation.

"Like *you* told me about the offer *you* accepted, after the fact?"

"So that's what this is all about? A little childish, wouldn't you say?"

"You know what they say, 'tit for tat'."

"Since when did we get on opposite sides?" I fume. "And who the hell are 'they' anyway?" I say, thinking *no tit for that.*

"Can't you just be happy for me, like you expect me to be happy for you? ... I'm going through a rough patch, okay? Seriously needed a pick-me-up."

Oh-oh, mid-life crisis has hit him early. Should've guessed, with all the menopausal symptoms he's been experiencing lately – hellova lot worse than anything I've ever seen in a woman. ... Anyhow, think Jillian, think fast to diffuse what is rapidly growing into an ugly situation. I blurt out, "I would've bought it for you myself with my advance, if you'd only given me a chance." Still no response. Half smiling, half staring at his crotch, I add, "You *do* realize that you don't need to compensate for anything!" Told you I say stupid things, just to avoid tension.

Jeremy half smiles back. We hug ... until my next question. "So, who was that leaving here, just as I was coming in?"

"Nobody."

"She sure didn't look like nobody to me." This I say with frustration building up inside me.

Jeremy says, "Nobody you need to be concerned with."

That did it – my patience does have its limits – sorry Grammy. "That's the best you can do?" I snap. "The woman is seen leaving *my* house – I think I have the right to know what she was doing here?"

Jeremy just stands there, head dropped down in shame, like a kid caught with his hand in a cookie jar – or a guilty man caught with his hand in a cookie. Bet he can feel my stare, 'cause after the longest pause, he finally says, "It's not even worth talking about," barely audible. Believe it or not, this is an improvement upon how he usually acts when I need clarification ... in desperate hope of avoiding misunderstandings. Normally, he just runs at the first sign of emotion, like cheap mascara.

The way I'm feeling right now, that may not be a bad idea for myself. In all my dealings with men, I know one thing for certain, when a man says he doesn't want to talk, it generally means he doesn't want to talk. Too pissed to hang around for this, afraid that I'll say things that I might regret later, I do the only thing I can – I walk out, slam the door hard enough to make the whole house shake behind me, and take off for work. Perhaps the girls will be there.

*   *   *

I race up to "The Cocoon", equipped with an emergency tub of Ben and Jerry's black cherry ice cream. "What the fuck am I going to do?" I don't bother with a bowl, just grab a big spoon from the cutlery drawer and plunk myself on the couch. I'm sobbing into my ice cream when I hear footsteps coming up the stairs. Moments later, the door swings open – it's Cyn. Part embarrassed, part relieved, I say a quiet "Hello," maintaining intense eye contact with my ice cream. One look and Cyn's certain that something is horribly wrong – see, I told you that women have reading feelings down to an art form.

Cyn plops on the couch beside me and gives me a genuine hug. "What's wrong, Sweetie?"

I sob, "It's Jeremy. I think he's having an affair."

"What the hell are you talking about?"

"I'm such a fool for burying my head in sand, even though all the signs were there – him being cold and distant ... needing more and more time by himself for his "hobbies" ... secretive e-mails and phone conversations ... unexplained VISA bills ... never letting me in on anything, just keeping me in the dark all the time ... not touching me as often as he used to, and certainly not as imaginatively as he used to, rarely complimenting me anymore ...."

"Stop, you're making me dizzy! You need to calm down – all that stuff is hardly proof that he's getting it on the side. To me it sounds like standard bored husband stuff, who is taking you for granted and can't be bothered to share his life with you anymore."

"I know, I know. I must sound totally paranoid to you, although he did cheat on Cathy with me, and had a reputation long before that – even his mother swears that I'd be foolish to think that his dick is safe with me. ... But this goes way beyond all that."

"You're scaring me."

"I'm scaring *me*. And it's about time. Too bad I had to actually run into her for that to sink in – but what an eye opener!"

"Run into whom?"

"The old bag hussy who was leaving our house as I was coming in. Of course Jeremy refuses to tell me who she is and what the hell she was doing there."

"That's odd. There's got to be another explanation. Could she be a massage therapist ... a psychotherapist ... or something else like that," she tries. "Some guys are embarrassed to admit to shit like that."

"She didn't look like any therapist of any kind that *I've* ever known of."

"Gimme more details," she says, almost chocking up. In all the years that I've known Cyn, I've not once seen her cry, tender as she is deep down. It just wouldn't match up with her tough exterior. She's the one who is supposed to keep it all together for the rest of us.

Watching her face waiting in anticipation, I say, "She looked like a fifty year old hooker – or a crack whore."

Furious, Cyn says, "If he was going to fool around, did he have to be so original about it? You'd think he'd at least have the decency to pick a twelve pound, anorexic embryo – like any self-respecting man his age – one that we could all hate, instead of some old cow who must make you feel just awful!"

"I wish it were that simple."

Cyn tries to do what she does best – side with me compassionately, while using humor to get a smile out of me. "Men are like laxatives – they irritate the shit out of you." No smile. She continues, more seriously this time, "Doesn't he realize what he has with you? How could he be so stupid?"

"Easily, I'm sure," I say, embracing the cynic in me.

Cyn grabs the spoon out of my hand, takes a big

gulp of ice cream for herself and says, "What are we going to do?"

"I've had my heart broken before – I'm sure I'll get over it."

"Well it's hardly over yet. We need to find out more. Want me to go home with you, to have a little chat with him and straighten things out?"

"No thanks – though I probably should go home and get to the bottom of this." I hand Cyn the minuscule remains of my ice cream and head out, before I lose my nerve.

I hear her yell after me, "Be firm. You give the guy an inch, and suddenly he become a ruler."

*   *   *

I start to drive home, quite upset, nearly clipping a biker with my Porsche. The back of my head and neck is all pins and needles, from the close call. When will I learn never to drive when I'm that upset? I pull over and compose myself. ... After a while, I complete my drive home.

*   *   *

I park my Porsche beside the Z4 and march in.

Jeremy greets me at the door: "We need to talk."

Of the many things that my touchy-feely, emotion-loving, feminine side knows, one thing's for certain: no conversation which begins with "We need to talk" is ever going to be a pleasant one ... with one exception, I suppose. When Jeremy proposed to me, it wasn't on bended knee. It was a serious "We need to talk" conversation, where he had me going with "I'm not happy with how things are going between us anymore" – could've fooled me, since I thought things were pretty damn good. But then came the grande finale – "So, I guess it's time for a change ... that is, if you'll agree to marry me." ... Back to reality – somehow I don't think it's a proposal this time. All the same, I have to give him a chance to speak up, instead of jumping to all the wrong conclusions. God, please let me be wrong with this one!

Jeremy says, "About the girl you saw leave here before – it's not what you think."

My heart wants to say "That was no *girl*," but my head spurts out, "Go on."

"Go on, nothing – it's just not what you're thinking."

"Well, what is it then?"

"Nothing to worry your pretty little head over," he says, giving me a condescending kiss on my forehead.

I'm fuming now, for him making it sound like he's actually doing me a favor ... protecting me even, by keeping me in the dark. Well fuck that! I snap, "Until you tell me what 'it' is, or who *she* is, I will worry, dammit! ... Wouldn't you, if the tables were turned?"

"Not really."

Don't know which lie I hate more, the "Not really" kind or the "That's different" kind. For the record, it's *always* different with him, and *never* his fault. At least he didn't compare my paranoia to my mother this time. In all the years that he's done that to me, I haven't once compared him to anyone – or said anything nasty for that matter, like he does. But he can't seem to find it in his heart to be at least as respectful – he's the only guy I know who can play both defense and offense, often at the same time. ... All this, after I've stood by him through so much, keeping my hurt feelings to myself. ... Seeing that we're done here, I simply walk away. Wonder what Grammy would've done?

I'm just about to pour myself a glass of something that burns the throat going down, to know that I'm not dreaming this, when the phone rings. The call display tells me it's Alison. I guess Cyn must have called her – how else would she know that I'm back? I pick up, and sob, "Hi Hun."

She sounds surprised to hear my voice. "You home already? ... I mean of course you're home." Why, who else was she calling?

"So Cyn never called you?"

"Nope. Should she have?"

"Why else were you calling then?" I ask impatiently.

She hesitates and then says, "I was just going to leave you a message about the Chanel warehouse sale – you know, to ask you if you'd like to go with me? I handle the account for one of their local VPs, so I have this exclusive pass for me and a friend."

"Maybe a bit of retail therapy is just what the doc ordered," I sob, quite unsure of myself.

"What's wrong – you sound awful. Did you get sick while you were away? ... Small wonder you're back early."

"I'm not sick, okay? I just found out that Jeremy's been up to no good behind my back, right in our home. Of course he's not willing to talk about it. ... Oh yeah, and I almost forgot, he just bought himself an expensive car without consulting me. ... The car I can handle, but an affair – how predictable is that?"

"Calm down, I'm sure it's nothing," she says.

Of all the things that I anticipated Alison would say, that was definitely not it! At the very least, I expected her to call Jeremy a bastard, followed by her diatribe on men and mixing relationships with sexuality – but never *this*.

"How the hell can you say that?" I ask, enunciating each word clearly and slowly, like I'm talking to a foreigner, just in case she didn't understand me for some stupid reason.

"Trust me on this one – I think you're just over-reacting."

"Is there something I'm missing here?"

"Don't know what to say, other than you have nothing to worry about."

Unless she's planning a surprise party for me with Jeremy, and that hooker was my strip-o-gram, I don't know what to think anymore. What if Alison was actually calling *Jeremy* before, not me? If so, what about? Could she possibly know something? Nah – don't wanna go there. But don't want to continue this conversation either.

"Is *that* it?" I snap, my mind racing a mile a minute – better that, than my mouth. Maybe she'll provide Jeremy with the perfect alibi. I'm sure that would make a great side business for her – providing alibis for cheating hearts, since they resonate with her philosophy on keeping sex and relationships apart.

I say, "I just need to be left alone right now!" and hang up.

Chapter 6 – *A Little Pick Me Up*

Whoever said, never confide in your girlfriends, 'cause in the name of friendship they'll talk you out of anything – a good husband, a great job – should have also added "and talk you *into* anything", 'cause believe you me, if it weren't for my partners in crime, I wouldn't be driving out to a Botox party right now.

I look to the left and to the right, making sure that no one sees me pull up into a cosmetic surgery clinic, tucked away in the woods as it is. You see, I'm a Botox virgin, unlike the others, who've been there, done that, and are now hooked. Normally, the thought of having botulin toxin injected in my face would scare me to death. But seeing how happy my comrades are with their results, far be it from me to be a "party" pooper. Besides, we can all use a little "pick-me-up" every now and then, can't we – Jeremy has his Z4!

I park my Porsche in the shady parking lot and look at myself in my rear-view mirror. Using my index fingers, I pull up my brows just a wee bit, then pull them apart to get rid of the two little worry lines in the middle. Next, I pull apart my cheeks, while lifting them up ever-so-slightly. I feel like a little kid making scary faces, only the face that looks back isn't scary at all – it's a younger version of me. I decide to go for it – the free consultation in any case – before I lose my nerve. The girls did say that there was needle waiting with my name on it, one that could treat lines deeper than Barry White's voice.

Uncertain as I feel, I'm now inside the clinic. Wow, the decor is impeccable! I feel like I just walked into Caesar's Palace in Vegas – only the marble sculptures in here are fitter, thinner, without an ounce of saggage. The carpet is a rich burgundy, the walls a marble faux finish in gold and ivory. And then there's the vaulted ceilings, painted to look like a perfect sky, soft valence lighting bringing it to life. I'm quite impressed – if someone's gonna mess with my face, might as well be someone with such attention to aesthetic detail.

As I step inside the waiting area, I'm greeted by Adonis in a tux, a cosmetic surgery marvel I'm sure – no one is born *that* perfect. He takes my jacket and leads me to an overstuffed, emerald love-seat, nestled amongst lush palm trees and a tranquility waterfall. Next, he offers me a drink, reciting about ten different choices of flavored, bottled water – no booze at this party, not if you're shooting up other toxins. I ask him for cucumber flavored water and grab an album on the side table, to peruse *before* and *after* pictures of famous Botox clients. I wonder if they can inject some into my boobies, to perk them up a bit? Or inject some butt fat into my lips? Wouldn't that be ironic – Jeremy kissing ass every time he kisses my lips. It will be the only butt fucking he'll ever get – *if* I decide to blow him – not the other kind that he's been pushing a lot lately.

My revere is interrupted by a cackling bunch walking my way. It's the girls – the whole lot of them – and my favorite tall, dark and handsome man. What the hell is Dan doing here, I find myself wondering. Instead of the usual hugs and kisses, everyone goes Hollywood on me, with faux, air kisses. Just as well, 'cause Alison looks very uncomfortable around me – as she should.

The girls barely plop into matching chairs around me, when Cyn blurts out, "So, did you talk to the bastard?" I nod. "Well ... what did he have to say for himself?"

"Not much, other than how wrong I was in my assumptions ... and how I was over-reacting when I had nothing to worry about."

"Over-reacting? What a bastard! How can he say that after he got caught?" Cyn hisses.

Alison finally adds, "Would you cut the guy some slack – it could be as innocent as he says it is."

All heads swing in her direction, with the speed of light. Darla says, "What the hell has gotten into you? If he's innocent, why can't he just explain away the misunderstanding and put her mind at ease?"

Alison is really pissed now, being outnumbered. "Yup, leave it to your girlfriends to talk you out of a perfectly good marriage."

"How nice of you to not act like my girlfriend, in that case," I say sarcastically.

After the longest ten seconds of dead air, Dan finally blurts out, "On behalf of the lesser half of the species, guys do stupid things – we pass gas to amuse ourselves ... get excited about the size of our dump." This time all heads swing over to Dan, looking even more confused than before, wondering what the hell he's talking about. He notices, and starts up again. "What I'm trying to say is ... when it comes to us acting crazy, especially around women, it's rarely as complicated as anything you might imagine. ... All I can say is, no man in his right mind would ever want to lose you, Jillian."

"Obviously *my* man would. Why else can't he just be honest with me?"

"'Cause you'd be *really* pissed if he said, 'Honey, I'm going through a mid-life crises and might need to be validated by other women – maybe even try out some stuff – but hey, if I don't get laid, you shouldn't give me a hard time over it'."

"Yeah right! ... Even though all that bullshit might *un*-validate me in the process."

"I know what you're thinking – if I was pretty enough, exciting enough, listened more, complained less, spent more time doting on him, and all that other stuff you girls worry about unnecessarily. But the bottom line is, it has *nothing* to do with any of that. Just ask Hugh Grant."

"Since Hugh isn't here at the moment, pray do tell, what else does it have to do with in that case?"

"A whole bunch of guy stuff, as you see your life winding down and realize this is it – stuff that has absolutely *nothing* to do with anyone else."

"*Guy* stuff? I got news for you – don't you think *I* feel disappointed in *my* unfulfilled dreams?"

Cyn cuts in with, "Honey, you're forgetting something – we don't dream from our dicks."

Dan laughs, "You would, if you had one. It's the whole 'why do dogs lick their balls' thing – 'cause they can."

"Okay, Mister, since you claim to know man-kind so well, what does it mean if he says 'We're just hanging out, not having an affair'?"

"In guy-speak, that means – in as much as I'd like to sleep with her, I won't ... 'cause I cherish my relationship with you *way* more than that."

"Why would he want to sleep with *her* in that case?"

"We're men ... so we want to sleep with *every*body, but the important thing is that we don't. ... Haven't you ever drooled over a dress, only to put it back 'cause it was too expensive?" Everyone stares at Dan, as if to say "and?".

"Did you feel guilty desiring something you couldn't have, if you never closed the deal?"

The way I'm feeling right now, I could sure use some guilt-free thoughts around Dan – who gives a damn about a stupid dress? I save face with, "Even though that's *completely* different, you're suggesting I just lay low, until I'm certain that I truly have something to worry about?"

"Bingo!" says Alison, beating Dan to the punch.

Our chit chat is interrupted by Dr. Brown, a skinny doc – make that very skinny, since he can easily make Randy look huge by comparison. He's friendlier than any doc I've ever known – no boundaries here. He clears his throat, claps his hands in a chop chop mode, and says, "Gather up everybody. Time to get to know each other better." ... After everyone is seated in a circle, he asks us to go around the room, introduce ourselves, and share what special occasions are coming up for each one of us – the ones that we're hoping to be in tip top shape for.

I share my need for a post cheating husband pick-me-up – no, the pep talk didn't take – only to get a no-no-no finger gesture from the good doc, followed by, "I recommend you do this for yourself, not anyone else – least of all, someone who doesn't deserve you."

Cyn goes next, sharing her penchant for young flesh, and wanting to look at least as good. Darla too is now courting her own young sweet thang and wants to feel "uplifted" for when she meets the fam on the weekend. And Alison just loves to spend money on whatever is vogue and will make her look hot – why, I'll never know.

It's now Dan's turn. He says, "I'm just here to offer a bit of immoral support. If the girls have to sit up straight for six hours, unable to bend over, I'm their beck-and-call guy."

My mind conjures up a wicked image of Dan bent over, but I quickly shake my head to rid it of its lascivious thoughts. I know, I know, you're probably thinking that whole goose gander thing, but I don't believe in grudge fucks. Besides, while men can feel better if they get laid in such situations, women generally feel worse. ... Fucking aside, if someone has to help me slip out of my heels or into my car anyway, it might as well be Dan.

Dr. Brown – "Call me Bobby" – starts off by taking Darla into the treatment room. I'm too much of a chicken to volunteer to go first. Besides, I'm not sure what I'd like done, just yet. I ask the girls, "So exactly which parts can he fix?"

Alison jumps in with, "Frown lines, worry lines, crow's feet, opening up the eyes – you name it, he can do it. ... Even if you want to fix deeper laugh lines that are nothing to laugh about – but that's a different injectable. ... And then there's a whole nip-tuck menu – why work your ass off every waking hour of your day, when you can easily have it fixed by a surgical knife while you're asleep."

"How about the boobies, or tightening up my pink parts down below?" I say, half-jokingly.

Cyn responds, "You can tighten up your pink parts *yourself!*"

"Is there a do-it-yourself kit for that?"

"You know what I mean. You *do* do your Kagel's, right?"

I know full well what Kagel's are, but I put her on the spot in any case, to get a "rise" out of Dan.

Cyn makes a fist and says, "You know, squeeze release, squeeze release, harder and longer as you get the hang of it."

I hope and pray that Grammy isn't watching this – sharing such secrets in front of the opposite sex goes way beyond letting them find out that we actually shave our pits ... and aren't naturally Barbie-smooth. I smile mischievously, "We're all squeezing our love muscles right now, aren't we?" hoping to shock Dan ... and Grammy, if she happens to be watching – that'll teach her!

Dan shakes his head in disbelief and gets up. "I think that's my cue to sneak off and get some coffee for all of us – this place only has bottled water and herbal tea."

"But many fla-vors," I say flirtatiously. If Dan's skin wasn't so dark, bet he'd be beet red right now!

It's now my turn to go in. Boy that was fast – I guess Darla's beautiful skin barely needed any tweaking.

I feel like a pin cushion – after having what feels like millions of needles injected into me, every which way. This had better work! For what it's worth, the fillers have already taken effect in my smile lines and lips, which are now curling out and looking quite plump – not Angelina Jolie plump, just teen plump – who knew that people would actually pay good money to get a fat lip.

My eyebrows have also started to lift up – hope I don't end up looking like Spock, when all is said and done. Don't go there, Jill, the girls swear by Dr. Brown – sorry, Bobby.

One by one, we're pinched, poked, and uplifted. True to his word, Dan takes care of us. He offers to buy us manicures and pedicures, to help keep us upright instead of uptight. We agree, under the condition that he join us – not that it's a hard sell, the female-lovin', metro-sexual that he is!

Dan's totally game and suggests that we all squeeze into his Lexus SUV. ... As I'm about to climb into it, It occurs to me that I forgot my new book in my car – *Sex Tips For Straight Women From a Gay Man.* I'd once read that bedroom boredom rarely happens to individuals – more often than not, it happens to the couple. Meaning, if you're dissatisfied, chances are, so is your partner. Whether or not, I felt that every relationship can use a little pick-me-up and bought the book earlier today ... just in case. Sure hope that Jeremy and I can work things out and seal the deal with a genital reunion. ... I start to descend from the SUV as stiffly as I was trying to get in, saying, "Be right back."

Dan asks, "Where do you think you're going?"

"Just have to pop into my car for a second to grab my book. I hate the outdated magazines they have at the nail place."

"You'll do no such thing, Miss. Gimme your keys and I'll get it for you."

How I love being addressed that way – sure beats Ma'am. But I'm not crazy about the idea of Dan bringing *that* book to me. ... Oh hell, he'll see me read it in any case. Reluctantly, I hand over the keys to my Porsche.

Dan holds up my keys and laughs, "Okay Girls, I'm off. You're on your own."

A few minutes go by. What the hell is taking him so long? Hope he isn't flipping through the book. I feel my face go hot with embarrassment, as I finally see him head back our way, book bag in hand. Without as much as a word or a wisecrack, he hands it to me and we take off. Wonder what kind of a driver he is? They say that you can learn everything you need to know about a man by the way he drives – betchya Dan's fast, confident, and courteous, unlike Jeremy's reckless, self-centered ways.

*   *   *

Half an hour later, we arrive at the nail place, looking like the cast of *Riverdance*, stiff above the waist, respecting the no bending rule. I catch a glimpse of myself in his side mirror and feel amazing! Once inside our favorite Korean nail place, we take over the entire joint, sitting side by side on vibrating chairs, feet soaking in jetted spas. I can't believe how awesome this feels. The aesthetician starts to rub my feet with mint jelly, putting me right to sleep. But the Guardian Angel that Dan is, he's not having any of it – it's his self-appointed job to keep our heads vertical. He wakes me up with a real eye-opener. "Come on sleepy head, it's time for a little sex talk. ... Hey, as long as I'm here anyway, I might as well teach you girls a thing or two – no charge." He then winks at me and goes on to say, "Should be right up your alley."

Betchya he flipped through the book and has been biding his time to savor this very moment. "Isn't that Cyn's job?" I ask coyly.

"What would you rather – a man or a woman teach you about blow-jobs?"

Darla laughs, "That depends – are we blowing men or women in this lecture?"

"Men," laughs Dan. "Sorry, Hun, you're a little outnumbered."

Darla teases back. "And what would *you* know about blowing men? Given one a blow-job lately?"

"Duh! We're talking advice from the horse's mouth, on what feels good? Isn't it better that way, Jillian?" The last bit is a definite dig about the book.

102

I blush, "That's awfully cocky of you, but what the hey, show us what you got. ... Wait, I take that back – just teach us what you know from a guy's perspective."

Dan takes a rolled up face towel and pretends it's a penis. Using his hands and mouth he teaches us everything from the juicer to the cockscrew. While we all laugh our heads off, the Korean girls just drop their heads down and converse feverishly in their native language. For anyone who has ever wondered whether or not they talk about their clients, this time I'm sure of it ... and rightfully so.

Alison watches Dan's complicated moves and says, "That looks like a lot of work."

Cyn says, "Hence it's called a blow-*job*."

The Korean girls aren't impressed. Out of respect for them, I say, "Come on guys, let's talk about something else."

Dan suggests we play a little game. Starting with me, we are to share the happiest memory of our lives, with one minor caveat – if we were to die, we'd have to live out that memory forever. So much for getting married, giving birth, best orgasm, scariest roller-coaster ride, most succulent meal, etc, etc. Naturally, I decide to go with something lower key, like the picnics Jeremy and I used to go on. Hey, what better way to include great conversation and R&R with gourmet sex and food! ... How I miss those picnics. I wonder if we'd indulged more often, would we be better connected?

It's now Cyn's turn. She picks the time when she took her kids to Disney and they ended up talking for hours, as they waited excitedly through various lineups.

Darla picks the first time she was true to herself, sexually.

Alison picks the first sleep-over she had at her place, when we spent the entire night innocently chatting about boys – long before cynicism and jaded views took hold, thanks to being hurt umpteen times, I'm sure.

Oddly enough, Dan picks the night at "The Cocoon", when we threw our private surprise party for Darla's fortieth – a wink at me confirming that he's just yanking my chain, albeit quite effectively. Go away Grammy!

Three hours fly by quickly, between blow-job demos and special moments. One thing is for certain – life isn't necessarily about big gestures that would be hard to sustain, more like the little things that bind us to those we love. Gosh how I wish I could believe in Jeremy ... and our marriage, recapturing what we once had ... yes, including blow-jobs, now that I have new skills to try out. Maybe the bed tremors weren't so bad after all. If only I could trust him again. ... Why is it that we stray so far away from that giddy feeling that tells us that we can't survive without someone? ... *When* do we stop seeing the good in them?

* * *

With the drive there and back, and the three plus hours at the spa, we're now close to the six hour mark. Time to go home and face Jeremy with my new face ... or maybe not. At least the kids will be amused, with me being unable to frown at them.

* * *

I drive straight home and pull into the garage – kids must be out, 'cause their cars aren't here. Once inside the house, I smell my favorite food – Jeremy's homemade cannelloni. Barry White is filling the house, as is the special scent from the incense that we bought in the little Indian place down the street from us. I'm half expecting some crack-whore to knock me over on her way out, when Jeremy walks up to me and asks if he could have this dance. I let him take me into his arms – better that than have him inspect my face closely.

Can't remember the last time he held me like that, cheek to cheek. Alas, I pull back, to look into his eyes. I gaze, and gaze, and gaze, looking for lord knows what ... and then I find it – the same warm feeling we used to share through our picnics. He strokes the side of my face with his hand, ever so tenderly, and I find myself kissing it gently. Jeremy leans down into me, to kiss me back, but then stops short ... almost as if asking for my permission. I let him – I need to know what I'm feeling inside.

My breathing quickens, part pain, part longing. There's so much still left between us, so much worth fighting for, especially if Jeremy truly hasn't done anything uncontainable. Hey, don't knock denial until you've tried it – it's the ultimate form of optimism.

Wish I knew the truth.

The music stops, but we keep dancing. ... Eventually, Jeremy scoops me up into his arms, like he did so many years ago, and carries me over to the picnic he's laid out on the floor, right in front of the fireplace. The glow of the fire is much brighter than the dim lighting I've been hiding in so far. Jeremy studies my face and says, "You look very different tonight – brings back memories of happier times." Whether it's my new face or the vulnerability in my eyes, I don't know, much less care. "Dinner will be a while – can I interest you in some cheese and grapes?"

I let him cut me a thin slice of brie and wrap it

around a grape, just like old times. As I put it into my mouth, he moves behind me and sits as close to me as possible, spooned up into my back. He's now rubbing my neck and shoulders – I find myself aching for so much more. As I nuzzle into him, like a cat about to purr, he kisses the top of my head and says, "I can't believe how beautiful you are," – not younger, just beautiful. Then again, young doesn't seem to be his criteria, based on what I recall from a few days ago. I tense up. Don't go there, Jill – you're ruining everything. ... But dammit, I can't help it!

"You seem so tense. Would you like me to massage the rest of your body?"

"I'd like nothing better than to get rid of all this tension, but not the way you're suggesting. ... I really need to know that you trust me enough to share openly with me, and that I can still trust you after that."

Jeremy walks over to the sofa and plunks himself in the corner, head hanging down in shame, cradled into his palms. "I really don't want to get into this, but I want to lose you even less."

"Then talk to me, dammit!" I say, showing my frustration through my inflection. Lucky for him, I'm unable to frown. I wonder how many relationships could be saved by Botox keeping people from frowning at each other.

Jeremy finally musters up enough courage and says, "Okay, I guess I owe you that much. ... The woman you saw the other day is a Pro Domme."

"A pro what?"

"A Pro Domme."

"Meaning?"

"A professional Dominatrix."

"What?"

"You heard me."

"And what the *hell* were you doing with her? ... You want pain – the way I'm feeling right now, I'd be more than happy to cause you some *serious* pain."

"There you go, jumping to conclusions again. ... It's not always about pain, you know. True, some people are into hardcore S&M and are looking for it. But most people are like me – just interested in trying out a little bondage and discipline. It's the ultimate theater where you can lose yourself in something different ... embrace dark parts within yourself ... perhaps even get punished for your screw-ups. ... We're just talking a little costuming and some slap and tickle – pretty harmless stuff."

"Is *that* it?" I say sarcastically, wondering if there's any truth to what they say about a man's sexual preferences tying into his philosophy on life.

I wonder what Grammy thinks of Jeremy now? Knowing her, she'd probably expect me to play along.

Grammy once told me that whenever Grandpa asked her to try out something unsavory, she just learned to acquire a taste for it. She said it was like marmite – kinda gross at first, but okay once you got used to it. I wonder how Jeremy developed *his* taste?

"Honey, I go through my days in rote, like a zombie – living the *predictable* life of a man with loads of responsibly ... only to face one disappointment after another. I guess I just needed to experience something different to feel alive – not sexual, just different. ... So you see, it's not like I was cheating or anything."

"Let's not go there, okay? Firstly, the Zombie thing is your own doing – you thrive on chipping away at accomplishments. Secondly, aren't *you* the guy who agreed with Harry from *When Harry Met Sally,* that if a man is doing *anything* with a woman, he's bound to be thinking sexual thoughts? Finally ... and most importantly ... why couldn't you have asked *me* to try that out with you?"

"I would've, if I thought you'd consider it, without judging me ... or thinking that I'm a pervert."

"How presumptuous of you to think that of me."

"Oh come on. It's not like I didn't try to test the waters."

"What the heck are you talking about?"

"Remember that night, after I delivered Mrs. Johnson's baby? I tried something a little different and you immediately slipped into your own little world, assuming the most heinous things, I'm sure. You're our worst enemy."

I know he's referring to the night when we tried some rough stuff and I drifted into dreamland, thinking about how much fun "The Pleasure Palace" was going to be. But now I find out that *he's* the one who was assuming the worst of *me*. I guess that explains why that night never repeated itself. Furious, I hiss, "*I'm* our worst enemy?"

"Okay, then tell me, if I'd asked you to go the whole nine yards with me, would you have gone for it?"

I think hard, searching deep within myself, unsure of how far I'd be willing to go. "Who knows – but it would've been nice to have been asked."

"Would it *really*?"

"You'd be amazed at what I'd be willing to try out."

"Really?"

"Really! ... How about clearing up your calendar next weekend and going away with me – just the two of us." Better me than someone else, right Grammy?

"You mean that?"

I barely say, "You bet," and the oven timer goes off. ... Phew, saved by the bell.

What was I thinking? What did I just get myself into ... do I even know?

I guess it's just as much my responsibility to salvage this marriage as it is Jeremy's. At least the talk helped me see that – wonder if Jeremy realizes that a good long talk can cure just about anything. ... I am now more committed than ever to make this thing work.

Brace yourself Honey, the lusty girl you married is about to make a major comeback – equipped with some new blow-job skills and serious blow-job lips! ... Now if I could only have someone give me a few tips on spanking Jeremy's sorry ass. Dare I ask Cyn ... or maybe Alison, since she did suggest it back when? ... How the hell did she know that Jeremy would like that? It's almost as if she was somehow in on it all along, right down to the "innocence" of the crack-whore incident – sorry, the Dominatrix incident. I wonder what she's holding out on me? Whatever it is, I'm not going to worry about it right now – there's sex in the cards.

Chapter 7 – *In-Laws and Out-Laws*

I think back to the night that Darla came out to her parents, feeling the pressure from Danielle. You'd think a girl who didn't want to be kept secret would already have her own house in order. But guess what, Danielle hasn't told her parents either – all the Goldstein's know is that their lovely Jewish Princess got engaged behind their backs and is now bringing home the fiancée. When will we learn that after-the-fact-shock-value isn't what it's cracked up to be? But being the great friends that we are, we're all headed to their retirement community in Florida, to support Darla when she's delivered at their doorstep in the wrong sex, colour and religion. Wonder what will shock them the most? One thing is for certain, they're expecting a nice Jewish lawyer who they can say *mazel tov* to – possibly over a big showoff party – not a Black, Catholic Dyke who'll bring out the *oye ways* in them.

Seeing that the trip is going to be challenging enough, we decide to charter a Beachcraft – it's one of those deals where they're training someone on their first passengered flight, so you get to fly along for the price of fuel. Now I know what you're thinking – this is supposed to *relax* us, not take our anxiety through the roof. Rest assured, the guy already has over five-hundred flight hours under his belt and a supervisor above his belt.

As I step inside the plane, I realize that I've been traveling the wrong way all this time – this baby is first class the whole way. It feels like a living room where we can actually face each other comfortably, instead of having the guy in front of you land in your lap, and the kid beside you puke into said lap.

As I'm trying to figure out all the bells and whistles on my seat, a six foot two hunk takes my hand in his and shows me how. Of course Cyn is drooling and asks him to ring her bell too. Wish Jeremy was with us – the way I'm feeling right now, I'd be willing to give the Mile High Club a go. ... Oh, in case you're wondering, my wastelands are definitely starting to turn into wetlands again.

The flight is now well on its way and we're coasting along smoothly at an altitude where we can unbuckle and relax – though looking at Danielle, she's anything but. I ask her, "What's wrong?"

"Hope you brought black with you, 'cause I have a funny feeling that we'll be attending my funeral."

"They're not going to kill you."

"Maybe not physically, but for all intents and purposes, I'll be dead to them the minute they find out. ... And I'd be willing to bet that they'll even keep a *shiva* for me."

"What's that?"

"Eight days of mourning ceremonies which follow a funeral."

"To make sure the funeral takes?" I try to joke, to lighten her up a bit. But she's not smiling. She looks as serious as they come. Told you I was no good with jokes.

Randy interjects, "At least you won't be getting guilt messages in your voice mail like Darla has been, from her parents. They leave them during the day when she's bound to be at work, giving her something to come home to. ... The one time that she was working from home, she picked up the phone and they hung up, knowing full well that she has call display. Talk about cowards."

"Hey, at least they're still acknowledging her existence. Take it from me, the Catholics have nothing on us Jews when it comes to guilt."

Darla rolls up her eyes and grunts, "Wanna bet?" I can tell that she's pissed at the irony of the whole situation, after how her birthday party was ruined, thanks to intense pressure from Danielle.

Randy chimes in, "As long as we're comparing, I got news for you both – Chinese parents definitely take the cake. ... My brother had to die for it ... and *I* might as well be dead too, as far as they're concerned."

"What are you talking about?" asks Danielle, in an irritated voice. Her expression has the telltale signs of someone who isn't taking Randy terribly seriously – he *is* a drama queen after all.

"Didn't Darla tell you?"

"Tell me what?" she huffs.

"The whole deal with my brother, Wayne?" he chokes up.

"Is it going to make me feel better?"

"Probably not – though you'll agree that nothing your parents do will quite match up."

"In that case, spill already."

"My older brother was also queer and obviously didn't wanna get married – not to someone without a cock anyway. But since he was supposed to carry on the family name, my parents pushed and pushed and pushed, even though he wasn't having any of it. ... Eventually, they had the bloody gall to actually arrange a marriage for him, when we went to visit our relatives in the Hakka community in Calcutta – that's Chinese dwellers in India, mostly involved in the leather trade. Anyhow, my brother had taken his 'best friend' – a.k.a. lover – with him ... so all hell broke loose when he found out. He issued an ultimatum and my brother promised that he'd take care of it. Long story short, Wayne talked to the girl and told her everything, offering her immigration and a fab lifestyle on the family mullah, in exchange for keeping his secret and giving our parents a Chinese grandson. Of course she'd have to figure out a way of getting pregnant on her own, without expecting Wayne to provide the swimmers – not the old-fashioned way, in any case. ... A-n-y-how, the girl agreed and Wayne hugged her to show his gratitude. Unfortunately, his idiot lover was spying on them, misinterpreted the hug, and decided to go for a murder suicide ... shot 'em both and himself right then and there, without bothering to talk first. I'm guessing he felt that if he wasn't going to have Wayne, he'd better make damn sure that neither would anyone else." Randy is now crying and we're all stilled by silence. After the longest pause, he sobs, "But even though my brother had to die for it, my parents never accepted what *really* happened. I tried my damndest to explain it to them, but they fuckin' refused to listen. ... And before *I* could come out, I was kicked the hell out – under the stupid pretense that I was dishonoring my brother's memory. ... Cowards, I tell you! They knew damn well what went down that night and where our little ret e tet was headed next." Randy pauses to wipe his eyes and pulls himself up a little higher in his chair. Following a deep breath, he finishes up with, "But no matter, despite all their bullshit, I turned out *great*, thanks to my friends."

Tears are welling up in Danielle's eyes, probably more for what lies ahead of her, than what lays behind Randy. But the sentiment is appreciated by him nonetheless, expressed by a big hug, as she says, "I'm so sorry, I had no idea," sounding quite genuine.

I of course, slip into my own little world, battling

my *own* demons. While Randy and Darla miss their fathers and Danielle is worried about losing hers, I wish I never had one – for all the times that he touched me like he shouldn't have. I'm not talking all out sexual abuse, just enough of thigh stroking to creep me out and make me wanna die. I felt so ashamed and confused that I didn't know who I could turn to. Besides, speaking of it would've only made it all too real. So I started to use food for comfort ... to fill the emptiness inside ... and to reward myself when nobody else would. You should've seen the weight collect around my thighs, midriff and upper arms. If only I'd turned to the girls instead – I probably wouldn't have fallen into the cycle of depression ... weight gain ... insecurity ... more depression, all the while cleaning like mad, so I myself could feel clean. ... The only time I felt normal was when I'd escape into my own little world – yup, I started back then – after everyone went off to bed. I'd put on my headphones and dance to ABBA, pretending that I was a famous star, one with enough money to move as far away from him as possible. I figured, money may not buy happiness, but it sure as hell could rent it ... along with some peace and dignity.

"Penny for your thoughts," says Cyn.

I shake my head and say, "Oh nothing." Maybe someday I too will have the guts to tell my story. For now, it will have to stay locked in my mind, where even Grammy can't access it.

Looking at our downcast faces, Alison tries to save the day with, "Don't mean to sound insensitive here, but could we please talk about something else? ... Trust me, you don't wanna get me started on my theories about love and sex. ... Whoever said 'love hurts' had it all wrong. Personally, I think it's sex-related shit that ends up hurting way more."

Cyn laughs, "Why, what kinda sex have *you* been having ... and who with? ... Is his thing bigger or smaller than a bread box?"

Randy lisps, "Does it matter?" bending his index finger to make it look like a limp dick. "And as far as size goes, I don't think *that* matters much either."

Alison laughs, "*That* horny huh, that any cock'l'do?" Seeing an affirmative from Randy, she holds her right index finger and thumb fairly close together and laughs, "Even if was an incey wincey one?" Another affirmative. "Bullshit! The whole size not mattering thing's gotta be one of the biggest lies of our century."

"Steven has a nice one. ... Honestly, this trial separation thing is cramping my style ... although he did say that *if* he comes back, it'll be for the whole nine yards. ... But the way I'm feeling right now, I'd be willing to settle for his nine *inches*."

The hunky flight attendant's gaydar must've picked up a signal from Randy's randy mind; for he pops up out of nowhere and starts to pour champagne for everyone, getting particularly close to our homo-sapien, shamelessly undressing him with his hungry eyes. ... Poor Cyn!

Moments later, the champagne starts to kick in and we become as giddy as ever.

Cyn takes over the conversation with, "I know we're not supposed to talk about parents, but it'll make you happy to know that mine are truly the craziest."

Danielle takes Darla's hand and gets comfortable in her seat. "Do tell."

"For starters, they were hippies – free love, pot, key parties ...."

"Key parties?" Danielle asks, dating herself as a

young sweet thang.

"You know – the guys put their car keys in a basket, the girls pick them out at random ... and then end up going home with the guy whose keys they have?"

"Swapping?"

"Don't look so shocked, Danielle, they'd probably think that *you're* the one who's screwed up."

"Anyhow, that's not all of it. The worst part was, I didn't realize that my mom was the only mother who hung around the house topless, until it was too late."

Alison interrupts, "I still remember the day you found out that other mothers actually wear clothes around the house. You came over, stared at my mom's dorky outfit and asked her if she was headed out. She thought you were complimenting her clothes. But then you had to go and ruin it, by telling her that wasn't it ... you were just curious 'cause she was wearing a top."

We all laugh, and Alison says, "I wasn't allowed to go anywhere *near* you for the next two weeks ... until Dad offered to drive me over one day. His schpeal to me – 'If the lady wants to go around with her top down like a convertible, it's her damn business'."

"I can see why you became a sex therapist!" comments Danielle, knowingly.

"You mean, to figure out why my parents were so screwed up? ... Nah, I kinda was into sex all by my lonesome."

Randy laughs, "I know – I caught you that way once, remember?"

Cyn reaches into a nut tray beside her and throws a cashew at Randy. "It's not like I was weird about it or anything – did you see me tie myself up first? ... But if you're going to be Mr. Big Mouth anyway, let's see if you can actually put your mouth to good use?"

"Meaning?"

"Help me plan for a racy bachelorette party that I'm hired to do next weekend – sure could use some ideas."

We're all getting into it now – helping Cyn plan. Randy suggests a male stripper and offers his help, but Alison poo-poos the idea in favor of a Rabbit Pearl – the ultimate gizmo with more pleasurable attachments than a Swiss army knife. I keep my mouth shut, 'cause my suggestions for lingerie feel lame by comparison. ... Of course Cyn is way ahead of us all – why she asked for our help, I'll never know. She announces, "I'm thinking of including a little toy party along with my instructional lecture – has the potential for a new side business for yours truly."

Alison smirks, raises her glass, and says, "I'm all for side businesses – the racier the better!"

If I didn't know better, I'd say truly spoken like someone who already owns the T-shirt on that issue. ... At least we're laughing again.

Danielle says, "Would you also make it your business to teach them how to take care of their pink parts?"

"As in, how to *stimulate* them?"

"No, as in how to keep them nice-looking. I don't know about others, but I'm partial to a Brazilian myself, even though most dykes I've dated prefer to keep it *au naturel.*"

"Just don't send them to get waxed where I used to go, okay?" I add, laughing my head off.

Danielle deadpans, "I'm definitely missing something here, aren't I?"

Randy says, "Are you gonna tell her Sweetie, or shall I?"

Afraid of how he might embellish, not that the story needs it, I figure it's a hellova lot better if I fess up myself. One deep breath and I go for it. "Ok-ay, if you *must* know. ... Since I'm too tender to do anything for a couple of days after a bikini wax, Jeremy always likes to have a go at it just before I get it done. ... Anyhow, this particular Saturday afternoon, following a particularly delish sex-fest, I was escorted to the seedy back room to do my usual business, with a salon full of people out front. What I hadn't realized was, all that playing had left my nether lips looking Angelina Jolie full. One glance and the aesthetician shouted out to her assistant at the front of the salon, in a heavy Korean accent, "Julie, she make sex. Lips too puffy. Come stretch out pussita so I wax paw-pulee." Needless to say, my blushing pussita went from a just-relished pink to a crimson red, with the pussy posse tugging it every which way into submission. Naturally, nobody in the outer area rushed out before they took a good look at the girl who'd just "made sex" before getting her bikini wax."

We're all howling now. Randy swears that the story gets funnier each time. You betchya, since it's not his goods that we're talking about. I wonder if they did stuff like that back in Grammy's day?

The plane is about to land, so we've been instructed to buckle up. Just as well, I don't think Danielle could handle another story. Besides, she doesn't need *that* much information about us.

*   *   *

A short limo ride lands us right in front of the Goldstein estate rather quickly. Palm trees and magenta bougainvillea bushes are swaying in front of an over-sized, yellow stucco bungalow, with a great view of the harbour. We knock on the front door and are promptly greeted by Mrs. Goldstein – a skinnier version of Dr. Ruth, right down to her bottle dyed hair – dressed up in a pale blue velour leisure suit. She holds out her bony hand – studded with loads of rings, liver spots and blue veins – to shake ours. One by one, we're introduced to her. Once we're done, Mrs. Goldstein looks behind us, searching for the groom I'm sure. As we close the door, she asks, "Aren't we missing someone?" her smoker's voice making her sound a bit like Marge Simpson.

Danielle says, "Nope, everybody's here," only to watch her mom give Randy a distasteful once over. She's probably wondering if it's him, being the only guy in our posse. Little does she know that she's gonna *wish* it was him!

Unhappy as she looks, Mrs. Goldstein walks us through a high-ceiling hallway with shell pictures and a ceiling fan, to an art deco family room – plastic covering every vulnerable surface – leading to a gorgeous lanai and pool out back. As we plop ourselves on the chairs by the poolside table, Mrs. Goldstein's patience finally runs out. She blurts out, "So where the hell is my future son-in-law? Isn't he coming?" giving Randy a dirty look, making it clear that she can neither fathom nor accept him as such.

Danielle asks her to have a seat, patting the cushioned chair beside her, while Randy interjects, "Don't look at me like that – don't you think I'm good enough for your daughter?"

"Hell no!" is all that she bothers with.

"Mom, you're such a racist!"

"Who said anything about race? It's religion that I'm concerned about."

"How do you know that Randy isn't Jewish ... or Darla for that matter – just 'cause their skin colour is a little off?"

"There's no *way* either one of them can be Jewish!"

"Sammy Davis Junior is Black and he's Jewish."

"Sammy Shmammy my ass – now where's my future son-in-law?"

"There you go assuming things again. I just said that I was bringing my fiancée – I don't believe I ever specified that it was a *male* fiancée."

"*Oye way* – you trying to give me a heart attack or something?"

"No, Mom, just trying to introduce you to my fiancée ... as promised."

"Enough already – where is he?"

"*She* is right here – it's Darla."

Mrs. G. puts the back of her hand to her forehead, like she's about to pass out, eyes rolled up to the skies. "Have you lost your mind? After *every*thing I do for you, I have to live for *this*? Why didn't you just shoot me instead?" Oh-oh, looks like we're headed for a full blown, meet the parents freak-out. Took her *that* long?

Darla cuts in, "Your daughter and I really love each other and hope that you can be happy for us."

Never before have I seen that brutal an expression, which says, 'Ohmigosh, she's Black, and there isn't a damn thing I can say about it without appearing racist'. But to my shock, apparently Mrs. Goldstein can and does. Without any hesitation whatsoever, she fumes out, "I'd hoped for a nice Jewish guy, but I could tolerate a non-Jewish one – at least I can convert him. But a *shiksa*? I haven't even accepted your brother's *shiksa* yet – and she's not even Black."

And here I thought that the gay part would be more challenging! I guess if you're going to break a rule anyhow, might as well make it worthwhile. Like the Jewish saying goes: if you're going to eat pig anyway, let the lard drip all over your chin.

The shocked look on everyone's faces is definitely worth the price of admission. I'm pretty sure that in all her years of being subjected to such ignorance, Darla has never come across anything quite like this. To Danielle's credit, she grabs Darla's hand and says, "Let's go ... we don't need this!" with the conviction of a you-can't-fire-me-I-quit moment. ... So much for my black dress and the funeral I was promised.

We all follow Danielle out the front door, with Mrs. Goldstein shouting, "You're dead to us. Don't bother coming back. ... Ever! ... I'll bury you and give your inheritance to your brother and his *white shiksa*." ... Has anyone ever told her that as diverse as we all are, our differences account for less than one percent of our entire genetic code, with colour being the tiniest fraction of that? Personality on the other hand, takes up a bit more code than that. But right now, the only code I can think of is *code red* – an emergency situation is definitely in full bloom, with temples flaring like nothing I've ever seen before.

Just as we're rushing away from the scene, we run into Mr. Goldstein coming in – a man of short stature, he could easily pass for a more rotund version of George Castanza's father. Looking a bit confused, he takes off his thick, horn rimmed glasses and does a double take, not sure why we're headed in the wrong direction. Danielle is way too upset to stop, so she just waves at him, "Hi, Dad ... bye, Dad," and continues to head out to the edge of the driveway. I'm on my cell, trying to get the limo guy to come back for us – darn, voice mail.

Mr. Goldstein says, "What's going on?"

"Why don't you ask *Mom*?"

"'Cause I'm asking you. ... Besides, she's too crazy to give it to me straight."

Danielle continues her march along the curb side, Daddy in tow. Since he's not going away, she decides to give it to him straight – the man did ask for it. "I'm a dyke, okay?" she sobs. "And my fiancée is a Black, Catholic woman, not a Jewish man, as you'd all hoped."

Poor Mr. Goldstein looks confused, as he should – that's quite a bit to swallow without any warning. But bless his heart, he says, "Please come inside and let's talk about this. Dyke or not, you're still the only daughter I got."

"That's going to be a little hard to do, 'cause according to Mom, I'm already dead."

"That's just Mom. Us guys never have problems with the lesbians," he winks, trying to give us an awkward smile – gotta hand it to him for doing his best to lighten things up a bit.

Danielle says, "I'm not stepping in that house unless I know that *both* me and Darla are welcome, and that she'll be treated with the respect she deserves. ... She's a well-regarded attorney, not to mention someone who I plan to spend the rest of my life with; but Mom just treated her like a complete and utter loser."

"Lawyer? That's even better," he tries to joke.

"Your Mom and I always worried that you'd end up with a starving artist."

"I'm sure a *male* starving artist would still be more welcome around here."

"Let's not be so harsh on Mom, okay? It's a lot to take for someone in her condition. ... And knowing her, she's probably thinking that she's looking out for you, wanting the best for you."

"Well she sure has a rotten way of showing it."

"I'll grant you that. But come on, let's give it another shot with her, shall we?" he says, pulling Danielle's arm to drag her right back up the driveway. I of course, stop trying to reach our driver, at least until I know what's going on.

Looking at Danielle, I'm not sure what she's going to do? But it's gotta be her decision. So the rest of us try to make ourselves scarce, finding a shady spot under huge palm fronds by the side of the house. Darla says, "Go on, talk to them, I'll wait here." Having gone through the pain herself with her own parents, I'm sure she's likely to be a lot gentler on Danielle than she was on her. Being mature also helps.

Time stands still as we wait and wait and wait. Not one word is uttered amongst us, since we're straining our ears to catch the conversation inside, through an open window nearby. I take a peek and see some action. Looks like there's some crying and a lot of hugging going on. Good, I love hugging.

Danielle finally comes back out to share the scoop with us. "You think *I* gave them a mouthful – talk about the mouthful they just gave me," she sobs.

Darla takes her hand and asks, "What's wrong, Honey?"

"Just found out that Mom's been diagnosed with lung cancer – but since it's only a very small area, the prognosis is pretty good."

Gotta get her off those cigarettes I'm thinking, when Danielle drops the next bomb. "*Any*way, she'd planned this huge engagement party for me, with about a hundred of her closest friends and enemies. Dad said that it's the only thing that's kept her going through all of this. ... *So*, here's the deal – she says that she'll try to accept us privately, if we'll respect her publicly."

"I'm even afraid to ask what that means, but do go on, if it'll keep your funeral at bay," says Darla. Yes, do go on, I'm thinking, we're all "dying" to know.

"She asked if we'd help her save face by going ahead with the party, pretending that the *fagola* is the fiancée, not Darla. In exchange, she'll never put us through anything like this again."

Told you, she'll *wish* Randy was the fiancée, once the truth comes out. I ask, "So what are you planning on doing?"

Before she can answer that, Darla turns to Randy, "Think you can pull it off for one evening?"

Always a good sport, Randy grabs his crotch and says, "You betchya – me and the boys are definitely up for playing the man for one night!" making it clear that he's ballsy enough for the challenge.

Danielle hugs Darla for being so understanding. To which, Darla responds with, "Save it, just trying to make a good impression."

"I wouldn't hold my breath if I were you, but thanks

anyway."

I stare at Randy leaning against the wall, looking as gay as possible, and shake my head. ... I'd really meant it when I told you that if there were degrees of gayness, he'd be right at the top. It would be easier to get the pope to cross-dress than Randy to un-cross-dress. ... Better get started, we have our work cut out for us.

Mr. Goldstein suggests that Darla and Danielle stay in her old room, instead of going to the hotel that we're all booked into. Darla thanks him and offers to stay in the guestroom instead, to make it easier on everybody. She must really love Danielle to make such a sacrifice.

* * *

Back at the hotel, I go for a facial, while Randy, Cyn and Alison take off to buy a more masculine outfit for him. ... An hour later, I look at myself in the mirror to see if my skin is indeed like a baby's bottom, as per their promise. Yikes, they forgot to tell me the part about the diaper rash. ... I guess if this is the worst thing that happens to us all weekend, we should consider ourselves very lucky! Tomorrow will tell, whether or not the in-laws and the out-laws can actually get along.

Chapter 8 - *The Frog & The Princess*

We gather up in the hotel lobby to head out to the Goldstein's, for the infamous engagement party. I'm nearly blinded by the brightest thing which hits my eye, in a heavily chandeliered marble lobby no less – Randy in a chartreuse jacket, atop some funky looking pants. Shocked, I say, "Is this the best you could come up with?"

"Don't you like it?" he says, doing a little catwalk and curtsy thing, to show me an even gaudier backside.

"If you want to look like Kermit the frog, maybe?"

Cyn laughs, "I can just see page six – 'The Frog and The Princess take over Florida', or should it be in the crime section, since it is a fashion crime after all."

"Misdemeanor at best. ... Hey, at least I'm covered and wearing a silk jacket – what more do you want?" Randy snaps.

Always the responsible one, Alison says, "Can we take this outside? Our ride's waiting."

I shake my head in disbelief as we walk to the cab. "How could you guys let him get away with that? I thought I could trust you. Should've known better and come along myself!"

We all squish in together, trying to make sure that we don't crush whatever the guest of honor is wearing, while he informs me, "Hey, Sweetie, if I'm paying for it, I wanna get some use out of it afterwards. Why do you think I turned down being one of your bridesmaids?"

*   *   *

Fifteen minutes later, we're at the Goldstein's. Mr. G. takes one look at Randy and says, "There's no way you can pass for a lawyer. You're not *mensch* enough. We'll just have to tell everybody that you're one of those artsy fartsy guys who Danielle is known for dating – though mother may have already shown off about the lawyer bit." ... I'm left wondering if the other guys that Danielle "dated" and brought home were also *fagolas* being passed off as boyfriends, to appease her pushy parents.

Randy high-fives Mr. G. and says, "Sounds like a plan. I'm much better at playing a starving designer than a lawyer any day. ... You could even say that I've got it down to an art-form." The latter he says, while batting his lashes. Is that eyeliner he's wearing?

Whether or not, Mr. G. doesn't seem to care. He pats Randy's back and says, "Good, less screw-ups that way. At least a *schmatah* designer is supposed to look and act like a *fagola*."

"That's metro-sexual to you," laughs Randy. ... Thank goodness they're on the same page.

Other than Darla's long face, the evening is off to a good start. Even Mrs. G. appears to be at her best behavior. She must, considering all the trouble she's gone to, to arrange the perfect evening. Truly, she spared no expense in going first class the whole way. She's got scores of candles and flowers floating in the pool, and tons more decorating the tiki torch stands that are mounted into the beach sand embracing their property line. As the sun sets upon them, everything turns bird-of-paradise orange.

A twelve piece oldies band starts to play a waltz, hoping to entice people onto the gorgeous dance floor that's been laid out. But it's still too warm for that. Yet, despite the heat, we're surrounded by gorgeous ice sculptures and wait staff in tuxes. One is headed our way with the finest crystal, loaded with the finest something-or-the-other, I'm sure – looks like a full-bodied Merlot. I grab a goblet and try to down some in a big gulp – gotta put away a few to make it through this evening. "My gosh, what is this stuff? Grape juice? Or something even less recognizable than that?" I whisper to Cyn, practically spitting out the nasty tasting concoction.

Looking at my horrid expression, Danielle comes over. "So you think you're a connoisseur and yet you can't recognize this?" I nod. "Well you haven't tasted anything until you've tasted non-alcoholic, kosher, Jewish wine."

"At least it will keep Randy in line," I smile.

"Speaking of my charming fiancée, where the hell is he?"

Randy pops out of nowhere, wraps his arms around Danielle and air kisses her. "Did I hear my name? ... I'm right here, Dah-ling."

"I was worried that you'd abandoned me already."

"Are you kidding? At least not until midnight. I turn into a flammer then. ... Although, the waiter over there looks quite tempting, even as we speak. Better have your way with me while you can, Sweetie."

Danielle slaps his ass, "Don't you *dare*! ... You're straight tonight, remember? And only allowed to gawk at babes."

Tall order, since the entry into this joint requires that you be 65 or older – they're checking IDs at the non-alcoholic bar. But in all fairness, there's loads of divas walking around, dressed to the nines in various forms of tight-fitting animal skin. When I'm their age, I just hope that I can fit that tightly into my *own* skin. I look at their chiseled features and comment to the girls, "They look am-- a-a-a-zing for their age. You'd think that they were all beauty queens in their time."

Cyn grunts, "Or just able to afford the best darn plastic surgeons that money can buy, in the present time. Too bad they can't do a whole heck of a lot for upper arm jiggles ... a dead giveaway, if you ask me."

Alison points to a small cluster of ladies and says, "They all look like they have the same surgeon on speed-dial – just check out the similarity in their nose jobs."

I say, "Surgeon schmurgeon – what I'd like to know is, how do you get such youthful skin?"

Darla finally opens up her mouth. "Who needs estrogen when you can have alpha-hydroxy!"

Whoever they are, however they got their looks, Randy is in fashion heaven. Everyone loves him and he's loving them right back, with his charming comments. He's probably the only guy in the room who can recognize their designer-wear, along with the year – when it comes to Prada, Gucci, Chanel, and Dior, you'd better be wearing next year's fashions right now! ... Never thought he'd be such a hit. He's practically one of the girls, and making plans to go shopping with them tomorrow morning. I guess all my worrying was for naught – then again, what else is new?

As we watch Randy do his thing, a bony guy with wispy white hair, punctuated by some major liver spots, drives up to Darla's butt in his motorized wheelchair and stops. He takes a good look at eye level, and decides to give it a smack. Normally, she would have a few choice words; this time, she settle on, "I desperately need a *real* drink, if I'm to survive any of this."

A vintage woman in a Chanel suit walks over to Darla and says, "Hi, I'm Sara – without an H." She then proceeds to rummage through the contents of her classic quilted purse – with the two C's – and pulls out a designer mickey with something strong in it. Without a comma of hesitation, she has the top unscrewed and is now topping up Darla's virgin Mojito with the good stuff. "These girls have become so boring ever since they started with their health conscious Pilates, Atkins, and no-booze programs. ... Not me. I figure, at my age I've damn well earned the right to be unhealthy."

Darla mouths a "Thank you," and takes a swig. She then smacks her lips and says, "Not bad ... not bad at all."

Like little kids who wanna get in on something that's been taste-tested and rated as yummy, Alison, Cyn and I also hold out our drinks to her. ... We're all topped up now ... and sticking close to Sara without an 'H' and loads of designer 'C's! As we get to know her better, turns out that she and her hubby are bigwigs in the *schmatah* business. They've got two, exclusive designer wear boutiques in Naples and another one in South Beach. Of course this has Alison's full attention – don't know where the girl gets her money, but she sure as hell spends it like she's dying tomorrow.

After an extensive inquisition on what they carry, Alison suggests that they should consider throwing in some of Randy's pieces into their boutiques, just to test drive something different.

"Randy has his own line?" ask Sara.

"He has some gorgeous prototypes, but needs some serious cash to launch a full blown line," I add.

The quilted purse opens up yet again, for more top-ups and Sara's business card. "Give this to him and have him call me. The Goldstein's have been our best friends for so long, it would be a shame not to give their future son-in-law a chance to show us what he's got."

Darla fires us a dirty look. I'm thinking, oh-oh, what have I gotten everybody into? Randy only agreed to play the adorable son-in-law routine just this once. But the fashion slut that he is, I have a feeling that he'll wanna play along a bit longer, if it meant designing for money versus exposure. ... Now how do we get Danielle to play along, just until he can pull it off? Darla will be a cinch – she's always wanted the very best for Randy.

But despite her heart in the right place, Darla still looks upset ... and from the looks of it, going into binge mode. As a gorgeous waiter passes around some Thai spring rolls, she takes a handful on a napkin and asks him if there's any peanut sauce to go with them. You'd think the girl made a bad JAP joke, the way Mrs. G. goes ballistic when she hears that. "Peanut sauce? Don't you know that Bubu has a severe peanut allergy? She can't even *smell* them."

"Sorry, I didn't know that."

Mrs. G. squeezes Bubu – her freshly blow-dried lap poodle – tightly in her arms, out of harm's way. "Honestly, some people," she says, walking away from us, "We don't even let Bubu as much as *look* at a peanut."

Memo-to-self: never bring around a Charles Schultz book to the non-peanut gallery at the Goldstein's.

Thank goodness that Danielle sees the commotion and heads our way. Her mom bumps into her on her way over and tries to pull down her ultra-short skirt, to cover her up a bit. One more inch and we'll be in full view of the crystal G-string she was bragging about, right above her butt-crack. She's so not what I expected a hard-core lesbian would look like – maybe a porno lipstick lesbian, but not a real one. I guess it just goes to show you.

Anyhow, our bouncy babe has now joined us. "I think this calls for some real booze. Anyone up for it? Dad's got some chilling just for us in the trunk of his Seville." *Now* she tells us?

The five of us disappear into the garage, to get some reinforcements. Poor Sara's stash has already run dry, thanks to us.

As Danielle tries to uncork a vintage Chardonnay, Darla wraps her arms around her waist from behind and nuzzles into her neck greedily. It's the first bit of movement we've seen from her all day. She's been pretty quiet ever since we got here. "I'm not sure how much more of this I can take, Honey. ... I just want this to be over already, so we can be a real couple again. ... Feels like a lifetime ago, since we were last intimate," she says. I'm thinking, me too. If Jeremy was here, I'd even settle for a same ol' same ol' deja-fuck, just to be doing it again.

The moment is broken. We're being missed, 'cause I hear a croaky Marge Simpson voice yell our way, "You'd better not be doing what I think you're doing in there." I wonder if she means drinking or lesbian-ing? Either way, we have our orders to go back and mingle.

As we head back, Darla says to me, "This is too much for me, maybe I should just take off."

I say, "Must be the hardest on you, standing by the sidelines like that."

"That and the fact that if one more person asks me if I'm Halle Berry, I'm gonna punch them out. ... I guess we all look alike to them."

"Well at least they picked someone gorgeous. And if one's vision is a little off, you could pass for her – a nicer version of course," I smile.

"Nicely done," she smiles, and then reluctantly huffs, " Fine, I'll go back and give it another shot, for Danielle's sake." I'm sure this is not at all what Grammy meant, when she said you must always stand by your man.

We're back in the land of the three Rs – rouge, red lips, and Restylane. The waltzes have picked up to swing now, with a lot more action on the dance floor. Randy decides to leave his ret a tet. "Sorry Girls, as much fun as this has been, if you'll squeeze me, I must have a dance with my fiancée." And with that, he heads our way, grab's Danielle arm and escorts her to the dance floor, for a performance of a lifetime.

Everyone's oohing and aahing, watching them together. Soon, you hear a familiar cling, cling, cling of glasses, with everyone cheering on to get them to kiss. Whoever heard of a pre-wedding kiss like that? ... Between a gay guy and a lesbian girl no less. Looking at them, you'd think love was definitely in the air, along with the stench of rotten lies ... and mothballs. But their act is so believable that it unnerves Darla just enough to make her take off in a huff. I chase after her, only to have her leave me in her dust, as the Seville screeches away. Not a smart way to win brownie points with future in-laws, stealing their car like that. Knowing Darla, I'm sure she'll bring it back just as soon as she cools off. At least I hope she will.

A couple of hours later, all the merry-making finally draws to an end. After all the goodbyes have been said, the caterers paid off, the flaming torches dismantled, Danielle finally notices that Darla is missing, just as Mr. G. notices that his Seville is also missing.

"What the hell is going on?" gasps Danielle.

I respond, "I think the whole charade got to Darla. She left in the Seville right after the notorious kiss."

Mr. G. just shakes his head and walks away, without as much as a word, hands thrown up to the skies in a 'why me?' gesture.

Randy pouts, "You *try* and help out ... and suddenly everybody's misunderstanding you. Doesn't she know that vaginas just don't do it for me? I tried one once, but I think I dislocated it."

I say, "You know how it goes – you tell a thousand jokes, but nobody thinks you're a comedian; one unexpected *kiss* and suddenly your whole sexuality is in question. But you gotta admit, as far as kisses go it certainly was an awesome one – and there weren't any vaginas involved." The last bit I say, remembering the dynamic kiss that Dan gave me that night at The Cocoon, also sans any vaginal appearances. ... Truly a lifetime ago. My revere is interrupted by my buzzing purse.

Cyn teases, "What you got in there Girl? A vibrator perhaps?"

"I wish," I say and reach in for my cell. It's a text message from Darla. She wants me to meet her at the crab shack near the hotel, alone. How the hell am I going to get there discreetly? ... Everyone's looking at me now. I say, "Just Jeremy missing me."

"It's about time," says Cyn, while Alison just rolls her eyes up into her head.

The gang wants to head out to a late night bar for some *real* drinks that don't need to be sneaked around. Lord knows we've earned the privilege. In as much as I myself could use a few, I feign fatigue and excuse myself, insisting that I take a separate cab back to the hotel so no one has to go out of their way to drop me off – never mind that I'm not going back to the hotel at all. We call for two cabs and head our separate ways, leaving Danielle at her parents, for when Darla returns. Too bad her cell phone is off and no one can reach her.

*   *   *

A quick fifteen minute cab ride later, I'm at the crab shack. It looks like a typical seafood place, with various fishing nets hanging off the ceiling – standard plastic sea fare trapped within them – and a few mermaid-shaped poles here and there, keeping the tin roof from coming down. At this hour, the place looks pretty desolate, so it's not hard to spot Darla at the bar. She looks at her watch as the bartender places two huge marguerites in front of her. "I hope one of those is for me," I say, giving her a hug. Looks like she's been crying.

I place my arm reassuringly on her shoulder and ask, "What's up, Honey?"

"Whatever's shared here stays here?"

I do a scout's honor motion with my right hand and say, "Mum's the word."

The attorney that she is, she goes straight for the facts. "Do you remember Rita from when we were in high school?" she asks, her right leg shaking restlessly.

"Your housekeeper's daughter?"

"Yup, that's the one." Big sip.

"Of course I remember her, clearly. You two seemed pretty tight back then."

"You have nooo idea how tight."

135

"Meaning?" Big sip.

"Meaning, she was my first love."

Shocked, I put my hand to my mouth and say, "Never would've guessed in a million years."

"Of course not – we did go out of our way to keep it a secret. And everything was fine until my parents started to feel that it wasn't right for us to be so close. So they fired Mary, shipped them away somewhere, and refused to tell me where they went." Major nose blow and major sip.

"Do you think your parents knew?"

"Who knows – they do like to wear blinders. I suppose it could be that, or just the fact that I was associating with someone 'inferior', when they'd done everything in their power to upgrade me to an upper middle class lifestyle."

"Go on." Big gulp.

"A while back, Danielle forgot to turn off her computer – her browser was parked at one of those 411 web sites that search for lost connections. Any-way, when I went to close it for her, I realized that she was trying to hunt down her first love. ... Made me think of mine ... so I entered Rita's name out of curiosity – to see what she's been up to, where she's living and all that crap." Following another big sip, she sidetracks, "I still remember the innocent way we discovered each other ... all those gentle kisses and soft caresses. ... The first time she had my nipple in her mouth, I practically screamed from ecstasy. And then her fingers found their way between my legs and gave me feelings I'd never experienced before. I learned how to do the same for her. And of course from there on in, it was our little secret – one we shared together over and over again."

Since we're heading dangerously close to the too-much-information point, I cut in. "So all that time when you were cheerleading, you really had no interest in the boys who were hounding you?"

"Nope, just Rita. Naturally, I was totally devastated when my parents separated us. Took me forever to get over her. ... After the longest time, I chalked it off to childhood experimentation and tried my best to fall for a man who my parents could love, adore, and approve of.. And you know the rest," she sobs.

"So did you find Rita on Danielle's computer?"

"Yes, and she lives right here."

"Are you planning on seeing her?"

"Kinda late for that."

"Why? Is she married or something?"

"Nope, 'cause I already saw her earlier tonight. ... When she heard that I was coming into town, she wanted to hook up for old times' sake, but I told her that I didn't think it was such a good idea. ... Then, when all that stuff happened with Danielle ...."

"You decided to look her up."

"You got it."

"And?"

"And I'm quite confused now. I barely walked in the door and all the old feelings and passion came rushing back. I'm embarrassed to say that ever since I found her again on the Internet, I've been thinking about what it would be like. And know what – it was everything I ever fantasized about and then some."

"And now you don't know how you feel about Danielle ... or Rita for that matter. ... Do you think it could've been just a grudge fuck?" Who'd blame her, after everything that happened, and whatever else Dan was talking about a few weeks ago.

"On the way over I was open to the possibility, but when it actually happened, it was a hellova lot more."

"So what are you going to do?"

"I don't know – just can't face Danielle right now. ... Please do me a favor and drive back the Seville to the Goldstein's and give Danielle this note," she says, handing me a letter.

"Then what?"

"Then I'm going to take the next available flight back home – not returning with you guys. Sorry!"

"I understand. You do what you have to do, Honey. I'll take care of the rest." Looking at her concerned face, I add, "And what was shared here stays here."

"Thanks. What are you gonna say to everybody?"

"Just that you're getting cold feet ... 'cause you're not sure that you can handle being treated like that?"

"Think they'll buy it?"

"Why not? And whether or not, you know they'll always love and support you in *anything*."

"You're the best friend a girl could ever have."

I give her a big hug and say, "You'd do the same for me." I finish what's left of my drink and say, "I guess I'd better head off – I have a car to return. You gonna be okay?"

"I'll be fine. Call me after you get back into town."

"You got it. Love you, Honey!"

*   *   *

I'm now driving back to the Goldstein's, terrified of running into them. I order a cab to pick me up in exactly twenty minutes from the time I leave the crab shack – don't wanna stick around and get grilled by Danielle. The chicken that I am, I leave the car keys and the letter in the mailbox and take off before anyone comes out.

*   *   *

At about three in the morning, I hear voices in our hotel hallway. I guess the gang's back. Randy is singing, Cyn is trying to sing, and Alison is telling them both to shut up, 'cause her head is pounding all on its own. I'm really not looking forward to the shopping trip tomorrow, knowing full well that I'll have to lie when they ask me if I know anything about what went down between Darla and Danielle.

It's now the next day and Randy's already taken off with the ladies who lunch and spend, for lunch and a spending spree ... on them. The deal is, if he helps them dress to impress, they'll pay him back in kind. Alison's also taken off on her own, to check out Sara's boutique, leaving me and Cyn to our own devices. While the two of us love to spend like the best of them, we still believe in stores where the amount of fabric isn't inversely proportional to the price. And thousand dollar racks have approximately ten items on them, putting each at about a hundred bucks, versus one hanger that'll still have to bring in the same thousand bucks. I guess around here, less truly is more.

*   *   *

A short cab ride later, Cyn and I arrive at an outdoor mall, with stunning waterfalls, exotic birds and lush vegetation sharing space with impeccably dressed clientele – matching tans and identical honey blonde hair setting them apart from the tourists.

As I try out an infinite number of things, I feel like a college kid; only with a ton more money, so I can actually afford to *buy* something this time. ... Two hats, five pairs of shoes, and three outfits later, I've spent over five thousand bucks, and Cyn isn't that far behind. Dunno when I'll have the occasion to wear half these things, but right now I *have* to have them. Like I told you before, I'll probably feel guilty a year from now, when all the tags are still attached because I haven't worn anything once – but right now, none of that matters. All that matters is, I can't afford to pass up on anything that makes me feel good about myself. Talk about retail therapy – gets faster results than my shrink any day.

*   *   *

As we head back to the hotel in a cab, Cyn asks me the dreaded question. "So, did you ever find out what happened to Darla last night? Not seeing her today I'm assuming that the lovebirds are probably working out some stuff. ... Do you know if they'll be joining us later?"

"Doubt it."

"Okay, let's have it, what happened ... what do you know?"

"She left to go home last night."

"WHAT?" Cyn shouts.

"You heard me. No big deal though, just a cold feet situation."

"No big deal? How the hell can you say that? ... Okay, what aren't you telling me?"

"There isn't much to tell, really."

"Did they fight after she got back to the Goldstein's?"

"I don't think she ever made it back."

"This is *huge*! Come on, tell me the whole scoop already."

"I don't think even Darla knows the whole scoop just yet."

"She got *that* upset by the kiss? Hellooo, this is Randy we're talking about? A cock-smoocher with no interest in pussy whatsoever ... just doing her a *favor*?"

"I'm sure it goes deeper than that."

"You bitch, you know exactly what this is about, don't you?" My eyes are downcast, my face still – I'm even afraid to breathe or swallow, lest I give something away. One look and she continues, "And you're not going to tell me, are you?"

"You of all people should respect the therapist client privilege."

"Whoa! Last time I checked you were an English major and she wasn't cutting you any checks for girl talk."

"You know what I mean – the whole confidentiality thing."

"Just say yes or no in that case. Is the sex lousy?"

"I don't know."

"'I don't know' wasn't a choice – just yes or no."

"You're wasting your time."

"I know lousy sex would definitely be a deal breaker for me," she says, trying to change the subject.

Nice save – gotta hand it to the girl, she knows when to quit. "How about with you?" she asks.

"When I was single, I always had this thing – if I couldn't imagine my mouth around a guy's dick, or his hands on my body, it was definitely a deal breaker."

"So the decision was made *after* you guys were already naked?"

"No! You just get this sense, based on how the person looks and smells ... particularly how their hands and feet look. ... Don't you ever get that feeling?"

"Smells, definitely. Not sure about the feet. ... You *do* realize that the whole thing about big feet meaning big cock is nothing more than a myth, right?"

Before I can answer, our cab screeches to a halt in front of our hotel, scaring me to death. The East Indian cabbie looks in his rear view mirror, shakes his head in disbelief, and says, "Cab ride over. This is not the porno – you disgusting girls must leave cab immediately," in the thickest accent imaginable.

We giggle, pay the fair, and head back to our rooms, arm in arm. Don't know how she does it, but she always manages to make me laugh ... and I her. Just hope that I can do the same for Darla, once all is said and done.

And put a silly grin on Jeremy's face, during our upcoming sexperimentation weekend! Too bad I returned the keys to "The Pleasure Palace" – my new trashy lingerie will have to do for now. ... I can't help but remember the first item I ever owned in that genre.

The night before I married Jeremy, Grammy came into my room, to do what Mom should have done – have "the talk" – clutching a brown bag like it was contraband. Nestled within, was a tarty black nighty that she'd bought me at K-Mart, made out of the scratchiest lace that money could buy – probably wanted to make sure that I don't fall asleep on my wedding night. As I held it against my body in front of the mirror, she instructed, "Put this on tomorrow night, and then let him do whatever he wants ... even if it hurts."

Shocked that she thought I was *that* innocent, I decided to have some fun with it. "What's supposed to hurt?"

"You know, when he puts his thing into your ... your ... ehm ... hole."

"Grammy, I don't want anyone putting anything in my hole," I whimpered.

"Just be glad that I told you what no one bothered to tell me," is all she had to say, before kissing my forehead and hurriedly making her way out of my room.

After the special night in question, I led her to believe that I allowed Jeremy to put his thing into my butt-hole, because of our little talk, even though it hurt pretty bad. *Jeremy wishes!* She was pretty disgusted and stopped speaking in code after that. Poor Grammy!

Chapter 9 - *Good On Paper*

Call me anal retentive, call me OCD – that's Organized, Clean, and Disciplined to you – but I pack for a trip well in advance and unpack the minute I return. This time is no different. I plop my suitcase on the bed to change over from my Goldstein trip necessities to my upcoming, sex-capade weekend accessories. The new heels are definitely coming along, since they match oh-so-well with my never-before-test-driven coquettish-wear – I kinda planned it that way.

You see, ever since I told Jeremy that I'll be whisking him away for a weekend of sexperimentation, I've been collecting all sorts of naughty goods. Thus far, I've managed to find a stunning leather corset that actually looks pretty amazing on, an equally awesome red silk teddy, a very special disciplining officer's uniform, a cheerleading outfit, a Geisha kimono, and one of those tarty, peekaboo numbers – who needs the blue pill when you have baby blue slut-wear – all to get a rise out of Jeremy. Just hope that I can develop the nerve to pick up a paddle for whipping his ass, and some clit cream to whip my own pink parts into shape.

For what it's worth, I've been doing my Kagel's religiously, wondering if prep H or eye cream could speed up the tone and tighten process. By the time we leave, I expect to be as ready and easy as a "just add Jeremy" recipe. ... And in case you're wondering, yes, I'm getting quite excited myself. Truly, all this planning has gotten me more aroused than I ever imagined – beyond the retail therapy way.

With my stuff all organized into my three-quarters of the suitcase – yes, I believe in a fair division of closet and luggage space – I decide to throw in some sexy things that

I'd like to see Jeremy in. "I wonder if he still has the little leopard thong he got last Christmas, as a gag gift from his adoring Ob-Gyn nurses?" I rummage through his underwear drawer to see if it's still there, along with other things that make his bulge look ... well, bulgier. To my shock, tucked amongst his by-the-pack *Fruit of the Looms*, I find a large pair of women's underwear – granny panties to be exact. If I hadn't seen them for myself, I would've never believed it! "What the fuck is this?" I say, stretching out the elastic waistband to max capacity. ... "I guess the bastard hasn't stopped his hanky panky after all!" Talk about a mood breaker. No amount of clit cream or Viagra will be able help us out of this one ... not this time. Damn you, Jeremy!

Part of me just wants to keep on packing and move out. I wonder if there's any truth to what Cyn once shared: most people move out emotionally long before they move out physically. The way I'm feeling right now, I could do both, without awaiting sentence. But it's never that easy, is it?

I so want to give Jeremy the benefit of the doubt, but blood is rushing in my ears, trying to make it to my brain, so I may think from my head for a change. Dare I confront him? What good will that do? I've heard it from too many women in my shoes, in as much as we want to know all the gory details so we can grasp what happened, it never helps. I guess I should've known better – he did have a history of cheating before we got together, indicating that he's not entirely immune to it.

I'm now having trouble breathing. I should be trying to calm myself down, or get the fuck out of here. But instead, I find myself tidying up our bedroom. Reminds me of all the times that I felt fucked over by my Dad, and I'd do whatever it took to regain order in my life. ... As I smooth out the gold damask comforter, I feel warm tears stinging in my eyes. "When you make love for the last time, you never really know that it's going to be last time, do you?" I say out loud, thinking back to *our* last time – yup, we managed to sneak it in, post-talk, pre-Florida. We lay right here in each other's arms, our bodies melting into a tender embrace. He placed soft kisses on my neck, which led to hungry sucking on my nipples. His knowing touch and passionate attempt made me feel like nothing could touch us, ever again. But obviously something has!

What could I have done differently? ... Don't know, don't care anymore! But one thing's for certain, I know what I *should* be doing right now – get the fuck out, for some fresh air and to gain some fresh perspective.

I leave the kids a quick note to say that I have to go away for a bit, and make my way out of the house in a hurry, before I run into someone. I reverse my Porsche out of the driveway as fast as I can, knocking over our just-emptied trash bins. Normally, I couldn't resist the urge to put everything back neatly, and make sure that the Porsche is okay; today, I don't give a shit and drive off.

*   *   *

As soon as I'm on a side street, in the opposite direction from where I could run into Jeremy, I pull over by a park bench and take a seat on it – can't risk driving like this again.

I imagine my life without Jeremy in it. Pain rises from my gut to my throat, like bitter bile. I bend over and puke out my guts, to rid them of anything that might cause strong feelings for him. I try to convince myself to look at the positive side, acknowledging that happiness is an active choice for the most part. I cloud my mind with silly visions – eating what and when I like, watching silly shit on TV without being ridiculed for it, and doing my own thing without having to wait around for him, while he indulges in bullshit that's always more important than us. Wonderful as the freedom sounds, sadness starts to take over again.

I need to stop this right now and talk to someone other than myself – but who? Generally I'm the first call when weird things happen in our clique, since I'm the only one who allows people to unload, without feeling compelled to share an opinion. In this case, I guess I have no choice but to go with the opinions. ... I call Cyn and ask her to grab Alison and meet me at "The Cocoon". Don't wanna bug Darla or Randy just yet. They've got enough relationship bullshit of their own that they have to deal with.

*   *   *

As soon as I get to the "The Cocoon", I make myself a huge martini and down it in one big gulp. In as much as I could use another one or two or ten, I resist the urge. ... I look at my watch for about the millionth time and tap it to make sure that it's working, since it appears to be stuck. ... "What the heck is taking them so long?"

After pacing back and forth like an expectant father, for what seems like an eternity – even though my watch seems to think it's just a few minutes – the girls finally come charging in. Cyn's covered in athletic-wear, hair tied up in a ponytail, Alison looks just as casual in her Seven jeans and a tight, black Dolce T – yes, her casual wear is still designer wear.

The two of them give me reassuring hugs, knowing full well that something's wrong. Why else would my eyelids look like puffy pink *Fruitellas*?

Cyn is the first to break the silence with, "What's wrong, Honey?" as we plop ourselves onto one of the couches – me in the middle.

"The monogamously-challenged bastard is at it again!"

I now have their full attention, even Alison's – hope she's more supportive this time. Judging by the concern-filled look in her eyes, I guess so. ... She strokes the side of my face with the back of her hand, and asks, "What has he done *now*?"

"I found women's panties in his underwear drawer. Sizable panties – don't know how I should take his 'love your figure' comments anymore, if *that's* what turns his crank," I sob. "Probably why he married me – the fat chick. ... Funny how I went through a lifetime of humiliation with so many people, when I could've been his 'it girl' all along."

Cyn is now fuming. "Stop that, Jilly. You're not a fat chick!"

Alison interjects, "And even if you were, so what?"

"I've been trying to keep it together for the kids, and because I do still love him, I think. ... Don't wanna flush everything we've built together down the toilet, after all these years ... but not sure how much more of this I can take either."

Cyn interjects, "You shouldn't have to put up with this shit. What is the man thinking?"

"Wish I knew. He's been acting really strange over the last little while. ... One day he's warm, the next day he doesn't give a fuck. I don't know if it's his passive aggressive bullshit, or if he's having mood swings."

Alison asks, "Have you tried talking to him?"

"He claims that as far as *he's* concerned, our marriage is perfect; it's everything else that's getting to him. For me, it's just the opposite; everything else is great, but the marriage is getting to me."

With the professionalism of a therapist, Cyn says, "Of course *he* thinks the marriage is great – *his* needs are being met. ... And don't worry about the kids. They're going to be taking off soon anyway, leaving you to decide whether or not you *want* to stay, versus *need* to stay, for them."

"The funny thing is, in as much as I'd like more from him, I can live with whatever little he has to offer, when he's stretched. But him ignoring me, while he makes time for other things .... Maybe I'm just not good enough for him."

Cyn says, "Nonsense! He'd be a fool to think that. Just look at him and then look at you."

"But what if that Hugh Grant thing that Dan talked about is really true?"

"Honey, if he starts acting like Hugh, have we got something for you."

"I already tried one of those – didn't work for me. Dunno how Charlotte developed the 'Rabbit' habit on *Sex and the City*, when I can barely figure mine out."

"We're not talking gizmos here, Silly," says Alison, and reaches into her purse to pull out a stack of printed emails. What the hell is she doing? I wonder. This is not the time or the place for her to show me her personals letters. The diversion may have worked for Randy, but not me. "Just take a look at these," she says, trying to hand over the stack to me.

Like a hot potato, I drop it back into her hand. "The last thing I want or need is your impotent men! ... Even though they're probably the only trustworthy bunch left on the planet."

"These aren't from *my* impotent men. They're for

you."

"What the fuck is she talking about?" I ask Cyn, fearing that Alison has finally lost it.

"When you were all bummed out the last time, feeling bad about yourself, we did one of those pro and con lists that you're famous for. And let me tell you, Girlfriend, you came across as one hellova lot better package than that asshole. ... Just look at you – you're hot, lovable, successful, smart, funny, sexy – while he's nothing more than a stubborn, lecherous drunk, with millions of problems. ... Granted that he's a doc and has a hot car, but no hot bod to match, unlike you – he's not aging very gracefully, is he?"

"*Hey*, he's still my husband."

"Well he'd better start acting like one – not like a fucking bachelor who wants to eat his cake and have others' too," hisses Alison.

"I hope so too, 'cause I can't imagine how I'd survive without him."

"Honey, there's billions of women out there doing just fine without him, so will you," says Cyn. She then looks me straight in the eye, to make sure that she has my undivided attention, and grunts, "A-n-y-how, since you're always claiming that we're biased when it comes to you and Jeremy, we decided to do a little experiment to give you some unbiased opinions."

I give Alison a worried look, and say, "I'm even afraid to ask."

Alison smiles, and says, "No worries – we just took out a personals ad for you and another one for Jeremy."

Shocked, I say, "Is *that* all?"

Alison continues, "It was just supposed to be a fun gag when we did it, to prove our point to you; but now I think the timing couldn't be more perfect."

Cyn adds, "'Cause guess what? Jeremy got only two emails, probably from a couple of desperate losers who'd be willing to put up with anything, just as long as they can nail a doc. ... You, on the other hand, got more than fifty, in just over a week."

"Gimme that," I say, trying to take the stack of letters away from Alison, while sucking up my tear-snots. "I must look really good on paper. ... Sure beats the responses I get for the employment ads I place for my catering company."

"Let me put on a pot of martinis and we can go through them together, one by one ... before you decide what you wanna do with the pig. ... I don't want you going back to him like you did the last time, just 'cause you think no one else will ever love you," emphasizes Cyn.

"How do you know that these guys wanna *love* me? They're still men – probably just wanna sleep with me ... and then I get to repeat the Jeremy cycle with them all over again. ... I'm thinking, until someone comes up with a love vaccine, I'm going to treat men like carbs and stay the heck away from them. They're both bound to head straight for your hips and then leave you in a state of ruin."

"Hey," chimes in Alison, "Do we have a convert to my philosophy on sex and relationships?"

"Not so fast, Sistah," barks Cyn. "If *anything*, you'll be *lucky* if they wanna sleep with you. The whole fucking thing is all ass backwards – we're at our sexual prime when men don't want us anymore ... not men our age anyway. Now younger guys of course are a whole different story ... and quite happy to keep up, if you know what I mean," she winks.

"And they don't complain, no matter what you do to them," I laugh, remembering all the times Cyn had treated them horribly.

"You know her philosophy," adds Alison, "Men are like tiles. Lay them right the first time and you can step all over them for the rest of your life."

Cyn laughs, "Stepping on them is not all that bad ... if only men were grapes, so you could actually turn them into something decent that you could have dinner with."

We are now laughing and acting almost as silly as the night we got high on pot – but still not high enough to look at the emails, tempting as they're becoming with every sip. You see, as broken as I feel, I'm not sure Jeremy and I are broken up just yet. I truly believe that a breakup requires far more commitment for it to take, than getting hitched – all *that* requires is going to the alter and sacrificing yourself. ... Next thing you know, you've become one. And it works out fine, just as long as *he's* the one, and you're both in love with *him*. What was I thinking, trying to carve out a life for myself? ... I wanna tell the girls that I'm not done licking my wounds just yet, but I know exactly what Cyn will say – then let these guys lick them for you.

Three martinis later, laced with loads of flattery – who needs Zoloft when you have girlfriends – I now have the courage to tackle the pile ... just out of "curiosity".

The very first email is from someone wanting to be my soul-mate. "Hah – spoken like a true Jeremy, though I think it was *my* fault that I misunderstood him. In hindsight, I think he meant sole-mate, since he intended on walking all over me. ... What a heel!"

Cyn chimes, "You know what they say – time wounds all heels."

"You mean 'time heals all wounds'."

"Nope, I mean 'time wounds all heels' – his pain will come."

"Trouble is, I think he digs pain. ... Hey, maybe that's what this is all about – him giving me something he *really* cherishes," I say sarcastically. "Though I wish he'd stop surprising me with it so often."

Appreciating the need to nip the pity party in the bud, Alison scans through a couple more letters on her own and hands one over to me. "Fuck that – read this one!"

It's not really a letter, more of a note – a noteworthy note at that. There in black and white, it says, "Would you like to join me for a drink and perhaps some sex afterwards?" We all break into hysterics. "Ohmigosh, a man who is actually willing to sacrifice himself for a woman my age, if he can get drunk first! ... Perhaps I should snap him up." I chuckle.

Alison picks out another one with an equally entertaining punch line: I'd give my right nut to go out with you. I laugh, "In that case, if it doesn't work out for us, he'd be perfect for you, Alison."

Cyn adds, "I want *my* men to have some major balls – physically and otherwise. To me, good ball size is more important than good cock size."

"You're not fucking the *balls* – what difference does it make?" asks Alison.

"It's an aesthetic thing – same reason they've gotta be manscaped."

"For me, it's the whole package," I add. "Sex is

just the icing on the cake – without a good relationship, it's just icing."

"And what's wrong with that? When a relationship sucks, you're supposed to go for zipless sex *and* guilt-free icing binges, are you not?" adds Alison. "Sure beats mixing 'em all up."

"Personally, I'd rather take the sex and skip the fattening sweets," says Cyn.

I jump in, "Are you kidding? When we feel bad, sex makes us feel worse; when guys feel bad, sex just perks them right back up. ... Even adultery has a gender bias. For guys, it may just be an extra that doesn't have anything to do with their relationship; for us, it can be because our relationship sucks, so it has everything to do with it... otherwise, why would we bother?"

Now the girls are irritated. Cyn gives me a dirty look, "Boy do you have a lot to learn. If I had to get stuck in a relationship with one loving dick for the rest of my life, I'd kill myself. I'd much rather have four or five on the go – that way if one can't be bothered to hang out with me, or do things that I like, there's always others that'll be more than happy to take his place."

Gotta love the girl for balancing things out. For every five-hundred-year-old guy who can get a barely legal girl, Cyn sure does her bit as the female equivalent; for every man needing variety, ditto. The only thing that she hasn't tried yet is the female equivalent of serial polygamy – supporting a series of exes, without the privilege of living together as one big happy commune. ... If Jeremy and I split up, I guess that'll be another strike against him – baggage, where money goes out instead of coming in.

Cyn jars me back into the here and now. "Earth to Jillian please."

"Just drifting off into my fantasy world, 'cause you girls are waaay too cynical for me."

"Hell no," says Alison, jumping to their defense. "Realistic maybe, but never cynical."

After entertaining various possibilities, and me *almost* forgetting about my predicament, we put the letters aside and log onto a hot-mail account the girls have set up for me. Beyond the customary offers of hot babes and penis enlargement – with appropriate pills, pumps and porn – I find tons of letters from various prospects, responding to a posting on a dating web site; again, thanks to the girls. To my surprise, not one of them looks like a serial killer or a complete loser. In fact, a lot of them are downright gorgeous. I say, "I wonder how old these pictures are, or the guys for that matter, 'cause stuff over the Internet can be all lies. Then again, so is my marriage." Watching the girls frustrated expressions, I try to make light of the conversation by adding, "Okay boys, lie to me ... especially if your wood grows bigger with each lie, like Pinocchio's nose!"

Cyn takes the opportunity to point out, "See, size *does* matter to you." We all laugh.

But in as much as the girls have shown me that this isn't the end of the world, I can't help but feel like my life is over ... I'll never be able to feel good again. My chest hurts when I breathe, probably because I wanna die. ... I know, I know, I've been here before, after my breakup with Rick ... just before I met Jeremy. Didn't think I'd survive that either, but I did ... and will again.

What if I'm wrong about Jeremy? Then again, what possible explanation could he have for those panties? One way to find out, I suppose. But I've gotta do it outside the house – the kids mustn't hear that conversation.

I turn to the girls and say, "Thank you so much for lifting my spirits and the old sagging ego, but I need some time alone." They understand and leave on cue. I call Jeremy next, and ask him to come over to "The Cocoon", pronto!

Jeremy walks in about half an hour later to find me on the couch, curled up into myself like a shrimp, eyes pinker than *Pepto-Bismol.* He sits down beside me and brushes the hair off my forehead with his fingers, looking quite worried. "What's the matter, Baby?"

Bluntly, I get straight to the point, "*I know.*"

If there were a picture in the dictionary by the word "guilty", I'm sure it couldn't do justice to what Jeremy's face looks like right now. Talk about admission of guilt. But even though I'm right this time, somehow it doesn't feel very good. Just this once, I wish I was happy instead of right.

"How did you find out?" is all that he can say, head hanging down in shame.

"Does it really matter?"

"I guess not... I never meant to hurt you."

"How could you think it wouldn't hurt?"

"Had I planned it out that logically, I wouldn't have done it at all."

"But the point is you did ... and it hurts like hell."

Jeremy tries to hold me – not a consolation prize I'm interested in. "Don't," I whimper and pull away. "I can't understand how anyone can expect an affair to turn out okay. ... If it's good, you end up resenting your family; if it's bad, you end up resenting yourself. A definite lose-

lose situation, where everybody can end up getting hurt."

"I know I really fucked up. I'd give *any*thing to undo this if I could ... but obviously I can't. I feel sick inside, that's why I've been all over the place – wanting to reconnect with you one minute, pulling away the next, 'cause I don't think I deserve you. ... For what it's worth, it's over now – has been for a while." Strange how Jeremy is doing all the talking, when generally it's the other way around. And no, it being over hardly heals the wound.

I sarcastically hiss, "How sweet of you. I guess if it's over, we really don't have to worry about having this conversation anymore, do we?"

"I deserved that. Go ahead, take as many shots at me as you like – if it'll help you feel better."

"*Feel better*? I don't think *any*thing can make me *feel* better," I sob. "But thank you for your generosity in offering me the shots. Just hope I don't miss you."

He stands up and starts pacing back and forth. "What can I say?"

It's amazing how he expects this thing to blow over, just 'cause it's out in the open and he's had a chance to unload his conscience. That's the toughest part of forgiveness, isn't it – the onus is always on the injured party. Well not this time! ... No matter what Grammy might expect of me.

"Look, Honey, I'd be willing to do *anything* to win back your trust. I'll see a therapist, stop drinking, come straight home after work, let you call me anytime you like – whatever it takes."

Wish I knew what the magical formula is, *if* there is one – I'd bottle it. ... I'm now dying inside, but I'm sure he doesn't want to see me that way. I mean, how attractive is that? And if the truth be known, I don't think *anybody* wants to see me that way – not even me. ... I want to close myself off from the rest of the world. But it's not a luxury I have, not when you share a household and two kids.

Some decisions will have to be made. But what? And how?

Bleary-eyed, I look at him and say, "I'm not sure if there's *any*thing that can win back my trust. All I know for sure is that I need some time to process this."

Jeremy says, "I'll stay in a hotel tonight," and starts to walk out the door.

I grab the granny panties from my purse and throw them at him. "Don't forget to return these to her, when you have your rendezvous at the hotel."

Jeremy looks very surprised and shocked to see the panties. I wonder why – the worst is already out? Sheepishly, he asks, "Where did you find those?"

"In your underwear drawer, when I went to pack for our trip."

"What makes you think they're her's?"

"Who else's would they be?"

Shamefully, he confesses, "Mine – I like to wear them when I feel like playing a submissive role."

"Oh God Almighty – this has nothing to do with the affair, does it?"

Holding the panties up in his left hand, he points to them with his right, a puzzled expression crisscrossing his face. "Is *that* why ... how *did* you find out about the affair?"

"You just told me."

"What an idiot I am," he says, slamming his forehead with his right fist.

"For getting busted, or for doing it in the first place?"

"Both," he says, shamefully walking out the door.

Like Grammy used to say, if you look for something hard enough, you'll eventually find it ... and it won't necessarily make you happy.

But the VISA bill charges finally make sense now. For every cheap bit of lingerie he bought me, every lame bouquet of flowers he sent me, the bills were always too high to justify the cost.

He must have been doubling up for her. What a genius way to make sure that I don't suspect anything!

Well fuck you, Jeremy – two can play that game!

An hour and six martinis later, I've numbed myself enough so the thought of Jeremy can't cause me any more pain – at least not for now.

I wonder what's worse – paralysis, or excruciating pain that tells you that you're still capable of feeling. ... Definitely paralysis!

Almost as if in rote, I log back on and start to have an on-line conversation with someone who really seems to be my speed.

Not that I plan on doing anything, but I play along anyway ... to see how far my numb mind will allow me to go.

To my surprise, things heat up pretty quickly and I find myself having cyber-sex with a total stranger.

I guess a grudge fuck isn't half bad when you're merely exchanging words, instead of bodily fluids.

Intrigued, I decide to take the next step and ask my amour if I may call him.

He gives me his private cell number. I dial. It's ringing. He answers with a sexy "Hello."

The voice sounds familiar – a little too familiar. I hang up!

*   *   *

I go home, slip into my bed – alone – and sob the night away, with my face buried into my pillow. I can't imagine anything hurting more than this.

The no-way-out feeling reminds me of all the nights when I cried myself to sleep as a teenager.

I knew at that time that Mom could hear me, but not once did she come into my room to comfort me. It's not like I was a baby and she had to break the habit.

Then again, if she'd come into my room, she'd actually have to get involved – not something you can do when you choose to wear blinders.

They say that we either become exactly like our parents, or the exact opposite of them – wonder where I fit in?

Chapter 10 - *New Beginnings*

The kids have been sent off on a long-awaited summer vacation through Europe, making it easier on everybody as Jeremy and I sort things through a trial separation – though I'm not exactly sure what the rules are. Are we supposed to be reflecting on what is, or dating others to see what could be?

Rumor has it that Jeremy has already started experimenting with the latter, with his all-too-eager nurses. Now that discretion is no longer an issue, why stick with just one when you can have as many as you like? After all, when it comes to research, sample size does matter – the bigger the better. Just the push I need to do some serious sampling of my own. Sure beats sulking and whining, especially since it doesn't look like Jeremy will come crawling back to me anytime soon, begging for forgiveness. ... Actually, if the truth be known, I'm *really* looking forward to my date tonight. I've wasted far too much time and energy on self-doubt and self-pity, making myself miserable. Time to move forward and make myself happy instead. I deserve it! Anything less would be *my* fault at this point, not Jeremy's, for being miserable that is. Yes, sir, my self-esteem is repaired and I'm ready to re-pair – bring it on!

*   *   *

I pull up into Mr. Articulate Stockbroker's driveway, to pick him up – hope he's as delish in person as he is in cyber space. But I'm not holding my breath. From what Alison's told me, more often than not, even the most yummy sounding guy can be a major letdown in person. Something to do with words counting for less than ten percent in reality and hundred percent in cyber space, where we fill in the blanks with our fertile imaginations – same reason why movies are rarely as exciting as the book.... I guess I'll find out soon enough ... according to Cyn, within the first ten minutes of meeting him, assuming I pay attention.

I walk up to the house, hoping for the best. Like any typical downtown home where land is at a premium, it's skinny and tall, with a pointy roof – like a gigantic penis. I take one good look at it and ring the doorbell with anticipation. A lady weaver bird would be impressed – like some humans I know, they check out the male's nest to see if he's worth mating with, before committing to anything. But that's not why I'm here.

Then exactly why are you picking him up, you ask? Because Grammy taught me never to rely on a guy for a ride on the first date. What if you need to bale? Worse, what if he's drunk? I had really only wanted to meet him at the restaurant nearby, but he insisted that I come over and see his penis ... I mean, his place.

The door opens up to a well-dressed, hunky guy. Boy would I ever love for him to show me *any*thing he wants. But following a polite hello and a handshake, Stu suggests that we save the grande tour for later. Dunno if it has to do with me showing up late, risking losing a reservation that took three weeks to get, or if it's just a ploy to end the evening at the very tip of the penis house. Stu claims that he sleeps there, for its pyramid-like health benefits.

No sooner do we slip into my car when Mr. Articulate – make that Mr. Gorgeous and Articulate – decides to take his shoes off and makes himself comfortable. "Aaah ...."

Words can't describe what hits my nose. I open up

my window and slide back my sunroof, to get rid of whatever the smell is. ... Nothing doing! I finally look at his feet and say, "We've barely met ... exposing our feet already, are we?" trying my best to sound flirtatious versus offensive, while still drawing attention to the subject at hand ... foot.

Stu strokes my thigh and says, "Would you rather I expose something else?"

Whoa, not what I was expecting at all. Even if, not a chance of me wanting to see or smell anything else now. I sheepishly grin, and say, "Feet are about all I can handle for now."

Stu wiggles his toes and says, "You know what they say about big feet?"

Not this again! What I really want to say is, "Foot size, no relation to cock size – foot odor, on the other hand ..." but I bite my tongue and go with, "Need big shoes?"

Thigh stroking intensifies, as Mr. Smelly Feet Guy informs me, "Wish *these* were big shoes. They've been pinching my feet all evening – no room to breathe." Right now, I'm not certain if *I* wanna breathe. But Smelly Feet Guy doesn't seem terribly concerned. Shamelessly, he puts on a sex smile, stares me straight in the eye, drops his voice a few octaves, and continues, "But I must say, I *do* like a girl with a good sense of humor – bound to be playful in other ways. I just *hate* uptight girls."

"Oh, I wouldn't be too sure about that – the playful part, that is. Never undress my feet on the first date." And with that, we pull into The Rose Club driveway and handover my car to the valet. As the red-jacketed guy takes over my Porsche, he really checks me out – my new-found sexual élan must be giving off the right signals. Eyes still locked onto mine, he hands me a claim ticket with a wink.

I'm praying that he doesn't think it's *my* feet that stink – kinda like when you get out of an elevator with just one other person, right after they drop a toxic fart, hoping that no one thinks it's you, while they make their best effort to look indignant.

Stu escorts me inside, and insists on pulling out my chair, even though the *maître de* had already started to do it for me. I sit down and pray that our shoes stay on. ... Of course you already know how that turned out – yup, the loafers are off again. I can't even begin to think of eating now, with that terrible stench covering up all the gourmet smells that I've smelled here before. Our neighbors don't look too pleased either. Sorry, Stu, you're not going to make the catch of the day!   I do the uncontainable, feigning a stomachache, hoping to turn the date into a rain-check situation. Mr. Smelly Feet Guy is not too pleased. He hisses, "Do you have *any* idea how long it took me to get this reservation ... and how *many* girls would kill to have me bring them here?"

"I'm sooo sorry, Stu. Why don't I drive myself home and let you call up one of those gals to join you? No need to waste a perfectly good evening."

No response – not that I expected any. Memo-to-self: add smelly feet to list of reasons to take your own car.

No sooner do I plop into my Porsche, I open up all of my windows and my sunroof. Too bad it's starting to get a little chilly, with a light rain. I get on the highway and dial Cyn on my cell. She answers to loud whooshing noises, and asks, "Aren't you supposed to be on a date? And where the hell did he take you anyway? I can hardly hear you."

"The date's over. *I* ended it. He has the stinkiest feet on the planet – I couldn't stand it."

"Boy you guys work fast! Whatever happened to eating before undressing?"

"The date hadn't even begun yet, when Mr. Smelly Feet decided to take his tight shoes off and make himself comfortable in *my* car."

"Where are you now? What's that noise?"

"That's the highway – I'm driving with my windows down, trying to air out the Porsche."

"That bad, huh?"

"Worse! Never knew that someone with such impeccable clothes could take the hygiene beneath them with such a huge grain of salt."

"Why don't you come on over and we'll dissect him over a few martinis?"

"Are you alone?"

"You gotta be kidding. Ever since Jonathan's gal pal's parents stuck her with us so they could travel alone, me and Rajiv haven't had a moment to ourselves."

"Be over in five," I say, and step on it. Hopefully the forceful winds will clear the air.

Oh, in case you're wondering, yes, Cyn and Rajiv Gupta have become somewhat of an item as of late. And if you were to look at them now, you could be easily fooled into thinking that our died-in-the-wool, confirmed bachelorette is falling in love. The irony? It's almost as if Cyn and Alison have swapped bodies, like one of those crazy switcheroo movies. While our sex-crazed Cyn is turning into a monogamous, domestic mush-ball, our sworn-off-sex Alison can't seem to keep her hands off her new beau – Clive.

The only one amongst us who's gone back to their

old ways, is Randy. Broken up that him and Steven are, he's anything but broken up over it. Yup, our boy is back to slutting it up ... and loving every minute of it. If only he could rub off on Darla – her heart is with Rita, her strange sense of loyalty with Danielle ... and she's too confused and messed up to sleep with either.

*   *   *

I pull up into Cyn's driveway and park. The door's been left unlocked for me so I walk in. Just as I make myself comfortable in her tiny little, black granite kitchen, she yells down from upstairs, "Your 'tini is chilling in the freezer. Be down in a minute."

I yell "Sure!" and make a bee-line for the freezer. Is that giggles I hear? I look over the serving window that connects the kitchen to the adjoining family room and find a kilted teen throwing herself onto Rajiv's lap, trying to tickle him. The man is resisting like crazy, even though the lump in his pants is defying him. What the hell is she doing? I wonder. But before I can investigate further, she's as well-behaved as can be – dare I say even sweet and dimpled, when Cyn comes down and said teen offers to help her in the kitchen.

Cyn introduces us, "Jill, I'd like you to meet Jonathan's friend, Melissa. Melissa, this is *my* friend, Jill."

We both smile, shake hands, and do a faux "charmed" gesture. I break the ice with, "So where's Jonathan tonight?"

"Oh, I don't know," she says, with a and-don't-give-a-shit attitude, sweet as she's trying to appear. The only thing that she does seem to care about is, a twenty-four year old, attractive, East Indian man, sitting on a couch nearby. She keeps smiling at him, unable to take her eyes off him.

166

I gesture to Cyn with a sideways nod, expressing, "What's with her?" Cyn just laughs and dismisses it. I guess if she's not too worried about it, neither will I. The old me would've driven herself crazy right about now, running stupid scenarios in her head. Actually, if the truth be known, the old me wouldn't even be here – she'd still be with Mr. Smelly Feet Guy, paying her dues politely. But the new me knows how to take care of herself, and have some fun.

And fun is exactly what I decide to arrange. I dial Dan on my cell, only to get his voice mail. In my most salacious voice ever, I say, "Hi, Big Boy. Wanna come over and play? I'm at Cyn's, but can be easily persuaded to meet you elsewhere."

Cyn laughs at me, "Oh no you don't. You're staying put. I have a funny feeling I'm going to need all the support I can get. Justin has suddenly taken an interest in the boys and has been hanging around a lot lately. He'll more than likely pop by tonight, to irritate the hell out of me and Rajiv."

Well that's certainly not something I ever expected. Why would Jonathan and Michael's father suddenly take an interest in them, after being away all this time? Unless ... his interest lies with their mother, since his girl-toy has ditched him – ditto for his booty call. Rumor has it that the poor guy can't afford much of anything these days.

My reprieve is broken by a buzzing text message on my cell. It's Dan: wat u waring? In bored mtg, wil leav sn. Can't be soon enough for me. You see, Dan isn't just gorgeous, he's like one of the girls. I can talk to him about anything under the sun – from deep and meaningful to funny and exciting. And he not only listens, but actually responds to me, with a great deal of interest. It's become the most important criteria for all of my relationships now, especially with men – if I can't imagine clearing my calendar just to have lunch with you, I'm certainly not going to clear any hairy landscape to have sex with you.

Cyn takes one look at my dreamy expression and says, "Go on, I'll be fine."

"Am I *that* transparent?"

"Let's put it this way; if I were ever to play poker or rob a bank with a partner, you'd be the last person I'd look up."

I hug her, say "Thank you," and make my way out to my car. I'm fumbling with my keys, while trying to dial Dan at the same time. He picks up. But before he can even say hello, I tell him, "Would be a shame to waste a warm pool. How about a skinny dip?"

"Will I need to rescue you like last time?"

"That depends ... but the way I'm feeling right now, I think I'm ready to take the plunge, fearlessly."

*   *   *

I suppose the plunge part did the trick, 'cause we both set a new record, pulling up into my driveway at the same time, from opposite sides of town. His red Ferrari looks so much nicer by my Porsche than the Z4. Okay, Dan, let's see how fast you can go from zero to sixty!

We both get out of our cars and give each other an awkward hug – the kind where bums stick out 'cause you're afraid of genital contact. You'd think we were teens the way we we're acting. I'm getting wet just thinking about what might happen; the pearl between my legs swelling up from the anticipation of a new lease on life. After all these years of burying my head in the sand, I finally made something wonderful out of the irritation – a brand new pearl, just dying to be discovered.

I struggle with my keys yet again, to let us in the front door. Dan swoops me up into his muscley arms and carries me across the threshold, like a bride. How symbolic! If I'm going to crossover the threshold into a new life, what better person to have that transitional affair with than Dan?

Once inside, Dan lays me across the plump couch in my living room, lights all the candles he can find, and opens up my favorite Merlot so it can breathe. I wish *I* could breathe!

He then disappears into the garden and picks some fresh gardenias for my hair. After making me feel like a Hawaiian princess, he pours me some wine and raises his glass; his brows mischievously rise along with it, to propose a silent, telling toast. Before I can cling my glass against his, I wonder if I'm about to make a mistake? But the feeling is very short-lived. Cling ... I find myself going for it, confident that I'll never repeat my old mistakes again. I can always make new ones, if I must – as long as they match a fresh new start!

The undressing begins, starting with my sandals. Dan takes them off ever-so-carefully and rubs by tired feet – promise you they're sweet-smelling. After the longest time, making sure that I'm fully relaxed, he finally moves up to my ebony chiffon blouse. As he opens each button, he kisses the exposed flesh beneath, sending electric shivers throughout my entire body.

Once all the buttons are undone and the sheer fabric falls away, he rubs my shoulders to relax me some more. Normally, I'd be falling asleep right about now, feeling freed from tension after such a long time. Tonight, sleep is the farthest thing from my mind – I'm about to start a dangerous voyage.

My breasts quiver from excitement within my black lace bra, my nipples feel harder than they have in a couple of decades. Why won't he grab them already? I so want to experience a spiritual awakening. According to The Dalai Lama, from contact comes craving, from craving the desire to grasp. ... But Dan is not having any of it – he just works around my aching nipples, getting close, but not quite grasping.

As his hand "accidentally" brushes up against my right breast, I let out a big sigh, letting him know how badly I want him to do more. ... It appears to discourage him; for he promptly moves away from there and starts to plant gentle kisses on my belly, eyes deeply gazing into mine. Oh God, please don't let him see my hysterectomy scar, attesting to my infertile bod. Or for that matter, the stretch marks around it – from when I *was* fertile. ... Almost as if he's reading my mind, Dan stops the teasing and starts to make love to me – my belly actually ... kissing each and every part that I've ever been embarrassed about.

I wonder if he knows anything about water retention – or for that matter, pie, ice-cream, or cookie-dough retention, since my body seems to retain them all, quite indiscriminately in fact. But it doesn't seem to scare Dan too much.

I finally realize how Shirley Valentine must've felt when her lover kissed her stretch marks, after her husband had ignored her finer points for almost a lifetime. ... Not Dan – he heads for those finer points next.

I was always quite proud of my breasts, which must be said are quite amazing. In fact, they practically define me – physically. Even when I wasn't sure about the rest of my body, I found my breasts to be quite worthy of showcasing – thanks to plunging necklines – and a major turn on for me!

Dan's chocolate hands undo my bra and cradle my pale mounds, his strong thumbs encircling the rose tips at their very peaks. A moan escapes me. I wonder if he realizes that I could reach ecstasy from that gesture alone. But Dan has bigger plans. He unbuttons my skirt and pulls it away with the urgency of our first kiss, many moons ago. Thank goodness that I made time for a bikini wax yesterday, since my other prospect did sound like someone I'd want to have lunch with. It would be a shame to turn down Dan, just 'cause the landscape hadn't been tended to – though according to Cyn, it inadvertently kicks up the ante on the chase. Then again, I don't want him to chase me any longer – just take me already, dammit!

Alas, the man reads my mind again, and goes back to torturing me with tender kisses and not so tender teasing.

Don't know how we finally got here, but at long last Dan rips off my thong and opens me up. I'm drenched with excitement. As he skillfully slips his fingers in and out of me numerous times, I start to tense up, feeling myself get close to the brink. Dan pulls out, not wanting me to come just yet, and starts to explore my hard pearl with his wet fingers.

It's now my turn to undress him. But I've forgotten how. It's been so long since I've done it – don't know what the rules are any longer. Feeling quite exposed myself, I say, "Hey, that's not fair. If we're truly skinny dipping, I'm going to have to see a lot more skin than just your face and hands."

Dan starts to unbutton his blue silk shirt, beginning with the cuffs. Impatient as I am, I decide to give him a hand – ripping off his belt and undoing his fly. I wonder if it's true what they say about African American men? I guess I'll find out soon enough.

I stare at him hungrily, as his boxers drop down to reveal the most beautiful penis I've ever seen – large enough to impale me, yet comfortable enough to show off my new blow-job skills, to my teacher no less. I find myself staring at it, shamelessly – truly, it was made for no other purpose than to make a woman happy. Its smooth, velvety chocolate skin is just begging to be stroked ... licked ... sucked – definitely a cock I wouldn't mind my sun rising to. Without a comma of hesitation, I drop to my knees – who am I to argue with Mother Nature? ... It tastes and smells wonderful – better than any gourmet delight that *I've* ever con-cock-ted!

Within moments, Dan's legs start to shake, his balls rise up high and taut – I know the moment of inevitability is fast approaching. I reach into my purse and find a condom – thank goodness for the piñata incident. ... I want to use my mouth to put it on him. But what if I can't be as slick as a porn star? ... Honestly, don't think Dan would care – he'd just appreciate the fact that I tried. One-two-three – it's out of the pack and slipped on his cock. No sooner do I pull my mouth away from it, Dan plunges it inside me ... forcefully. I'm ready for him to burst as soon as he enters me, hoping that he'll take the time to finish me off afterwards, using his very skilled fingers. Even if not, there's always my own fingers. But Dan surprises me yet again. He rides high and pumps against my clit in a circular motion ... over and over again ... until I'm writhing, moaning, and moving in rhythm with him. Please don't stop – not now – I'm thinking, when he looks deeply into my eyes and asks if I'm ready? It's not a question that anyone has ever cared to ask me before. I respond by gyrating harder than anything I thought possible, engulfing him deeper, my Kagel's milking him in ways that I can relish myself.

And then, it happens ... my very first climax ... with a man inside me!

Is *that* what they call an orgasm? To clear any shadow of a doubt, Dan continues to pump into me, until I go into a second wave of spasms ... and a third ... and a fourth one after that.

In all my years with Jeremy, all that the bed tremors represented was intimacy, and a renewal of the feeling that I'm still desirable to him. But never did I anticipate that I could actually enjoy myself like that *and* feel more alive and desirable than ever! I finally understand why it's called *self-*image, 'cause how you see your*self* is a critical part of the image you present to others!

I lay there, my legs quivering. Dan kisses my lips, finger brushes the clingy wet hair off my forehead, and says, "Thank you, my love ... that was truly amazing!" – a sentiment which can be trusted wholeheartedly, because of its post-ejaculatory nature. ... And with that, he slides off me, slips into the powder room, and brings me back a warm, wet towel. I'm ready to take it from him, to clean myself up a bit, but he shakes his head and says, "Allow me." Gently, he wipes me, using an extremely erotic motion. I'm so sensitive that I pull away, unable to take any more. ... And here I thought that it's just the guys who go into a refractory period; until now, I had no reason to think otherwise, having been left unsatiated far too many times. I'd use my fingers to get off afterwards, but never *fly* off like this ... feeling truly weightless – sure beats sinking with a heavy heart!

But Dan's not done yet. He walks over to the stereo; his butt looks firmer and more defined than anything I ever imagined – and believe me, I've been imagining it a lot lately. ... Is that Natalie Cole I hear?

Dan walks back toward me – his penis as gorgeous as ever, even in its resting stage – and offers me his hand. We dance – cheek to cheek, crotch to crotch. Ohmigosh, he's getting hard again! I don't know how much more of this I can take. I smile, "Perhaps a cold swim for now?"

"I thought you promised me a warm pool."

I giggle and escort him outside. We take the plunge – fearlessly!

After possibly the most wonderful night of my life – as of late, in any case – I lay in bed and think, who needs a Goddess Awakening weekend with the girls, when a man can do just fine? But then I catch myself – can't expect a lover to do the work that I haven't done for myself, especially since I find myself waking up from a dream. A lifelike dream, but a dream nonetheless. All that teenage style groping must've left me with a craving so deep, that I ended up dreaming about it, after Dan left – he didn't want to rush me into anything ... never closed the deal. His parting words: thanks for allowing me to make love to you. ... I suppose, for him, that's what making love is all about, not penetration or spasms – that's just sex, as Alison would put it!

Chapter 11 - *Sex Gods And Goddesses*

The girls and I finally arrive at the "Goddess Ranch" – looks more like a chicken ranch to me – after driving for six long hours. This had better be worth it!

I've been promised all kinds of pampering – including spa treatments – in addition to dance therapy and workshops that are to awaken the sex goddess within. Normally, you'd think that Cyn would come up with something like this, sex-obsessed that she is. This time, it's in fact Alison who's surprised us with the gift packages – told you the two girls seem to have switched bodies. I suppose with Clive in her life, she'd better wake up those sexy parts of herself that have lain dormant far too long.

Once we drive through the main gate off the main road, there appear to be no more roads – just rough terrain, with worn off grass marking the way. Thank goodness we borrowed Dan's SUV. The Porsche would have had an ass-ectomy by now, being so low to the ground.

A mile later, we seem to be arriving upon a hint of civilization, though I've yet to see anything human. Birds are chirping, crows crowing, a peacock is showing off its plumage, and horses are doing what they do best. In as much as I love nature, I love amenities just a wee bit more – a firm bed and functional plumbing being truly non-negotiable in my books. ... Since we didn't pack any tents or porta-potties, I'm assuming the stone cottage up ahead offers both.

My cynicism comes to a halt when we finally pull up to the stone building. It's nestled amongst lush trees, on the most glorious beach I've ever seen. Just beyond are beautiful mountains, known for their hot springs and waterfalls. I can't wait to get out of my clothes and soak in the natural hot tubs. From what I understand, they're rich in minerals that money can't buy.

We barely park the SUV and get out, when we're greeted by a rotund woman in her fifties, dressed in layers of colorful gauze and a matching head scarf, oozing goddess charm. Right behind her are four adonises, dressed in equally filmy summer-wear. With the warmest smile, she steps forward and says, "Hello, I'm Sunny, your hostess at the Goddess Ranch ... and these here are your personal assistants for the weekend." One by one, we introduce ourselves to Sunny. When she gets to Alison, she throws her arms around her in the most affectionate hug. "Finally we meet, after all this time," she says, kissing her on both cheeks. "I've heard so much about you. ... Rest assured that you and your friends will have the time of your lives – I'm going to see to it personally. It's my way of saying thanks for all the business you've given me over the years. You truly are my number one client."

Number one client? Tons of business? What is she talking about? I can't imagine Alison sending anyone out here. And with what money – a place like this has gotta cost a bundle! As I look at her questioningly, her eyes drop down. I've seen that awkward look on her face just one other time, the night I intercepted her weird text message. Maybe she's running a drug business on the side after all, I think, the new me titillated by the risk factor we might find ourselves in. But before I can drift off into an action adventure sequence, my personal assistant introduces himself as Swen and takes my bags from me.

I shake my right index finger at Alison, like a school teacher, say, "Don't even *think* about getting out of this one," and follow Swen.

Watching his firm body move sexily within his filmy cotton jammies, I wanna say, "Take me to your leader and do as you please with me." But I entertain a wicked grin instead, wondering just how *personal* the personal assistants get. After all, they *do* have to awaken the sex goddess within.

Once inside my room, Swen leaves me to my own devices. I open up my windows and inhale the most delish, floral scent in the air, connecting me to an endless sky, with moving murals in various shapes, sizes and sunset colors. I barely unpack, when I hear a gentle knock on my door. It's Swen, holding a tray of earthly delights.

"Do you like your room?" he asks, as he sits down a pitcher of something colorful and frosty on my patio table – the kinda drink that comes with a little umbrella at most bars.

I laugh, "What's not to like?" giving him my most flirtatious stare ever. Gosh, give the girl a little action just once, and she turns into a total slut with a one track mind! ... But did I have to give him such a cheesy line?

As if on cue – like I'm the first woman who's ever undressed him with her eyes – he responds suggestively, "In that case, would you mind slipping out of your clothes?" handing me a fluffy, heated robe. "I'll get ready for your massage in the gazebo." All this before we've been properly introduced and had our first cocktail together? But who am I to complain?

I slip out of my travel clothes, grab a quick shower, and come out in my fluffy robe. Diaphanous curtains are billowing out of the gazebo windows, thanks to a gentle breeze. As I get closer, intoxicating smells from aromatherapy oils and candles dance to enchanting music and hit my nose. I feel like a goddess already.

Swen holds up a large bath towel to allow me to slip out of my robe, and then gracefully covers me with it once I've made myself comfortable on the massage table. In as much as I want to stay awake and savor every moment, Swen's hands drug me into a deep sleep, my body into a deeply relaxed state. When I wake up an hour later, I have no recollection of what went down, or *who* went down – as if. But as wishful thinking would have it, I imagine Swen awakening the goddess in my pelvic *chakra*.

Swen takes my right hand and helps me off the table, towel wrapped around me. "Be careful that you don't get dizzy." Inebriated as I feel, I may just fall into his arms. But I guess it'll have to wait for another time, 'cause Swen says, "See you later," and is already off, walking away with a stack of used towels.

*   *   *

The dining room is aglow with a million candles – or so it seems. Five guest tables, with four seats each, are set up exquisitely, attesting to twenty works in progress. Haunting sitar music fills the air, as does the aroma of various grilled meats. Time to eat the grills and grill the girl who brought us here!

Alison barely takes her seat, when I pour her a tall glass of the resident papaya-passion fruit drink, and impatiently ask, "So how did you find out about this place ... and why did Sunny call you her number one client?"

Full of anticipation, Cyn and I lean into the table, eyes glued on Alison, to listen to what she has to say for herself. But she just brushes us off with, "All in good time."

"Oh no you don't! You drag us all the way out here, in the middle of nowhere ... to awaken our sex goddesses. I'm thinking you're trying to learn the ropes again, with your recently revived interest in sex ... and just want us to hold your hand. But then I find out that there's a long-standing history between you and this place. Makes no sense whatsoever, especially for a girl who didn't believe in sex all this time."

"I never said I didn't *believe* in sex – just not *mixing* it up with love. ... And now I'm not even so sure about that."

"Pray do tell, how all of this ties into that." Silence. I'm quite irritated now. So I continue rather impatiently, "Are we your best friends or what? We've shared every heinous detail of our lives with you, and yet you can't seem to trust us with anything."

Looking at the hurt in my eyes, she says, "Okay, fine, I'll tell you – but promise not to judge me?" I never realized that I came across as judgmental – first Jeremy, now her. I nod an affirmative, and then motion a Scout's Honor to doubly seal the deal. Alison looks at Cyn and says, "Remember how pissed my mom was when she found out about your mom's topless habit?"

"Yeah?"

"And she forbid me from going anywhere *near* you, even though it wasn't *your* fault?"

"Ehm."

"Well her prudishness didn't just end there. As it turns out, she wasn't putting out all that much, leading Dad into the arms of another woman. ... Funny thing of it is, when she found out, at first she didn't seem too perturbed by it. If anything, she was relieved that someone else was taking care of all that 'disgusting stuff' for her. ... Then, when Dad started to fall in love with the other woman, Mom begged him to stop the love affair. But she was still willing to let him get some on the side, as long as *she* was the only one he loved. ... She even went as far as suggesting that maybe paying for the service would keep things simple – who could fall in love with a whore – as long as he never expected to sleep with Mom again. ... Drew a clear cut boundary between love and lust."

Cyn helps her out with, "Hence your obsession with treating sex and love as separate entities."

"*That,* and the fact that I could honestly see Mom's point, having had my own heart broken every time sex got wrapped up with love and distorted all perspective. Turned me off it completely. I guess I was terrified of ending up like her – she hit the bottle pretty hard back then, with all the bullshit that was going down."

Shocked, I stroke her arm, part comfort, part permission to quit anytime she wants – still don't know how any of this ties into what I asked. But she's on a roll – maybe it just feels good to get everything off her chest, once and for all. "Anyhow," she continues, "once I was able to acknowledge sex as a business transaction that could actually *save* marriages, I was quite comfortable stripping my way through college, to support myself."

"That's why we were never allowed to pick you up from the bookstore you supposedly worked at?" I ask.

"You got it!"

"And you were never strapped for cash," acknowledges Cyn.

"While you were slaving away at minimum wage, I was picking up fifty dollar tips in my G-string. ... Naturally, once I became a 'respectable' accountant, I couldn't stand the drop in my cash flow. But since I couldn't do both, I decided to hire some collage girls to do it for me."

Puzzled, I ask, "Strip for you?"

"No, Silly. I opened up a highly specialized, high-end call girl service, to cater to special requests ... private stripping being only one of many. I figured it would cost the guys a hellova lot less than their marriages."

Cyn deadpans, "Sounds pretty fucked up to me."

"Thanks for not judging."

"Sorry – not really judging, just trying to get my head around your logic."

"Well my logic brings in six figures annually, for being a mere liaison. How the hell do you think I can afford to pay for Mom's expensive rehab ... and my niece's tuition at the private academy?"

Impressed, Cyn adds, "Not to mention fab clothes and some *majorly* fab bling. ... Six figures, huh? ... I'm definitely in the wrong end of the sex business."

I ask, "I still don't understand how this place ties in?"

"Wait until you see how sexy they make you feel here, both inside and out."

Cyn laughs, "Let me get this right – our very own Madame Mayflower has been training her girls here?"

"Bingo!"

We clink our juice glasses together, as if to propose a toast to Alison's venture. I ask one more question. "You said you cater to special requests – what kind of special requests?"

"Anything from closet ass-jockeys needing intelligent trophy girlfriends for a business dinner, all the way to ass-whooping and other things that my impotent men seemed to be interested in."

"Hence the huge 'yes' pile from responses to your ad?"

"I wasn't intending on recruiting them for my business – but hey, if I can't date 'em, might as well mate 'em with someone else, especially if there's big bucks to be made."

"Please tell me that the requests for ass-whopping didn't include my Jeremy in any way."

Alison's eyes drop down, her mouth seals shut. Sure explains why she was jumping to his defense back then, convinced that there was nothing more going on. The old me would never speak to her again. The new me doesn't want to waste any more emotion on Jeremy, and thus raises her glass to Alison, "Handled like a true businesswoman!"

"You're not mad at me, Sweetie?"

"Why should I be? *He's* the one who asked for it, and God knows what else!"

Alison hugs me, tears unloading the burden she's carried all this time. "I really had mixed feelings about it, but I figured at least this way I could keep an eye on what was going on. I swear to you he didn't cross any lines ... not with my girls anyway. Would've told you if he tried anything."

As we begin to dig into our almond mandarin salads, Darla finally joins us, looking tired as all hell. "Sorry girls, just had it out with Danielle over the phone. The girl can't *stand* me being away from her for even a minute. Can't live like that – told her as much. I've always been honest with her. Either she can learn to trust me or not. Anyhow, she broke up with me when she heard it put that way. In a way I'm relieved – gives me a chance to sort out my feelings for Rita, sans guilt ... not that I was *doing* anything guilt-worthy, with either one of them. ... Bring on the sex goddess training – I am ready!"

In as much as I feel for Darla, I can kinda see Danielle's point as well. Been there myself ... and let me tell you, trust don't come easy in that situation.

Following a dinner of various grilled meats and vegetables, we are treated to a fruit and cheese buffet. At it's very center is a decadent chocolate fountain. As I watch the velvety chocolate ooze and flow around a goddess sculpture, all I can think of is the chocolate hands that made me ooze and flow not that long ago. But before the orchestra can start playing porno music in my head, our hostess asks everybody to head outside for the moonwalk. I knew they offered dance therapy here, but little did I know that the Disco Divas would be actually strutting their stuff to Michael Jackson.

Thrilled, we all step outside.

Alas, there isn't a disco ball in sight, just a full moon, beaming down at us. Sunny asks us to form a circle, holding hands. She then instructs us to become really quiet and listen for the stillness and the tranquility around us. But all I can hear is a few crickets and the annoying humming of misquotes, ready to do disrespectful things to my bod. Don't they know that by the end of the weekend I'll be a goddess, able to strike them with my special sexual powers? I guess it hasn't taken yet.

As I try to stand still between Cyn and Alison, Alison leans into my ear and says, "Something just bit me down there."

"It's about time that we see some action there!" I mutter under my breath.

Alison gives my hand a good yank and whispers, "Stop it."

Sunny gives us one of those looks that makes me fear that we'll be expected to share with the rest of the class.

And sharing is what we do next: not our private little joke – something far more intimate than that.

One by one, Sunny makes each one of us go in the middle of the circle and share why we're here; what's challenged the goddess within? Being a fairly private person, I wouldn't normally dream of sharing with total strangers. But the darkness around us wants to become one with the darkness inside, making us spill our guts. There's laughter and tears, humor and seriousness, working together to bind us to one another.

Not long into the moment, Sunny announces, "Four types of women come to the Goddess Ranch. This group is no different. There are those who've struggled with low self-esteem their entire lives." Check. "Those whose self-esteem has plummeted recently, thanks to aging, bodily changes, divorce, or betrayal." Check. "Those who wanna own their sensuality and take it new heights, so they feel sexier." Possibly. "And finally, those who wanna charge up their love lives, either with an existing partner, or one they hope to seduce in the future." Check. "That said, the Goddess Ranch has set up various exercises to address each of those needs. I suggest that you pick through them wisely, to make sure that you reach your personal goals."

My hand goes up slowly, like a reluctant student. "What if you can identify with *all* of those categories?"

"Most of us do, to one extent or another – that's

why each exercise is offered more than once. Make sure you take advantage of that and plan out your schedule carefully."

As we walk back to our rooms, Cyn says, "I don't give a fuck what you all do with the rest of your weekend, but we're taking the 'Getting To Know Your Vulva' class together, first thing tomorrow morning. Not opening up *that* extensively to strangers."

I giggle, "Could it be that the Sex Therapist is feeling a bit shy?" Cyn slaps my butt, almost like she's reprimanding me. I impishly add, "And why *does* she need the class anyway?"

"Just wanna see how others run their classes."

"You bet. By the way, have you ever taken a good look at it?"

"Not really."

Alison says, "That settles it then. It's a rite of passage that we must share together."

Darla chuckles, "Glad *you* said that, not me."

Alison teases back, "You're not getting turned on by this, are you Darla?"

"What if I am?"

"You pig! You're just like a man!" laughs Alison.

"We both know a good thing when we see it." Wiggling her tongue at Alison, she continues, "And pussy is as good as it gets."

Alison flips her perfectly French-manicured middle finger at Darla as she says "Goodnight" and heads into her room.

"Cyn, have you ever experimented with a girl, since you're cool with everything?" I ask.

"Once ... in college."

"What was it like?"

"Hey, a warm tongue is a warm tongue. The sensation was okay – kinda like masturbation – but I definitely prefer cock."

"Me too," I add enthusiastically.

"Me three," says Alison.

Cyn laughs, "Honey, I can't even imagine you as a twosome ... or for that matter a onesome – three's still a long way away."

"So you think that I haven't been felt up lately? Well guess again – Jill knows for a fact that I have."

Cyn is looking at me with anticipation, hoping that I'll share some news. I choose to shrug my shoulders and keep the suspense going. After all, she'll find out soon enough, when she sees the cobwebs at tomorrow's unveiling.

*   *   *

Another day, another circle – the moment we've all been waiting for. Too bad that our personal assistants didn't stick around for this one.

But at least we have each other – not that that's helping one bit. I don't even go to clothing sales with communal change rooms, because of how judgmental women can be when you undress in front of them – men, on the other hand, are just grateful. But here I am, in a roomful of women, wearing just a robe, moments away from stripping down completely.

Sunny asks us to position ourselves on our "love cushions" – rubber floor mats, raised in the back like wedges. Once we're all nice and comfortable, she doesn't waste a single moment to make us *un*comfortable, insisting that we strip off our robes and open up our legs. Next, she goes around the room and gives us our little care packages. Each one consists of a mirror, a small silicone dumbbell, a towel, some lube, and a big-ass Hitachi wand – the mother of all vibrators. I think my parents owned one of those, though theirs was bought at a department store, as a back massager.

The class begins.

Step one: looking at our vulva and admiring how pretty it is. The woman actually expects us to name and describe it – a tough order to take seriously, if you ask me. Cyn compares hers to a bald eagle, Alison picks a turkey with an astronomical prattle. I don't know *what* to make of mine, with its multiple lips curled up like a giant pecan – sorry girls for breaking the bird theme, but I just don't see it in mine. ... We're all laughing our guts out, when suddenly we hear some whimpering in the corner. The oldest one amongst us looks horrified by what she sees. "Mine is so saggy that it looks like old colonial curtains – the ones that swag down. No wonder Harry is a two-pump-chump – how could *anyone* be expected to wanna hang around this thing?"

The laughter turns to silence. After the longest pause, the shy, freckled redhead in the corner stands up. With all the confidence she can muster, she points to her nether zone. It resembles a pale hunk of cauliflower. She takes a deep breath and says, "Just look at it – isn't it the oddest, ugliest thing you ever saw?" Dead silence. "I certainly thought so ... until my boyfriend convinced me otherwise. I'd never let him go down on me, because of how funny it looked. Then one day, we got into a big fight over it. He marched out without a word. I was convinced that it was over. But then he returned a half hour later, with various girlie magazines, and showed me what picture-worthy, star woo-woos look like – all uniquely different. Mine was no exception." If we weren't naked, this would truly qualify as a major group hug moment. But seeing that we are, Sunny decides to move on with her instruction.

Step two: opening up our vulva with our fingers, and stimulating it with the dumbbell in ways no man has done before. The upshot? We're all too busy looking at our own to be bothered with anyone else's. But I still can't help wondering if Darla is doing a better job than the rest of us, having seen a few up close and personal.

Step three: lubricating the vulva and manually massaging the clitoral head, until it's hungry for more. Wonder if Swen's massage included this last night? Would be a shame if I slept through something so delish.

Step four: buzzing the hell out of our pink parts with the mammoth tool – right to completion.

Jelly-legged as we all are, Sunny isn't about to let up on us. Confidently, she says, "Not a bad start. ... *Now* we move onto G-Spot stimulation. ... And after that, we'll learn to give ourselves vaginal, cervical, anterior fornix, urethral, nipple, anal, and blended fusion orgasms."

Well, that's certainly a mouthful I never expected. I'm thinking, I only recently experienced a vaginal one – don't know how much more of this I can tolerate. And what the hell is an anterior fornix anyway? Pretty sure I don't have one – I'd know it if I did. As for anal, sorry Sunny, but I've already had enough of my asshole. I actually came here to forget about him. So let's leave him out of this one, shall we? ... And if you mean the other one that's squished between my butt-cheeks, it's off limits too – we're talking strictly export business only, no imports allowed. I can't imagine anyone wanting anal sex, other than puppets perhaps – they're used to having things shoved up their asses.

Never being one to give up, Sunny makes damn sure that we all experience *every* single orgasm that our registration's paid for, my attitude notwithstanding. And boy-oh-boy, she's *good* – if I were to ever switch teams, she'd be my first choice. She even taught Cyn a thing or two, well-seasoned that she already is.

The class ends with an African fertility dance, to initiate us into pure sexuality, which just *is* – no games, no hidden agendas, just pure enjoyment in the moment. Sunny's final words to us make a lot of sense. "Intimacy should be treated like a child – a little bit of you, a little bit of your partner, brought together to create something that you can both get excited about. ... And when other things muddy the waters between you two, don't throw out that baby with the bath water." How many times has Cyn told us that too many people seem to do away with sex, the minute something else goes wrong – at least that's not one that anyone can accuse *me* of.

The morning session invigorated me so much that I can barely eat lunch.

High as a kite, I go to my afternoon class, to tackle my next challenge – dance therapy. The orgasm chemical – oxytocin, I think – must really be working, 'cause I seem to be falling in love with myself, for the very first time ever.

We start off the afternoon with something called NIA – non-impact aerobics that combine multi-cultural dances with forceful martial arts movements. I feel alive, energized; my body freed of its tension. The goddess in me is starting to awaken to new sensations that I didn't know I was capable of, thanks to our lithe instructor, Amanda. She's taking the time to teach each one of us how to move gracefully, while still feeling strong.

Next, we take our new found confidence to a strip-dance class and have an absolute riot. From lap dances on empty chairs, to pole dances for imaginary patrons, we've got it all uncovered. Don't think I've ever laughed this hard in my entire life, unable to keep up with Claudia, our sixty-something instructor. Just look at her shimmy and shake her behind to raunchy striptease music. She's putting us all to shame – from the way she grabs her jacket lapels to "squish them boobies", to sprawling across the dance floor like a cat, in the most obscene, take-me manner. Honestly, the woman is absolutely amazing!

I can't help but wonder what Alison used to do when she made a living that way. Too bad that she didn't join us for this one. Then again, "Giving Your Man Oral Pleasure" should be infinitely more useful to her, at this point in her life. Too bad she wasn't paying attention when Dan was trying to give us some hot tips – probably figured she had no use for them, back then.

As we wrap up, I find myself supporting my lower back with my right hand, like I used to when I was pregnant, knees equally sore. Guess I'm not as young and flexible as I once was. Then again, neither is Claudia – but it doesn't seem to stop her. Watch out world, this sex goddess is on the prowl – meow!

*   *   *

Our final day at the Goddess Ranch consists of total pampering, with loads of quality time with our personal assistants – facials, more massages, manicures, pedicures, and a soak in natural hot tubs, nestled beneath hot springs oozing out of tropical vegetation. Must say, they sure know how to heal them aching muscles, even though I can still swear that I dislocated my vulva.

It's now time for our farewell walk out of the Goddess Ranch. Sunny has set it up like a cat-walk. Each one of us must walk it like a runway model – one foot in front of the other, back straight and tall, just like the charm marm taught us – if we're to get our ribbons that is.

As we leave, Sunny reminds us of our mantra one final time: sexiness is not about the body you have, it's about the *attitude* you have toward the body you got! I finally get it.

Was it worth it? Absolutely! Would I do it again? In a heartbeat. Think Alison will hire me, now that I'm feeling oh-so-sexy, with all the right moves and manners? Not a chance! Though the thought of showing up at Jeremy's door the next time he orders up some ass whopping, delights me to no end. For now, my fantasies will have to do!

Chapter 12 - *The Child Inside*

The goddess within must've woken up with a roar, for she's frightened the bageebes out of the child inside.

Moments away from filming my first show, I'm terrified of doing what I do best – cooking – even though I have home court advantage, with the first show being filmed right here in my fair city. A sex show might have been easier, seeing that I'm now up to speed on what it takes to feel sexy. Then again, from what my co-host James Richardson has been telling me, it's often more about how you look on camera than what you know. Hope Laura, my makeup artist, can make me look as sexy on the outside as I've been feeling on the inside, my nervous belly notwithstanding.

I try to settle myself in a director's chair, in front of one of those huge makeup mirrors that's surrounded by big light-bulbs. But I can't seem to keep my legs from shaking. What did I get myself into? I'm pushing forty – not a time to be starting out at something new, even though forty is supposed to be the new thirty, and sociologists have us believing that for women, it's just the beginning.

Laura notices my unrest and asks me, "Nervous?" I shake my head in an affirmative – not the brightest thing to do when you're being air-brushed with foundation. Laura steadies my head and says, "Relax," part comfort, part irritation at me moving so much.

"You don't think I'm too old to be doing this, do you?"

"When I'm done with you, no one will be able to tell your age."

"Maybe – but how many TV hosts do you know

who started at my age and actually became successful at what they were doing?"

Before Laura can answer, James walks over and wags his finger at me, disapprovingly. "Did you know that Julia Child didn't go to cooking school until she was thirty-six – not 'cause she was passionate about it, but to amuse herself? ... And it was only after she turned fifty-one that she tried her first cooking show on TV, and became the first celebrity chef. ... Since then, she's published over a dozen cookbooks and been recognized for doing one of the most successful TV shows ever – earning her an award which represents the highest honor in public television, at age eighty-seven no less."

My mouth gapes open in shock. Good thing that Laura isn't applying lipstick on me right this second. When I finally regain control of my mouth, "No, I didn't know that," is all that comes out. Why would I? It's not like I went to cooking school myself, where they tell you stuff like that – I'm more of a bit-of-this-and-a-bit-of-that-home-cooking kinda gal. But I must say, while a part of me is relieved and even encouraged by Julia's story, another part is terrified, 'cause I've just raised the proverbial bar higher still. Luckily, I remember what Sunny said back at The Goddess Ranch, and give myself a mental pep talk, highlighting the importance of attitude.

And attitude is what the camera ends up capturing – lots of it – thanks to the adrenalin that's coursing through my veins. I'm talking a mile a minute, like I usually do when I'm at once excited and terrified. But James has no problem keeping up. If anything, he's having a lot of fun with it, whipping my witty innuendos right back at me – fast and furious – confident that I can handle it. The speed with which we're moving works to my advantage, wiping out any chance of me second-guessing myself. Like a quick game of tennis, I'm responding almost reflexively, making it easier to roll with the punches. Looking at us, you'd think that we've been doing this our entire lives, or at the very least, rehearsing for that long. *Spice of Life* may become a hit after all, though they might have to change the name to *Gourmet Sex*! ... The child inside is now comfortable enough to call me Julia, as I try to emulate her and do what we do best.

My hands are working almost as fast as my mouth – chopping, grinding, mixing – as James and I prepare a romantic meal, with loads of sizzle to titillate *all* the senses. We start off with oysters, nature's favorite aphrodisiac, move onto grilled chicken – served on a bed of arugula, with a side of warm goat cheese in puff pastry – followed by the *piece de resistance*, a fruit bouquet. Can you just see the opportunities for James to massage the breasts, stroke the slippery, clit-like suckers, lick the fruit juice off his fingers, while talking about the importance of each gesture in spicing things up in other ways? Well *I* certainly can, since I'm looking right at him, as he pulls it off oh-so-exquisitely. His flirtatiousness only adds to the oomph that daytime television is known for. I wonder what the audience are likely to enjoy more – the cooking lesson or the little show we put on for them? Hopefully both! After all, that *was* the idea, when the director picked James as my co-host – a cook, he certainly ain't. What a brainchild! ... I'm just glad that the kids are in Europe – they don't need to see their mother act like this. Then again, this is *my* chance at doing something I really enjoy.

Following the show and tell, James invites me out for a drink, to celebrate our instant success. He can't believe how well I did for my first time. I'm rather pleased myself and decide to accept. Like an excited schoolgirl, I'm practically bouncing when I say, "I'd really like that, but would you mind if I go home and change first?"

"Not at all, provided I can tag along and maybe go for a dip in that glorious pool that I've been hearing so much about ... that is, if you don't mind."

I say "Sounds like a plan" and escort him to my car. Since we're coming back anyway and I live only a few minutes away, why take two cars – unless of course he has smelly feet. Looking at him, I somehow doubt it – someone who looks and smells *that* expensive, must have feet to match.

*   *   *

Driving home, I'm feeling pretty good about myself and start to imagine what it would be like to be Julia Child? James just stares at me. "Penny for your thoughts?" he asks eventually.

"Oh, I just have this habit of drifting off into fantasy land."

"If I'm a part of it, I think I have the right to know what that fantasy is," he chortles.

I laugh and plead the fifth, since he *is* a part of my fantasy, but not the way he's sure to be imagining. For now, I choose to let his mind work overtime and change the subject. "Did you ever see the movie *Shirley Valentine?*

"Uh-huh."

"The man's gorgeous, sharp, funny *and* sensitive ... even though he can't cook to save his life," I tease.

"You got it. ... And not only that, but I'd be willing to bet that I know *exactly* why you're asking me about the movie."

"Oh really? This I gotta hear."

"Last time we traveled together, you couldn't enjoy any of this. You were too worried about hubby's needs and what he was thinking. If I didn't know better, I'd think that *he* was the star, not you."

"That bad, huh?"

"Stunning and sophisticated as you looked, with your to-die-for clothes and recipes, you might as well have been a simple Irish lass in a filthy apron, making hubby his chips and eggs."

"Boy, could I ever identify with that – on numerous occasions. That's probably why it's one of my all-time favorite movies."

"Tell me something – now that you've decided to take care of your own needs for a change, it's not all that bad, is it?"

"Not bad at all," I say, remembering some of the other Shirley Valentine perks that I've been enjoying as of late – like when Dan *kissed me stretch-marks.*

We're now pulling into my driveway. Lo and behold, it's full of cars, including a certain red Ferrari. I park right behind it and we slowly make our way into my house. "Hellooo."

The place is a hub of activity. The gang has decided to throw me a celebratory party – not their forte, but it's the thought that counts. I walk into the kitchen and immediately start to take charge – cleaning this, fixing that. Dan slaps my hand, gives me a glass of bubbly, and escorts me into the living room, sans James. "I want you all to myself ... at least for little while," he says, as we give each other mischievous grins, remembering the last time that we were in here. Boy if the walls could only talk! For now,

I'm glad that they can't – I'd rather not share that part with anyone, not yet anyway. Still feeling a bit creepy about misbehaving with Darla's ex, even though I know she'd be cool with it, and the don't-sleep-with-my-ex rule doesn't really apply when you switch camps.

My revere is interrupted, as is my sans-James moment, 'cause there he is, standing in the doorway to the living room. "Normally, I'm one to hang out in the kitchen during parties, 'cause that's where all the action is; but right now, the *living room's* looking like it could be a whole lot more fun. ... Are you joining us, or shall I join you two?" It's almost as if he's propositioning us. Randy did swear that James tipped off his gaydar – then again, he's been tipping a few things in me as well. Not wishing to ruin the orientation suspense, I decide to sashay to the pool, two eager beavers in tow.

The party is now in full swing, having moved to the pool, with different degrees of undress. As always, Cyn is the first one to go for a skinny dip, leaving a very conservative Rajiv with a terrified expression on his face. Don't know if he's more worried about his woman exposing herself, or the mere thought of having to do the same himself? ... The pressure is definitely on – we're all standing around the pool now, cheering him on to take the plunge. Always a good sport, Rajiv says, "What the hell" and starts to undress faster than the speed of light. His girly ankles and skinny legs lead to some not-so-skinny man-equipment, with pubes trimmed back like a freshly pruned bonsai.

The landscape has caught more than just my eye. Alison leans into me and says, "What has Cyn been doing to the poor guy?"

I laugh, "She always did say that a man is merely a

life support system for the penis. She's just making sure that it's free to breathe."

"And to think that *I'm* the one responsible for their introduction. I'll never be able to look at him the same way again, especially at work – serves me right, for mixing business and pleasure."

Alison and I are now in hysterics. Her own support system, Clive, decides to join us. "Looks like you girls are having way too much fun over here."

Quite unexpectedly, Alison blurts out, "You and I could have even more fun, if you weren't all covered up like that." Whoa, where did that come from? Not that I'm complaining – the girl seriously needs to get laid. Hopefully tonight's the night. Clive has been too much of a gentleman, from what she's told me – doesn't wanna be like all the other guys. I wanna tell him, "Trust me Clive, if you manage to get into her pants, you won't be *anything* like the other guys." But looks like I don't have to say much at all. The girl – sorry, the goddess – is doing fine on her own. Just look at her, trying to rip the clothes off of Clive's bod.

Clive fights a losing battle and then jumps into the pool as soon as he's in the nudenicks. But he doesn't jump alone – he drags Alison in with him, fully clothed. The girl's quick to peel off her Prada and throw it out of the pool, before the chlorine has a chance to get to it ... or so she claims.

Randy of course needs no excuse or convincing – he's only too happy to oblige on his own. "Thank Gawd I anticipated this and put on my waterproof makeup today."

The skin parade catches on with Darla – but she's only taking her top off. While the rest of us worry about our boobs racing down to see which one makes it to the waistline the fastest – not that I'm there yet – gravity seems to have skipped her entirely. If anything, hers seem to get perkier with time. Wonder if she has a Darla Gray nude in her attic?

All that's left on dry land now is, me and my eager beavers – but not for long. One by one we go into the Cabana and come out in skimpy swim wear. Dan is wearing his infamous blue *Speedo*. James has found himself one of Jeremy's hot little numbers – no, not the granny panties. ... I must say, it looks a whole lot better on him than it ever did on Jeremy – meow! As for me, I've slipped into a hint of a lemon colored string bikini, with three little knots barely holding it in place – yes, the goddess in me has finally made peace with the marks on my belly, showing off my life experiences.

As I slip into the pool, James and Dan slip in on either side of me, and start to pull on my strings. I pretend to ignore them and look across at Alison and Clive groping each other. They remind me of horny teens, when the anticipation is at least as exciting as the deed. I miss that stage. At my age, you just hope and pray that the movie is at least half as good as the commercial. Then again, why shouldn't it be? Just ask Goddess Alison – who just happens to be my age. And Dan, who happens to know how to make the movie sizzle.

I'm now ready to frolic like a teen, eager to experiment with new things. The anxiety in my gut is dousing me with that all-too-familiar rush. I'm totally digging this – the porno music has already started to play in my head. James must've noticed the look on my face, 'cause he ups the ante by pulling harder on my strings, challenging me with, "What are you hiding in there anyway?"

As if in cahoots, Dan says, "How about you take care of the top – I'll take care of the bottom?" not bothering to clarify if he means my bikini or what lies beneath. Here we go again, another threesome hint – this time from Dan. ... But it's sooo not what does it for me – quite anti-porno if you ask me – somebody stop the music, puh-lease!

While I don't have the guts or the inclination for what they might be suggesting, I sure am enjoying all the attention I'm getting, as each is trying to outdo the other. Just look at them go, right down to the bulge adjustments in their skives. Honestly guys, I think Freud had it all wrong – it's *men* who have penis envy ... of each other's penises. Us girls just take them in stride, knowing full well that no matter what you're trying to convince us of, where there's a phallus, there's bound to be a fallacy – you're not as big as you think, or as small as you fear.

Penis adjustment aside, neither Dan nor James is willing to leave me alone, not even to get a drink, afraid of being out-scored. If only you could hear their cheesy dialogue.

Dan runs his fingers along the curve of my right shoulder and says, "Being with you is such a privilege."

"And don't you forget it!" I laugh back, wondering if Jeremy ever saw it that way. ... Nah, he was more into taking me for granted, even though he'd swear that he was intending on getting around to me eventually. Yeah right – maybe if and when *he* felt like it. But it's not like it's *his* fault. The weather outside was always too nice to stay in and do me. Everything else was always too important and had to be addressed first. And heaven forbid if he should skip out on a chance to play out his hobbies. If someone called him, he *had* to make time – worse, he'd jump all over it as if it was his last chance. Too bad he didn't jump all over me when he *had* the chance! ... So exactly why am I wasting valuable time thinking about someone who never prioritized me – or for that matter even bothered to schedule me in – when I could be with men who actually give a shit? ... Why indeed! ... The goddess in me says "no more" and starts to splash around playfully.

Blah, blah, blah, poor James is waxing poetic and I've missed it all. Looking at my tell-tale expression, he laughs and says, "Fantasy land again?"

"Yup."

"You know it's extremely rude not to share."

"But if I share, it won't come true."

"That's only if you make a *wish*."

"Which happens to *include* us," Dan adds eagerly.

"Wish, prayer, wishful thinking, whatever ... don't wanna take any chances."

Dan teases, "Are you saying that you're only into sure things? 'Cause if you are, look no further."

Excitedly, James says, "Count me in also."

"Are you guys bi or something?" I tease back.

Dan smiles, "If it means wanting to make love to someone at least twice, then definitely I'm bi," winking to mark his territory.

"Hey I'd settle for just once, in or out of a bi situation," winks James.

Randy and Cyn are dangerously close, eavesdropping. I see them high-fiving each other, almost as if to say 'I knew it', 'me too'. Alison swims over to them and says, "The girl's doing alright, with not one but *two* prospects – and here you guys were worried about her." As she swims away, she decides to take some credit for it.

"Must be the goddess boot camp I signed us up for."

Glad *they're* feeling so good about *my* love life. Personally, I couldn't be feeling more awkward. Make that really, really awkward. I decide to pop out of the pool and go into my mile a minute mode – this time, cleaning feverishly. Dan decides to help, just like he did that one time ... with dangerous results. Needless to say, it's the very first time this evening that James leaves my side, not being terribly domestic himself.

The party starts to thin out – cleaning up will generally do that, with the exception of a few stragglers who just don't know how to take a hint. In this case, it's James and Dan – each hoping that the other will leave the building. Not a chance!

I change into my turquoise blue silk kimono suit, Dan into a fresh pair of jeans and T that he brought along, and James back into his shiny taffeta, made-for-TV suit.

Since everything is cleaned up and put away, and the boys don't look like they have any intention of leaving, I open up a bottle of Merlot and invite them to join me in the living room. As we drink our wine, Dan turns on the stereo, with some very sexy jazz tunes, bringing back another familiar memory. ... But what happens next has no memories for me whatsoever ... in any shape or form ... with *any*one ... not even in my rich fantasy life.

The three of us start to slow-dance together, with me in the middle, tender kisses covering my neck and face. I'm *really* nervous. I must stop this before it gets out of hand ... and into my pants. Lucky for me, I'm saved by the bell! I pull away before the ding has a chance to make it to the dong, and race to the door. It's Jeremy. Dammit, what's *he* doing here? In as much as I'd wanted someone to interrupt us, I could've gone the entire night without needing to see Jeremy's face. "What do you want?" I ask impatiently.

"Have I interrupted something?" he inquires, looking over my shoulder at the two handsome gents – wine and sex music looking all-too-obvious.

"Of course not. I never have anything better to do, except *wait* for you," I say facetiously.

"Look, we need to talk ... privately."

"Whatever you have to say to me, you can say it in front of them," I blurt out, making it sound like the three of us are an item.

"I'd rather not," replies Jeremy.

I open up the door wider and say, "In that case, we have nothing to discuss. You may leave."

"Very well then," he says, and starts to make his way in. I block him, making sure that he doesn't penetrate any further. "You want to talk out here?" he asks.

"Why not?"

"Alrighty then. ... Look, this whole trial separation thing was supposed to be just that – a trial. And I've reached a verdict – it's over – I wanna come back."

"How nice for you. But *my* trial has barely begun, and isn't *close* to reaching a verdict just yet."

"What do you mean?"

"You had your affairs, now I'm having mine." Ouch – that had to hurt. Where did it come from? More importantly, what's it supposed to accomplish? The goddess voice within me – which has successfully replaced Grammy's voice – says, *not a damn thing, Jilly, except for making you feel better.* I guess it must've worked, since I'm now smirking ... and loving every second of it. No more walking on eggshells, worrying about what Jeremy might think. Quite the liberating feeling if you ask me. Sorry Grammy, this is how we do things these days – you don't see doormats as often as you used to.

I hear a clink of glasses behind my back – I guess I inadvertently promised the guys something that I'm not sure I want to give.

Jeremy looks furious, shocked, hurt, disappointed, even pathetic – squirming like nothing I've ever seen before. "So that's it? You're willing to flush everything down the toilet just like that?"

Sarcastically, I snap back, "My sentiment exactly – should've thought of that yourself, before jumping into bed with someone."

"What's gotten into you, Jillian? There's no talking to you. I thought you'd be *glad* that I'm back ... thrilled, in fact. But you're acting like this new person I don't even know."

"Hey, it's not like it was *my* idea in the first place."

"That's why I'm so sorry ... and back to make things right again."

"Always about you, isn't it?"

Listening to us argue, soap opera style, James must've felt right at home, 'cause he decides to walk over and intervene, like a knight in shining taffeta. He clears his throat and says, "Jill and I seem to love the same movies." Following a long and suspenseful pause, leaving the rest of us wondering, 'And ...?', he dramatically continues, "And, I think she'll agree with me when I say that the one we hate the most is *Love Story* ... because of that stupid part which suggests, being in love means not having to say you're sorry. ... Personally, I feel it's gonna take one hellova lot more than just sorry – after how you've treated her." I'm impressed. I did not see that coming. Maybe it's a line from one of his shows ... but who cares?

"Stay out of it," is all the brilliant dialogue the good doctor can manage – after such an eloquent speech, no less. I must put a stop to this war between a real doc and a soap doc – the former doesn't stand a chance, when the latter can save sixteen lives, sow back a decapitated head, and revive a couple of people ... all in forty-six minutes or less. Small wonder soap docs are always more popular than real docs: just think Dr. Noah Drake – a.k.a. Joey Tribiani from *Friends* – versus Drs. Bishop and Varmus, Nobel Prize winners for cancer research.

I force myself to look serious and snap at them, "I think you *all* need to stay out," and point the three of them to the front door. Miffed as I appear, it did feel kinda nice to have James *stick* up for me, Dan give me the I-wanna-*stick*-it-into-you look, and Jeremy look terrified, willing to do *any*thing, if I'd only let him *stick* around. ... Talk about a *sticky* situation! One that *I'm* driving for a change, instead of just riding along or racing behind.

I suppose it's time I made a few decisions – though I'm certainly not going to rush myself! Never felt so powerful before. ... I guess for as long as men want to dip their tip, pussy will call the shots – though in Jeremy's case, I'm hoping it's a bit more than that ... and he'd better be willing to work with this "new person", as he put it.

Yes, part of me still loves him; the goddess in me wants to forgive him – through grace, not because he deserves it! All my life I've wanted things to change, as long as it wasn't me that had to change – but it needs to be, doesn't it?

Chapter 13 - *Out With The Old, In With The New*

I know *exactly* what you're thinking – my mind's made up ... and Jeremy doesn't stand a chance. After all, he did hurt me. But is there any guarantee that another man won't?

And he did take me for granted. True, but only with my permission. What about the underwear he always left sitting around in the oddest of places – excluding granny panties – and the mess he consistently made in my **O**rganized, **C**lean and **D**isciplined world? What *about* it? A mess on the floor hardly justifies messing up a relationship. But if I do decide to take him back, what will everybody think, after all the sob stories I've shared with them and all the support they've given me? If they truly care for me, they'll support me still – even if not, so what? It's *my* life – and I'm not about to apologize for my choices ... even if they turn out to be wrong. Besides, is there really such a thing as a perfect relationship? Grammy always said, everybody has problems – you just learn to live with them, like a bad back or allergies, trying your damndest to avoid aggravations. As for forgiveness – even though I haven't been able to forgive him just yet and wonder if I'll ever be able to trust him again, I'm tired of being mad at him; it isn't good for anybody, least of all me. Sade couldn't have put it better when she sang:

I won't pretend, that I intend to stop living

I won't pretend, I'm good at forgiving

But I can't hate you, though I have tried

I still really really love you

Love is stronger than pride.

There are people who reorganize their closets with every change of season, and people who hang on to inappropriate stuff, hoping to find some use for it one day. ... I happen to do both, in my own strange way. When it comes to the clothes in my closet, I belong to the former category. When it comes to hurts that are closeted inside me, I seem to hang on instead of moving on – at least I used to. Pretty silly huh, if you come to think of it? No one wants your past hurts – least of all you.

I guess what I'm trying to tell you in my long-winded way is, I've decided to give Jeremy a second chance; there's still a lot of unresolved feelings between us – I suppose after all these years, it's rarely all-or-nothing, is it? For the longest time I'd convinced myself that the passionate flame between us had died completely. Alas, it appears to be flickering away ever-so-slightly, like those last few stubborn candles on a birthday cake, mocking you. I need to know one way or the other, whether or not I'm truly done with him. But since I'm a brand new person now – a goddess who won't stand for being mistreated – Jeremy needs to date me all over again, to find out if *he's* still interested.

I call up Jeremy on his cell phone, adrenalin making my heart hammer away like a teenage crush. He picks up with a tentative "Hello", probably 'cause he's read my number on call display.

I go for shock value. "I've made a decision – out with the old, in with the new."

After the longest pause, laced with heavy, disheartened breathing, he says, "I'm very sorry to hear that. I'd so hoped that my offer to do *any*thing to get you back would've at least counted for something."

"Giving up so easily?"

"I can't fight anymore."

"Who said anything about fighting? I was just talking about getting rid of all the old bullshit, so we can work on a fresh new start."

Jeremy sounds relieved ... giggly ... possibly delirious, "When can I move back in?"

"Whoa, nobody said anything about cohabitation. ... Shouldn't we date first – get to know each other a bit better? ... I thought even sex wasn't expected *this* early – and here you are, talking about us moving in together already?"

"You wanna *date* me ... for real?"

"Of course, don't you wanna date *me*?"

"But we're already married."

"If you need to get a divorce first, I can always have an attorney draw up some papers."

"That won't be necessary. But I have to ask, where do you come up with this stuff – still reading those articles that tell you what's wrong with your life?"

Coyly, I say, "How could you possibly suggest something like that about me – I barely know you. And for the record, it doesn't hurt to read an advice column or two, even if you are a guy."

"Nah – men's advice columns only tell you what you already know: be sure to turn off the TV and call out the right name," he laughs, even though the last bit isn't all that funny, considering our situation. Maybe I caught my bad joke telling skills from him.

I play along. "Very funny. ... So, are you available this Saturday or not?"

"I'll make sure that I am."

"What if somebody decides to pop a kid – are any of your patients due this weekend?"

"That's what they make Ob-Gyn residents for."

"You could've fooled me. ... Oops, sorry about that – we just met, how could I assume that of you?"

"It's not like it's the first time."

Oh-oh, we're already falling back into our old patterns, thanks to me. I try to save the day with, "You must have me confused with somebody else."

"Touché."

"So, what time can I pick you up?"

"You wanna pick *me* up?"

"You got it – being the first date and all."

"Just in case I don't behave myself ...."

"Or have smelly feet."

"Smelly feet?"

"Private joke."

Jeremy starts off with "Are you talking with yourself again?" and then quickly switches over to, "I mean, are you one of those girls who likes to talk to herself?"

"Sometimes."

"I was in love with someone who did that a lot."

"Hey, Mister, did anyone ever tell you that talking about other chicks is so uncool, especially when you're trying to nail a new one?"

"Sorry, I didn't mean to offend you. Just wanted to

set the record straight that I find that sort of thing quite endearing."

"Did you ever tell her that? ... 'Cause she was probably under the impression that you wished she'd just *shut up*, instead of thinking out loud all the time."

"I thought we weren't supposed to talk about past girlfriends anymore."

"I can work with that," I say, pleased that Jeremy's finally catching on. ... But this is going to take some getting used to, even from me.

"So how's seven? And may I pick the place?" he asks enthusiastically.

"Seven it is – main entrance at the Hilton?"

"Yup, although I'll probably be there at 6:30, waiting impatiently, just in case you decide to show up early."

When it rains, it pours. Jeremy's gone from taking me for granted to getting all excited about making me his number one priority. ... Then again, he *is* dating somebody new. And like any first date, this one would rather not hear about his past mistakes.

*   *   *

All week long, I feel like a kid who can't wait until Christmas. But Saturday night is finally here.

I purge my closet of its usual suspects. An assortment of little black dresses is strewn across my now-invisible bed, each looking tighter and shorter than the next. I'm having a hard time choosing – don't want to look like I'm trying too hard, even though I am. This truly feels like a first date, when you want to make the right impression, 'cause you're setting a precedent for everything that follows.

I finally find a longish number – almost makes it to my knees, versus mid-thigh like the rest – and decide to stuff myself into it. Even though it's a size larger than the others, I still have to do some fancy moves to get in. I guess the ice-cream has finally caught up with me – part breakup ritual, part not worrying about every ounce any longer, now that I'm in goddess mode.

Alas, I look like a sausage, with not a curve left to the imagination. I take a deep breath, try to struggle my way out – even harder than getting in – until I look like a giant pretzel, entangled in a mass of black fabric. ... After some serious maneuvering – thank goodness for NIA training at the Goddess Ranch – I finally manage to slip out, with no more than a kink in my neck.

I swear to you that I used to be able to get into much smaller things – with a lot more finesse – back in my twenty inch waist days.

So what if it was more than three decades ago, when I measured in at twenty-twenty-twenty. I've acquired curves since then, and a couple of kids who I'm damn proud of. I even managed to get my figure back after childbirth – only problem is, I'd hoped to get someone else's, maybe Alison's. ... Desperate as I sound, I was never one to give up good food and wine for all the anorexia in the world. ... Okay Jillian, quit getting stuck in your mind again – time to move on, or you'll be late.

The next number I try on is a printed one – a bit more casual, not to mention kinder to the curves. Stretchy material that it is, it doesn't take too kindly to my bubble butt. I turn my head over my shoulder to look at it in the mirror. Fuck, I look like a printed couch, with massive cushions. Since it's our first date, I decide against it – don't want Jeremy looking for change in the crack.

Alas, I settle on my slimming black slacks and a creamy silk halter top. It's floating neckline shows off just a hint of cleave, if I move just the right way. Should be perfect if Dating 101 has anything to say about it – tease, without giving it all away. Hopefully it will tease Jeremy enough to transport him back to our college days, when he got a major kick out of catching a sneak peek. As for the pants, they're more for me – don't want to worry about how far back I can sit in my chair. You know how it is – if you're not *really* careful, your hemline seems to ride up, making your butt smooch the chair in unconscionable ways.

Anyhow, having settled on the perfect outfit, I throw on a string of pearls and a pair of black stilettoes, darken my berry lipstick and eyeliner, smooth out my hair, and look at myself in the mirror. I feel as ready as I'm ever gonna feel. Time to leave.

*   *   *

I show up at the Hilton, fashionably late – 6:45 – can't appear too eager. Jeremy is waiting, looking quite anxious with anticipation. One hand is holding long-stem red roses, not a reduced-to-clear grocery store special; the other, a nicely-wrapped gift. If he thinks he can impress me with that, it's working – well, it's a start in any case ... like tonight.

I open up the passenger side door to my Porsche and ask Jeremy to hop in. He slams it shut, walks over to my side, opens up my door, and asks the valet to park the car. I'm a little confused.

Jeremy smiles at me and says, "We're going upstairs for dinner."

"Upstairs? ... I don't do that on a first date."

"You don't eat dinner on a first date? ... That's too

bad, 'cause I made reservations for us in the penthouse dining room – window table, with a spectacular view of the city." I laugh a relieved laugh. He winks, "Why, what were *you* thinking?"

One thing I have to say for Dr. Briggs, he always manages to get the best table in the house. Everyone seems to suck up to doctors like they're huge stars – I guess if I were choking, I'd prefer a real doc to a star doc any day.

I wait for the menus, but dinner has been pre-ordered. I know that Cyn would be really pissed at not having a say, but I for one am quite excited about Jeremy taking charge, making a decision for a change. I wonder if he'll take charge of the conversation as well – the out loud part that is. While there's a cacophony of words being exchanged in my head, nothing seems to be coming out.

The waiter pours us some Dom and Jeremy raises his glass, "To new beginnings!"

I clink back, "To new beginnings."

"I must say, you look absolutely ravishing. I can't wait to get to know you better."

I smile.

And with that, Jeremy breaks into a series of first date questions, to truly get to know me better. After all these years, I didn't think there was anything left that he didn't already know about me. He did share most of my experiences over the last two decades. But his questions have more to do with how I felt, not what was going on ... and way beyond. He's even asking me about my childhood like never before, extracting intimate details that I never thought I'd have the courage to verbalize ... to anyone.

Whoever said that you learn ninety percent of what you're going to learn about a lover, *before* you sleep with them for the first time, hit the nail on the head. We slept together fairly early on in our relationship – hence the lacunae of missed information.

Jeremy and I laugh together when I tell him about the pumpkin hat that my mother always insisted on making me wear. He confesses he's already seen a picture with me wearing it, even though I'd forbidden everyone from showing it to him. ... But since he had to struggle with a similar evil, he totally empathizes. "Why didn't you tell me this before?" I ask.

"Felt too silly and trivial amongst the serious stuff that we seem to limit our discussions to." For the record, tonight is anything but – and the bubbliness has to do with a lot more than the bottle of champagne that we've managed to finish up so quickly.

I take one final sip, give Jeremy a knowing smile, and say, "What a shame. But I know the feeling – to this day, I blare ABBA when I'm alone ... and feel quite goofy doing it."

"I'd rather hear ABBA than a strained conversation, any day."

"Ditto for me, with Zeppelin."

"Wanna know what's strange? I thought I was happiest when I had my own digs in college. I could do whatever the hell I pleased, blare whatever music I liked, and leave my shit laying around with no one hounding me about it. But over the last few weeks, while I've been baching it, it doesn't seem to feel all that great anymore. It's really lonely and unnatural. ... Whenever I return to my suite, it's frozen in time. Other than the maid cleaning it up, no one else has been there. Worse, no one else will be coming – what a creepy feeling." Seeing that the conversation is getting way too heavy, he jokes, "I had visions of dying alone, with the maid finding my bloated body days later, thanks to my DO NOT DISTURB sign."

I tease, "I can just see a CSI team dusting your penis for prints, trying to figure out whether or not any sexual improprieties had taken place." We both laugh. But then I feel my face turn sad again. "What I would've given to get away from my parents and have a place of my own, back in my teens."

Jeremy looks at me and catches the tears that are now forming in my eyes. "You never did tell me why we never went over to your parents place for the holidays? ... You were always saving it for the right time, which never came."

I guess now feels as good a time as any. I let it all out, from my most painful memories to my most embarrassing moments through my informative years, including my ridiculous crush on Randy.

Then, just when I think it can't get any deeper, Jeremy moves onto what I see myself doing in the future. And here I thought that *I* was the thinker in the family! The last part, I must've said out loud, without even realizing it, 'cause Jeremy takes my hand and places the gift in it.

"Open it," he says, looking as excited as if it were a gift for him. It's Rodin's *The Thinker* – a miniature version. Jeremy says, "I've been doing a lot of thinking lately."

"And ...?"

"And I've come to realize that you're my one and only. All the other bullshit was just 'cause I wasn't feeling very good about myself – my life seemed so messed up, just as yours was taking off to exciting places. ... The right thing to do would've been to support you, like you did me when the shoe was on the other foot. But I acted like a brat instead. Please forgive me, Honey – you're all I've ever wanted."

"Let's not go there tonight, okay?"

"That's fine by me," he says, head hanging down in shame.

Over the next hour, I manage to finish most of my chateaubriand and roasted potatoes, while Jeremy just plays with his food, thanks to his mouth being busy with other things – running a mile a minute for instance.

I realize that he's undressing me, not out of my clothes, but the emotional layers of defenses that I've managed to hide under, all these years. Small wonder my dresses felt so tight! But if you could only see me now. I feel like a Russian *Matryoshka* doll – after all the outer nested dolls have been removed – delicate and fragile.

I'm feeling closer to him than ever, giddy from cocktailing first date magic with long-term comfort. We could've never come this far on a real first date – we'd still be playing the dating game, doing time in the introductory conversation stage, choking on fumes of superficiality. ... I won't lie to you – not all is forgiven *or* forgotten; but we do have a better understanding of each other now.

The emotional surgery must've exhausted Jeremy, 'cause he's starting to look sleepy – the circles under his eyes darker than ever. He flags the waiter for the bill and apologizes to me. "I'm so sorry Honey, but I *must* go to bed *right now.*"

I chuckle flirtatiously, "Told you I don't do that sort

of thing on the first date."

"No worries – all I can manage with a bed right now is sleep. Before dinner, I came off of a twenty-two hour shift, with a really tough case."

"We could have moved this to another night."

"Are you kidding? It's the only thing that kept me going."

I don't know what to say. Maybe Jeremy's a brand new guy also! His goodnight kiss certainly felt both familiar and new.

Chapter 14 - *Unusual Make-overs and Hostile Takeovers*

Don't know if it's my newfound mojo or James' shaggadelic attitude toward me, but we're rising on the charts, while our chemistry is flying right off of them. The reviews are awesome, even though I'm being referred to as "still sexy at forty" with a "maternal kitchen charm" – sure beats becoming invisible like all the female stars who fall off the silver screen, forcing their daughters to bed their male counterparts.

For the record, it's not just the ratings that are getting my undies all wet with excitement. My dressing room is studded with an array of flowers: chrysanthemums from my producer, lilies from Jeremy, orchids from Dan, and a panty bouquet from James – long stem roses made out of exquisitely folded lace panties. As I take it all in – a big smile spreads across my face. But before I can drift off into an elaborate awards ceremony in my imagination, I hear a knock on my door.

"Come in," I say enthusiastically, certain that it's more kudos.

The door swings open, and who should walk in but my producer Rochelle, with Lynda Jacobs – a seriously major, award-winning, executive producer. Rochelle introduces us – as if Lynda needs an intro – and makes her way out, leaving the two of us to talk alone.

I offer Lynda a seat in one of my canvas director's chairs and she plunks down right beside me, pulling her chair around to face me.

Since people like her don't have time for idle chit chat, she gets right to the point. "Jillian, I must say that I truly love your camera presence ... and the ease with which you handle the audience."

"Thanks – means a lot coming from you." Gulp.

"You have this warm way with people, no matter how trivial their cooking questions. Makes me wanna sit down with you in your kitchen ... and tell you my entire life story, over a cup of tea."

A nervous giggle escapes me – never was any good at handling direct compliments, in as much as I always craved them. ... The old me is dying to burst out with a trivializing remark, like, 'You're just being nice', or something equally condescending to myself. But the new me takes over the reins and says, "You're welcome in my kitchen anytime!"

Lynda smiles at me and continues, "What I'm trying to say is, I think you'll be perfect for another project that I'm working on – a breast cancer documentary – doing home interviews ... that is if you're interested."

"I'd be honored," is all that I can slip in, before she goes on to say, "And you being mature, will only help put our subjects at ease."

Mature? As in mentally or physically? Oh who cares? This is an opportunity of a lifetime, to become a part of something much bigger than all the trivial bullshit which relentlessly contributes to my mental drivel.

"Good," she says, looking quite pleased, and hands me a manila envelope. "Why don't you take this DVD home and take a peek at the initial footage, so you can familiarize yourself with the subjects and the subject matter. It's a heart-wrenching project, so I won't be offended in the least if you change your mind after watching it. ... 'Cause once you commit, you'll have to be in it for the long haul, following up with survivors and families through some of their darkest hours."

I say, "You have my word right now that I really want to do this," and take the package from her.

Lynda just smiles at me and leaves, without holding me to anything just yet.

My mind starts to wander. I can't begin to imagine what it would be like to lose a breast. Mine have always been my favorite physical asset. Even when I was at my heaviest and not feeling terribly good about myself, they made me feel sexy ... plus allowed me to pull off my weight. ... And now, post-hysterectomy, they're even more important to me – they're all I have left to make me feel like a woman on the outside, when my hollow insides scream "Fake!". It's almost like my marriage used to be – good-looking on the outside, empty on the inside. A tear escapes me. I'm determined to make everything come together – both inside and out. Wait until I tell the girls.

I call up Cyn with the good news. I know she'll be really excited, since she works with survivors herself, helping them rebuild their sexual confidence. ... Sure enough, she's thrilled and promises to hook me up with some interviews, provided I accompany her when she meets Rajiv's mother.

"Rajiv's mother? Why in the heck are you meeting her?"

"He wants to get married, pending her approval."

In all the years that I've known Cyn, she's *never* needed *anyone*'s approval. I guess she must really love the guy to go along with it. I tease, "Either some alien has taken over your body and you forgot to tell me, or Rajiv must be one hellova fuck!"

"No aliens, no hellova fuck. I just love how genuinely open and honest he is, sans the usual games. Any other guy would've told me how he can't wait to show me off to mommy dearest, but not Rajiv. He just told it like it is. How can you not love someone who is that straight up?"

"Can't say I blame you. Though didn't you say that honesty has ruined more marriages than infidelity?"

"I'll take my chances. Speaking of infidelity, how's Jeremy doing?"

"I think he's *really* trying. Though I'm still not sure if I'll ever be able to trust him again – or any other man for that matter. You know what they say – a man is only as faithful as his options ... and Jeremy certainly has a lot of those."

"Women cheat too, you know. It's human nature, even when we disapprove. ... Penguins are cobras are the only two species that I know of who mate for life."

"Duh! All penguins look alike – it's not like you're going to meet a better looking one. As for cobras, would you really wanna mess with one, by cheating with its partner?"

"Oh I've cheated with a few cobras in my time – but no more. Rajiv's dark cobra is the only one that's slipping inside me these days."

Beep-beep – call waiting – it's Randy.

I put Cyn on hold and tell Randy that we're talking about Rajiv's cobra, so I'll have to call him back. He says, "Fine, as long as you promise to find out how big it is. ... And hu-r-r-y – I have something big to share myself."

I say, "Would your big news have anything to do with you finding a cobra of your own?"

"Nope – it's w-a-a-a-y bigger than that. Just hurry, okay?"

I switch back to Cyn. "It was Randy, with some big news."

"What's going on with him?"

"Don't know yet. Have to call him back. And when I do, he wants to know how big Rajiv's cobra is?"

"What difference does it make? Randy's a guy – capable of exaggerating penis size to whatever he wants. Won't be the first time a guy's done that."

"Or the last," I laugh. "Is that why they're sooo good at reading maps – 'cause they have no trouble thinking of an inch as a hundred miles?"

"And we ask for directions, 'cause we've been misled too many times to know what an inch actually looks like."

We both chuckle and decide to hook up later in the afternoon, so we can head over to the Gupta's together, for an Indian high tea. Cyn's actually considering wearing a sari to impress Rajiv's mom, but I hope I've talked her out of it – don't want to give the wrong impression. The woman could easily misinterpret it as a sign that Cyn is willing to play by the traditional rules – the same rules which drove Rajiv into her arms. That said, I dearly hope that she doesn't go to the other extreme either, wearing something with a high cleave factor.

*   *   *

I pull up to the brownstone, to pick up some papers and hopefully catch up with Randy. ... He's sprawled across one of the couches in "The Cocoon"; his new designs neatly displayed across the other.

I barely walk in and he turns into a bumbling mess, talking a mile a minute. "I did it, Sweetie, I did it!"

"Did what?"

"Sold my designs – on consignment – to Sara in Florida."

"Does she know that you're no longer 'engaged' to Danielle?"

"No worries – she knows everything! We've been talking back and forth for a while now – I didn't say anything to you guys 'cause I didn't want to jinx it. But since it's a done deal now, we can talk about it as much as you like." As if – Randy will have to shut up first. "A-n-y-way, I ship out everything today and she'll have me do a fashion show at the end of next week. You *have* to come – it's the biggest day of my life ... so far. Huge, I tell you, simply huge. Sara's invited a lot of moneyed people – even a couple of possible investors."

Seeing that he's out of breath and I can finally get a word in edgewise, I give him a big hug and say, "I'm sooo happy for you. I've wanted this for you for-e-v-e-r. Hopefully it'll lead to even bigger things. ... I've been pushing my producer to meet with you, to try and put something together ... but she's always blown me off, insisting that at the very least you need to have a successful line *first*. Maybe this will do it."

Randy is now crying like a kid – forgetting all about the drama that usually accompanies his royal gayness. He looks small and fragile, without his flamboyant cover – almost like my cat, after I shaved its fur off, when I was seven years old. Boy did that ever piss mom off!

"Did you tell the others yet?" I ask.

"You're my first, Honey."

"I say this calls for a celebration. Tonight, my place, eightish. Call up any and everybody. ... Actually, better make that tomorrow night – I've made a commitment to Cyn this afternoon."

We exchange air kisses, I throw my papers into my briefcase and take off. On my way out the building, I run into Alison and Clive. She tries to stop me, "Do you have a minute?"

"Sorry, Hun, gotta run. Can we talk tomorrow night?"

"What's tomorrow night?"

"I'll let Randy fill you in." And with that, I'm off.

*   *   *

The Gupta household looks like it belongs in a Bollywood museum. Marble floors lead to golden pillars and silk swags. A gorgeous embroidered settee sits in front of the bay window, incense smoke curling into it from the table just behind. Opposite the settee is a gold brocade sofa, with red and blue silk cushions on either side, highlighting Mrs. Gupta like a well-decorated centerpiece. A rotund woman of about fifty, she's wearing a purple sari, exposing various love handles to show off the burden of the good life. A red dot in the middle of her forehead stares at me like a knowing third eye; gray hair pulls away from it, to give it breathing room. Hope Mrs. Gupta doesn't think that *I'm* the bride to be. Thank goodness Rajiv finally introduces us all – to clear any misunderstandings – while she pours tea into translucent cups, scattered about on the brass table in front of her.

Mrs. Gupta turns to Rajiv and says something in her native language, head wobbling from side to side like a bobble-head doll. He informs us that he has to run out to the store for some sweets and excuses himself. Following his rapid exit, the queen bee asks us to sit down on either side of her, so she can get better acquainted with Cyn.

No sooner does Rajiv leave, she glares at Cyn and gets right to the point. "Any girl who marries my son must know how to cook, clean, be willing to bear children, and take care of the family." *Whoa!* "But I'm getting ahead of myself here, aren't I?" Good, at least we're not rushing into anything. "'Cause before I can even *think* of bestowing that privilege upon you, I must know what kind of family you come from, what your parents do, how much money they have – enough to afford a decent dowry for my Rajiv? ... And of course *your* level of education, religion, languages you speak?"

Cyn's jaw drops down into her store bought boobies, leaving her speechless. I too am quite shocked, finding myself up to my push-up bra in unfamiliar traditions. Suddenly, Grammy doesn't look so bad by comparison. ... As Rajiv would say, "What to do, what to do?".

At least we don't have to worry about being speechless, when Mrs. Gupta can carry on a conversation all by herself. Without skipping a beat, she continues, "The fair complexion I like, the skinniness is no good. I read somewhere that anorexia keeps women from getting pregnant."

Cyn finally manages one word, "Pregnant?"

"You *can* get pregnant, can you not? How old are you anyway? You white people all look alike to me – can't tell your age, since you always seem to look older than you are. *Are* you older than Rajiv, or do you just look that way?"

Cyn swallows hard, trying to compose herself –

perhaps even bite her tongue before it's tempted to spill out a few choice words. But before she has a chance to answer, a woman of about six-hundred years of age walks in ever-so-slowly, clutching her walker for dear life. "Good, *DadiMa* is here – might as well get used to her, 'cause you'll be taking care of her. It will be good practice for when the babies come. She needs to be changed at least as often as a newborn," she chortles.

Cyn and I stare at each other in shock, uncertain of whether Mrs. Gupta's serious or joking. Cyn motions with her eyes, pleading with me to say something, knowing that I have a bit more self-control than her. But I'm not touching that one with a ten-foot sari. I simply shrug my shoulders in a don't-look-at-me fashion. Cyn does a sideways motion with her head, eyes gesturing to the door for a quick escape. But Mrs. Gupta grabs Cyn's arm to make sure she stays put, and asks, "So, how soon can you start?" as if she's hiring someone.

Thank goodness Rajiv is back and catches the last little bit. "Mummy, what's *wrong* with you? I thought you'd at least give her a chance, instead of scaring her away without even bothering to get to know her." Couldn't have put it better myself! To her credit, at least Mrs. Gupta didn't give us a grande tour for full impact – curry diaper marinating in diaper pail. Then again, the woman would actually need to move for that.

Cyn gets up and says, "No need to worry Rajiv, there's been a huge misunderstanding. My condo doesn't allow kids, pets or seniors – just goldfish. And even if they did, my eggs are far too old for incubation; my cooking skills limited to takeout food – just ask my two *grown* kids – the only reason I have a kitchen at all is because it came with the condo ... but I'm learning to cook up some damn good martinis in it. ... As for my parents, they're poor, nudist hippies, who raised me to work in the sex industry ... and since I'm not one of those adults who lives with them, doubt it if they'll pay you money to take me off their hands."

This time, it's Mrs. Gupta's jaw that drops down to her pendulous titties. Definitely time to go, before she recovers and throws us out. Cyn and I take hurried steps out the front door, without one more word being uttered, by *any*one. It's a good thing that she didn't wear a sari like she'd wanted to – I think she'd trip in it, the way she's dashing to her car.

As soon as we both get in, Cyn puts her peddle to the metal and takes off. I see Rajiv running after us in the distance. But it doesn't seem to matter to Cyn.

"Wanna talk about it?" I ask.

No answer.

"If he really loves you, and I think he does, he'll find a way to make it all work out."

Still no answer.

I give up and sit quietly in my seat for the rest of the drive, all the way home – not an easy thing for me to do. When we get there, Cyn still looks shell-shocked and drops me off without as much as a "Thank you" or a "Goodnight".

The house feels emptier and lonelier than ever. In as much as I like the independence, I wouldn't mind coming home to a lit house; music and food smells filling the air with signs of life; someone to greet me – someone who I could care for more than myself. But like Jeremy observed, everything's still and silent – frozen in time – just as I left it this morning, with not even as much as maid service. Jeremy's words are echoing inside my head – his wish to come back – twisting my neurons around this way and that. I decide to shift my focus to something else, before I'm tempted to drown my sorrows in Merlot and drink-dial Jeremy. ... The breast cancer DVD it is – sorry Jeremy.

One by one, I hear stories that are at once sad and encouraging. I hear of families that pulled together and families that were ripped apart; children who shaved their heads to support mom and children who got embarrassed by mom's peach fuzz; husbands who put their lives on hold and husbands who baled.

I'm balling my eyes out now, unable to fathom it. A part of me feels really guilty, for making a big deal out of things that don't matter much – in particular, body image stuff. So what if I'd carried a few extra pounds – the body I loathed was always healthy.

As I ponder various thoughts, more images roll by, my mind doing its best to block out their pain. And then, I see a woman plead with women the world over, to do their monthly breast exams – something I've never had the courage to do myself. "Early detection is the key," she emphasizes. I know I should listen, but I push the STOP button, since it's *never* going to happen to me!

Their pain is too much to bear. I need to take my mind off of it. I plug in my kettle in the kitchen, to make myself some tea. While I wait for the water to boil, I decide to get all goofy – it's not ABBA this time, it's Mrs. Gupta. I walk over to the mirror in the hallway and do my best Mrs. Gupta imitation. Not long into it, I hear a voice say, "You know you're being really silly." This time, it's *my* voice.

I take off my blouse, then my bra, and stand motionless in front of the mirror that was occupied by my rendition of Mrs. Gupta just moments ago. What a fabulous pair I have. I'm sooo lucky. Too bad I can't donate them on my organ donor card. ... My hands start to stroke the smooth curves which make for perfect outlines – gently at first, then harder. The ritual feels very sensual. But then, just as I'm about to tease my left nipple with my right hand, my breath freezes ... and my heart stops. I push harder. But the lump just lays there, relentless. It's gotta be a cyst, I'm sure. They can easily drain those, you know. I'll have it taken care of, first thing tomorrow morning.

The black night turns into a bright morning, without as much as a wink of sleep. How I wish I had Jeremy beside me. I do the next best thing. Tentatively, I dial my doctor, even though Jeremy is the only doctor I want to be with right now.

Hearing my predicament, the nurse reassures me that it's probably nothing, since I don't smoke, don't have a family history, and am barely forty. But she promises to get me in to see the doctor tomorrow nonetheless, just for my peace of mind. I'm relieved. The close call had a sobering effect on me. I don't want to waste another day of my life! I'm ready to give Jeremy another chance.

Feeling completely exhausted and nauseous, I end up moving our little get-together to The Lizard Lounge.

*   *   *

The evening blows by in a blur – must be the fatigue from not having slept last night. Everyone's voices sound hollow and far away, like a TV set that's been left on at the end of a long corridor. All I can barely make out is Randy's announcement. And I see Rajiv out of the corner of my eye, begging Cyn's forgiveness. Not sure if I heard him correctly, but I think he's willing to drop his condition – mommy dearest's approval. ... Ehm. ... Did Clive and Alison just announce their engagement? Nah, couldn't be –

not so fast. I must be hallucinating. ... I guess I'll find out soon enough. Just this once, I'm glad that *I* don't have an announcement to make.

I'm too tired to appreciate any of this. Lucky for me, everyone's too busy to notice. I clink my champagne glass with everyone else's – not sure what we're toasting, but I'm certain it's all good. Everything looks peachy perfect!

*   *   *

Another sleepless night, another dreadful morning. But at least my mind will be put to rest any minute now.

I lie on top of a cold examining table, and stare at the bright, fluorescent lighting above me. It puts me into a hypnotic daze – enough so that my butt exposing gown doesn't embarrass me, even as it rustles against the paper sheet and slides forward. Then, just when I think it can't get any worse, Dr. Bower starts to knead and squeeze my breasts like dough – Jeremy definitely has better bedside manners, at least when it comes to my breasts.

After what appears to be an eternity, Dr. Bower stops playing with my tits and starts tickling my pits. I'm giggling like a little kid, feeling quite foolish, praying that he'll be done soon. Nothing doing. I beg, "Can we stop this please – I can't take it anymore."

Dr. Bower finishes up promptly and allows me to change back into my clothes. *Finally*! ... As I go to put my bra back on, I see my nipples standing on attention, like soldiers ready to go to war. *Oh great*! Then again, what did I expect – even a gentle breeze has that effect on them – they're my stupid "on buttons", for fucks sake. If they're not turned on, nothing else gets turned on. How embarrassing! Though I'm pretty sure the good doc has seen it happen before. Even if not, it's the least of my concerns right now.

A few minutes later, I find myself sitting across from Dr. Bower; a mahogany desk keeping him a safe distance away from me. Following the deepest sigh – where was that when he was playing with my awesome pair – he says the most dreaded words, "I have some bad news."

"But you can take care of the cyst, no?"

"I don't think it's a cyst. I tried to move it around – feels like it's something more. ... And then there's your lymph nodes. ... I'd like you to do a mammogram *today*. If it turns out to be what I'm fearing, we might have to schedule surgery as early as next week."

What happens next is an even bigger blur than last night. I feel like I'm caught in a nightmare, unable to escape thick quicksand that's helplessly sucking me into a muddy vortex. Except I'm not outdoors; I'm stuck in a cold lab, my left breast smashed between two cold metal trays. Just tell me the results already, I'm thinking, convinced that it's all a big mistake. But the technician just glares at me. "The doctor will be in touch with you tomorrow. You may change and leave now."

I may leave now – that's it? ... And go where? ... To do what exactly?

No, I simply won't allow this. Nothing is taking over my body – I have so much to live for now ... so much to make right.

Wake up, Jillian. You're just having a terrible nightmare – will yourself out of it. And in future, you might wanna skip watching sad things so late at night. ... Now think sweet thoughts. Sweet, sensual, beautiful thoughts – of the long life ahead of you ... with Jeremy!

Chapter 15 - *Best Laid Plans of Mice and Men*

I've never been one of those people who sits by the phone, waiting for it to ring. If anything, I always laugh at how we've added cell-phones, e-mail, and instant messaging to our list of things to wait by, for a message that may never come...

But today, I have no choice but to join the multitudes of people who wait by the phone ... and wait ... and wait ... and wait. When will Dr. Bower call? ... I decide to take things into my own hands and call him instead. Why should a woman be afraid of dialing – it's the twenty-first century for heaven's sake!

I'm waiting for his chipper nurse to put me on hold for about an hour, only to inform me that he's in with a patient, when she returns. No such luck today – six rings later, I'm informed by a disembodied voice that the doctor won't be available until Monday morning, due to emergency surgery; but I may leave a message if I wish. I do and then hang up, hard, chipping the corner of my handset – that'll teach him! I now have two choices: stay home and sulk, or go out and make the most of my day. I pick the latter and decide to hook up with the girls, even though I'd declined earlier. I was supposed to go out with Jeremy tonight, but given my circumstances, I'm going to cancel – too complicated.   Hope I'm able to have a good time nonetheless, 'cause who knows how much time I have left to enjoy myself? What if I need to fast tract?

*   *   *

When I arrive at The Lizard Lounge, our usual TGIF hangout, the place is mobbed. I wonder what the hell is going on? Judging by the trashier-than-usual attire of the patrons, I'm certain there's a special event – perhaps even a private party.

I brush past a long lineup of people and find Alison and Cyn at the very end of the bar.

"What's going on?" I ask, wondering why they aren't seated at our longstanding, traditional table. Then again, the place is set up quite differently than usual. It looks like rows and rows of tables for two.

Alison says, "Speed dating – I guess we'll have to head elsewhere. We're just waiting here 'cause Darla and Randy should be here any minute. ... By the way, what are *you* doing here? I thought you had a hot date with Jeremy – wasn't tonight the night when you were supposed to make it official?"

"Make what official?" jumps in Cyn.

"Getting back together and everything else that goes with it."

"In that case, what *are* you doing here?" asks Cyn.

"I baled – told him I wasn't feeling well." Cyn glares at me. "Don't look at me like that – it's not like I'm lying either – my stomach's been churning all day. ... Just not sure if I'm ready to go through with it yet – especially the physical part." More intense glaring. "What? You of all people should know how that works. ... Every time I try to imagine myself with him, all I can see is various faceless women – with perfect bodies – doing things to him that I could never see myself doing."

Cyn barks, "For fucks sake Jilly – you either want him or you don't. What's with the back and forth shit? ... In or out – just make up your mind already. You can't have it both ways. You'll drive everybody crazy – yourself, Jeremy and the rest of us. ... I say do him already, to find out *exactly* how you feel – sex is the ultimate tie-breaker. ... Besides, it might just end up being *really* hot – passion doesn't get any better than when love and rage meet."

Quite sensitive for a therapist, isn't she? But not wishing to get into my real reasons for baling on Jeremy, I concede. "I know, I know ... I should make my up mind already ... but just give me a chance to process some stuff, okay?"

"Process *what*? It's simple – you either shit or get off the pot."

Boy she's in a nasty mood! I don't think I've ever seen her like this before. Usually she's the most supportive one of the bunch, her tough exterior notwithstanding. I convince myself that it's her *own* shit that's pissing her off – nothing to do with me. But since I've had it with her attitude and am in no mood for this, I take a jab at her. "Are *you* shitting with the Gupta's, off the pot, or undecided?"

"Fuck the Gupta's – not taking their shit ... though sure could use some pot. There, I said it – decisive enough for you? ... Can't believe I actually fell for all that sweet, caring, sensitive bullshit, just 'cause it was very different from what I'm used to. ... Yesserie, he's different alright. Unfortunately it's not just me who he wants to take care of – it's his whole damn family."

Alison teases Cyn with, "Maybe *you* should stick around for the speed dating thingy."

"Been there, done that, not bothering again."

I say, "This is news. I didn't know you did that.

What was it like?"

"Why, you thinking of trying it ... in case you decide to get off the pot with Jeremy?"

I lie, "Maybe."

"Don't bother – it's musical chairs where you *don't* want to sit down. ... Kinda feels like going to a supermarket on sample day – you taste stuff and keep moving on. And the odd time you decide to actually buy the crap and bring it home, you end up asking yourself 'Why in the hell did I do that?'"

"That bad, huh?"

"Worse. ... Let me see, I had my pick of a misogynistic professor who thought *A Clockwork Orange* was the best movie ever, a geek with a greasy mullet and backnee...."

"Backnee?"

"Back acne. ... And then there was the guy who was between jobs – told him I was between boyfriends and would look him up when he settled his job situation. ... Oh, and I almost forgot about the guy who kept looking at his Rolex, hoping I'd notice ... and when I didn't comment, he actually asked me if I'd ever dated someone who owned a Rolex before? Luckily, I was saved by the partner-switching bell – it rang just as I was about to ask him if it was made in Taiwan?"

We all break out in giggles. I look at my own watch. I've set somewhat of a new record here – didn't think about my sick breast even once in the last seven minutes. Now if I could only do that another three hundred or so more times, I could easily make it to Monday morning without a hitch.

Back to the girls – the distraction thing is working

well. I ask Alison, "You never did tell us how your whole dating thing turned out – with the impotent guys – or for that matter how you eventually ended up with Clive?"

"Remember the special guy I told you about, a while back?"

"The bigwig whose name you couldn't share with us, 'cause you didn't want it getting out just then?"

"That's the one. He'd told me that his separation hadn't been made public yet, so he wanted to keep it hush-hush. What he neglected to tell me was, it was such a well-kept secret that even his wife didn't know anything about it."

"Married and forgot to tell ya, huh?"

"Yup! Figured it wouldn't count since we weren't planning on fucking anyway, because of the whole impotent ad thing."

"So why go out with you?"

"Still needed his ego stroked."

Cyn interjects, "The bastard! Told you that ego stroking is more important than libido stroking – I even put it in my book. ... Were it not the case, more than half of the affairs would never happen."

"You're not kidding. Thanks to my ad, I think I met *all* the guys who needed their egos massaged, more than anything else on the planet – I guess if your dick's not working, what choice do you have? Talk about overcompensating with serious egomaniac tendencies, even though buying a penis car would be so much easier."

I ask, "What do these egomaniacs do ... to overcompensate?"

"Anything from insulting the waitress, to ignoring

the homeless; showing off their assets, to showing *me* off as an asset; pissing me off by ordering my food for me, to actually wanting to piss on me."

Cyn interrupts, "Serious control issues."

"Ya think – and that's just the beginning. The list is endless. ... But my favorite one was the guy who kept talking about himself all night long, not once bothering to ask me about myself. I thought, maybe he's just trying to impress me. Two hours later, when my eyes glassed over, he finally noticed and apologized. 'Sorry, I've just been talking about myself ... let's talk about you ... so what do *you* think of me?'"

"He had to be kidding, right?" I say.

"At first I thought so too, figuring the guy caught himself nervously babbling on, and then at least had the decency to address it with a great sense of humor. But when I giggled in response, he told me he was serious. I said, 'Does it really matter what I think, especially since we're not going to be hanging out with each other anytime soon?' and left. The upside: at least I didn't have to walk sixteen miles to the end of the parking lot where he'd parked his Viper, 'to make sure nobody dents it'. ... Frankly, I'm surprised that someone hasn't already, since he has pissing people off down to an art-form. ... On a happier note, I picked up a lot of new clients for my special call girl services."

I can't believe this. The dating scene sounds so discouraging, with or without a penis car. I hope Clive is a different story. I ask Alison, "What's the deal with Clive?"

"Yes, Clive," she smiles encouragingly. "Believe it or not, I met him at a church function."

"A church function? What the heck were you doing

at a church function?" asks Cyn, in a state of complete and utter shock.

"I take my mom once in a while. It does me good – no matter what I'm doing, I feel dirty doing it." We laugh. She continues, "Don't laugh – when you're not having sex, it's good to feel dirty in other ways."

"So what happened?" I ask eagerly.

"I was sitting in a corner, bored out of my mind ... actually more like bummed, after the whole married guy thing. Clive must've noticed, 'cause he walked over and said, 'I know what you're thinking – finally I'm going to get picked up by a great big hunky guy. But I'm sorry to tell you that I'm just a wee little Florence Nightingale, trapped inside this body, dying to come out to rescue you.' ... I laughed and told him that I wasn't buying into it, unless he could truly rescue me out of there. ... We left the function, went for a coffee, and then walked and talked for hours. I totally lost track of time until mom called on my cell, to find out what happened to me. When I told her that I'd gone for a long walk with somebody I met at church, she said she'd take a cab. So we talked some more – next thing you know, we're caught in the middle of a glorious sunrise, cradled in park swings."

Cyn adds, "Of course you insisted on keeping the whole thing *pure*?"

"Wasn't *my* choice. For the first time in God knows how long, I thought I could actually fall for someone ... even do some truly *impure* things to him. ... I guess he must've read my mind, 'cause right then, he swung around and asked my permission to kiss me. ... Wet my undies in a split-second, over that will-he-or-won't-he Hollywood moment. ... And then, when we finally got to it – the kiss – I went weak in the knees. What a damn good kisser he turned out to be. I thought if he can do that to my *mouth* ... well, I just wanted him to keep going. ... Definitely someone I'd wanna break my no sex rule for. Yup, a full-bodied relationship with him could be quite intoxicating."

I tease, "I take it he wasn't anything like the Hoover guy you told us about?"

"Nope, just soft and sensual."

Now I know what you're thinking, that my mind is probably playing porno music, having wandered off to the mega-kiss that *I* received not too long ago. I wish – but that couldn't be further from the truth. Not feeling terribly sexy right now. ... Nope, I'd rather concentrate on other people. It's w-a-a-a-y better than focusing on myself – reduced to a gigantic, lumpy boob, overshadowing everything else ... like one of those floaty things at a parade.

My pity party within myself is interrupted by Darla and Randy's rambunctious arrival! She drops a bunch of papers on the table in front of Alison. "Here's the initial proposal – now you're *sure* you want to sell?"

"I have to, for a lot of reasons – the least of which is, don't think that Clive will understand."

Cyn asks, "Exactly what are you selling ... and what does Clive have to do with it?"

"My side business."

"Like hell you are! With the kind of cash flow you're raking in, I'm sure Clive won't mind. ... It's not like *you're* doing anything yourself."

"I know, it's just the nature of the business – pretty sure it won't sit right with him. But I have to admit that I've been really torn – gone back and forth on it many times – but still think it's the best thing to do ... for *many* reasons."

Cyn asks, "So exactly who are you handing over your steady income to?"

"I have a couple of prospects. Darla is just writing up the initial proposal to make sure that it's worth my while."

Cyn snaps, "Oh no you don't. I want you to think good and hard about this ... and if it's still what you want, *I* might be interested in buying you out."

Shocked, I interject, "Back up! ... You're not serious, are you Alison? For as long as I've known you, you've never let a guy dictate *any*thing to you – hence the abstinence clause remember, to keep your head on straight?"

"Told you when you mix love with sex, everything goes crazy," she laughs.

"So the fast is finally broken?"

"I wish. After all this time, I can't *stand* waiting another minute – I'm ready to explode. You'd think the guy would be all over it ... but he doesn't believe in pre-marital sex."

"Neither did Rajiv, but he got over it. ... So how are you going to handle your non-virgin status with him?" Cyn teases.

"Are you kidding, I'm a born again virgin – after all this time I'm sure my hymen has grown back, like a piercing without an earring in it. ... Honestly, I don't understand what the big deal is anyway. The way some religious people act, you'd think that after God created the human body in it's perfect form, he turned it over to the devil to slap on the genitals."

"I still think it's a big mistake to plan everything around *his* comfort zones, with or without genital involvement," grunts Cyn.

"If the truth be known, I'm considering the deal as much for myself as I am for Clive – just don't have enough hours in the day for everything I want to do. I figure I've enjoyed being ridiculously successful all this time ... have my own cash, car and condo ... time to try out something new – and we're not just talking about my relationship with Clive. Blowing a healthy wad of cash also takes a fair bit of a time and commitment," she laughs. "Bottom line: it's not like he's pushing me – he doesn't even know anything about it – I'm doing it because *I* want to, for my *myself*."

Cyn says, "I've already tried all kinds of *new* things – nothing's as reliable as cash. ... Actually, the more I think about it, the more I want to buy you out – that is if you're still interested."

I jump in, "Wouldn't that be a conflict of interest, since you're supposed to be helping people deal with that stuff, not make it available to them on the sly?"

"Conflict shmonflict – I could always become a silent partner and have someone else run it for me. It's not like I'll be offering it to my clients, like an alternative on a menu. But if someone would rather go for it, instead of trying to deal with it, who am I to stop them? At least like this, I'll get their business either way," she laughs casually.

Randy cuts in with, "Girls, girls, aren't we forgetting something here?" Looking at our confused expressions, he continues, "Like planning for only the most crucial fashion event in history? This stuff can wait – my stuff is *the* most important thing that we should all be focusing on right now."

Randy, if you only knew! I figure now is as good a time as any to break the news to him. "About that – sorry, no can do. Something's come up."

"What could be *more* important than supporting

me, through the fruition of my life-long dream?"

"Trust me Hun, I want to be there with all my heart, but I *can't*."

Now they're all looking at me, probably wondering what could possibly keep me from being there for Randy – I've always been his number one fan.

Randy pouts, "Then find a way – I'll never speak to you again if you don't come with me."

Don't know if I'm over-reacting, or if it's just the proverbial straw, but I find myself losing it, tears gushing out of my eyes as I sob relentlessly... Feels good to let it out, finally.

Everyone looks shocked, as they gather around me, trying to make body contact – arm on shoulder, thigh-stroking, lifting my chin up to read what's going on, etc, until Cyn finally breaks the ice with, "What's up, Sweetie?"

"I have a breast lump that may be cancerous. More than likely, I'll have to go in for surgery next week."

Cyn throws her arms around me and gives me the most tender hug. "I had no idea. Why didn't you say something? I feel like such an idiot for reaming you a new one, when you must be scared out of your mind."

Alison asks, "Does Jeremy know?"

"Nope. And I don't want you telling him either. I'm not going to reconcile, only to fuck up his life."

Darla is pissed. "What are you talking about? You can't assume that he'll see it that way. Shouldn't you at least be straight with him and let *him* decide for himself?"

"This is how it's going to go down, okay? I could never take him back, unless I felt I have something to offer."

Now Cyn is furious. "Just 'cause you might be ill doesn't make you lesser of a person – you'll be offering him the same girl he fell in love with, only better. The girl he wants to fall in love with all over again."

"And what about the lust part? Am I supposed to offer him an amputee and expect him to get excited about it?"

Darla is crying, "This could have happened to any one of us. Is that how *you'd* see us?"

"Of course not!"

"Then what's the problem? ... And what possible excuse could you come up with to take back the new marital vows you wrote for him – the ones you e-mailed him already?" asks Randy.

"Fuck, I forgot all about that. Hope he hasn't read my e-mail yet."

Group hug. Followed by group tears. Followed by everyone heading over to my place for a group pajama party.

Alison offers to pick up some gourmet pizza and beer, Cyn's bringing over the entire *Sex and the City* collection from the video store, Darla's going to stock us up on ice-cream and *Krispy Kream* donuts, and Randy's bringing over his make-over kit to do our nails and hair. I didn't mean to take away from what they had in mind for tonight, but it sure feels good to have them by my side. It's not the three Fs that Jeremy and I were planning – film, food, and fucking – but it's right up there!

*   *   *

Speaking of Jeremy, guess who just showed up at my door, with chicken soup no less. Good thing I'm not out there, partying it up – as if it's even possible. A bowl of

Valium would have been more appropriate than a bowl of soup, but hey, it's the thought that counts.

Lovingly, he says, "I was hoping to nurse you back to health. You did say in sickness and in health." Fuck, he did read the damn letter. All blood drains out of my face, leaving me quite pale I'm sure. Jeremy comments, "You don't look right. Want me to take you to the hospital?"

"I think I just need to go to bed. Would you mind?"

"Boy you move fast – I thought you'd at least want some candlelight and wine before going to bed," he teases.

I smile and point him to the door. "Alone, thank you very much." And with that, I send him away.

I send Jeremy away!

Thanks to the gang, I manage to make it through the weekend, right through to Monday morning.

I call Dr. Bower again. To my shock, the hold part lasts less than thirty seconds, this time; and then, it's the great one himself who pops up on the line. What service! I must remember to send him an extra bottle of wine at Christmas.

But wait, he sounds sad, like he's about to tell me that he may not *make* it to Christmas. I ask, "What's wrong, Dr. Bower?"

"Normally I don't do this sort of thing over the phone, but since time is of the essence, I'd like you to clear your calendar for the rest of the week – I've booked emergency surgery for you first thing tomorrow morning. ... Naturally, we have to do the pre-op lab work ASAP *today*!"

I'm speechless.

The lump in my throat won't let me talk. Just hope that the lump in my breast doesn't keep me from living.

Maybe it's *me* who won't be making it to Christmas. ... Dr. Bower must be wondering what happened to me, 'cause he starts the "Hello, hello, are you there?" thing.

I sob, "Yes, I'm still here. ... Are you sure?"

"Am I sure you need surgery, or am I sure of the diagnosis?"

"Both!"

"Yes on the first count, no on the second."

"So there's still hope?"

"There's *always* hope ... even if it's malignant!"

"What are the odds?"

"Can't say for sure – that's why I want to do this right away. ... Best case scenario, why make you worry if you don't need to? Worst case scenario, let's not waste any time."

I honk into my Kleenex, "I'll be at your office as soon as I can," and hang up.

What am I going to do?

Just a few weeks ago I thought that Jeremy's infidelity was the worst thing that could ever happen to me. I wanted to die.

And now, I'd give almost anything to live and not have to go through this...

My insides burn, like I've swallowed glass; my stomach wants to throw it all back up.

I know there are many who've already gone through

this and come out stronger – just not sure if I'm one of them.

Thank goodness that Randy has offered to hold my hand through this, though I'm not very happy about him changing his plans – he's waited his entire life for an opportunity to show off his designs.

But to him, his place is by my side, even though the girls are going to be there in any case.

Cyn's moving in with me until I feel better – claims it will finally give her a chance to finish her book.

Darla is taking charge of the food situation, since 'Cyn can't cook worth shit'.

And Alison's looking into aftercare, support groups and stuff like that, should I need it. She's really good at that sort of thing – got her mom squared away in the best rehab facility in a jiffy, and took over her niece's schooling when her parents couldn't afford the education which would allow her to apply her gift.

I guess I never realized how lucky I truly am, until now.

Left boob or not, I can finally see it. It's amazing how much you grow up when you learn that a little bit of padding – give or take – isn't the worst thing that can happen to your body, as long as you're still alive.

Especially when you have so many people who love you – who've *always* loved you and *always* will – minus a boob or plus a few pounds.

I guess it's true what they say about the best laid plans of mice and men.

Chapter 16 - *Growth*

Tuesday morning, bright and early, I find myself in a blue hospital gown, hair tucked back into a blue disposable hat – quite the different fashion statement from last night.

A mere twelve hours ago, I felt like a star, immortalized by boudoir photography. Randy pulled a few favors to capture me in every bit of coquettish wear that I'd bought, for a sex trip that never transpired. It was his way of making sure that I never forget how sexy I am.

Needless to say, I was positioned in ways that would highlight my sensuous breasts. Randy teased me with, "If you don't hurry up and get well enough to stand in front of the *Spice of Life* cameras real soon, I'll be posting these semi-nudes on the Internet." The way I'm feeling right now, *I'd* be willing to post them *myself*, if I could only hang onto my body just the way it is.

Fear shudders my spine, sending shivers up and down the back of my neck. I pray that I come out of this alive ... there's lots I still need to do. I've wasted too much time worrying for naught – had no idea just how lucky I am. All my life, whenever Grammy said, "Hope you find whatever makes you happy," I wasn't sure *what* that was. Now I know – just hope it's not too late. God, please let me make it through this – I have so much to live for, so much to make right!

I'd really wanted to go to church this past weekend to say a proper prayer, instead of my rhetorical one liners – the orders I dish out to God on an as-needed basis – but I felt ashamed. You see, I've always treated church as something about *me*, not a Divine Being. The odd time I went, I walked in thinking: this is it, the time that something miraculous will happen to me, giving my life an exciting purpose, while taking away all of my problems. *I mean why else would you go to church, right ... other than to get your problems fixed?* And then, when I didn't feel all that different, I acted the way I would when a date didn't work out – 'cause the guy wasn't the knight in shining armor who could fix my problems and make me happier. I guess I missed the point entirely, on both counts – the part about enjoying the experience itself; the divine connection which brings out the best in you and carries you through anything.

Can you see why I felt embarrassed about going? Wish I'd made at least one trip to give thanks for the many blessings I've received.

But blessed as I am, I want to change the way I live my life ... and not just for my own sake. I have so many people to be thankful for – above and beyond those closest to my heart. My producer was not only gracious enough to let me take as much time as I needed, she was willing to keep it quiet for now.

I know I'll have to get into it sooner or later, but right now doesn't feel like the right time – need to find out the extent of the collateral damage first. Ditto for others finding out. The girls tried to push me into calling the kids and Jeremy – especially Jeremy – but I begged them not to make me. "The kids don't need this – it will ruin their trip. As for Jeremy, that remains to be seen."

My core feels cool and nauseous, as I receive the anesthetic; my lids get heavy, even as I try to hold them open, while trying my best to count backwards.

Next thing I know, I'm waking up, a breathing tube inside my throat, various other tubes going in and out of other parts of my body. I try to talk, but the tube won't let me. God, please don't let me be in a vegetative state – I don't even *like* vegetables. ... A nurse comes by to check my vitals. I grab her arm for dear life, hoping to get her attention. She talks about me in third person. "Mrs. Briggs is coming around."

A flurry of activity takes place all around me. Some things are pulled out of my body, including the breathing tube, while new things are pushed in to take their place – an anti-nauseant IV tube being a case in point. Then why do I still feel so sick? I wanna upchuck ... find out how things turned out ... feel *both* breasts on my chest. But my entire chest is numb – can't feel *either* breast – the bandage across it telling me it's all over.

When my speech is finally restored, I ask one of the nurses, "How did it go?"

"The doctor will be with you shortly," is all she says, before turning away in a matter-of-fact way. I know she's done this a hundred times before, all in a day's work, but it's the biggest thing that's ever happened to me. I'm kinda stuck in it like a tire stuck in mud, unable to move onto anything else.

The clock on the recovery room wall is stuck – somebody change the batteries please. But I find myself staring at it anyway – hypnotically – while my lead head drools all over my pillow. It's not like I can read or anything, to pass time – then again, time appears to be standing still. ... After about a hundred hours go by – make that twenty-four minutes according to stuck clock – I finally see Dr. Bower. At least I think it's him. Could also be St. Peter, since he *is* wearing a white gown. At least I didn't end up in hell, thanks to my shenanigans with Dan – even though Jeremy and I were on a break then. Don't go there Jilly – this has *nothing* to do with it. One in eight women will get cancer – no matter how great Dan is, he couldn't possibly get around *that* much. If anything, it's stress, not sinful pleasure, which may play a part – just about anyone who's been diagnosed with cancer, can pin point something immensely stressful within the past year. And although you've had your fair share, you don't even know if it *is* cancer yet, instructs my inner voice. ... But if it is cancer, and I can't blame myself, who else can I blame? A Devine being? The environment? Jeremy, for stressing me out all these years? What if there is no one to blame, 'cause this is no more than a freak of nature – what am I supposed to do with my anger then? These things are supposed to happen to *other* people, not me. Somebody had to have made a mistake – maybe St. Peter. ... I look up to the heavens with my eyes and wonder *why me*? ... I want to throw something at someone ... just as soon as I can figure out who's responsible.

As the man in white approaches, he doesn't need to say all that much – I can see it in his eyes, just before his lids drop down. "Sorry, Jillian, we had to remove the left one, but I'm happy to say that we were able to save the right one. ... Also, since we caught it before it made it to the lymph nodes, your prognosis is very good." Oh joy oh bliss, now I can be lopsided – can't even buy myself a matching pair ... and this is supposed to be a *good* prognosis? Even though my breathing tube is out, I can't utter a single word. Not one word.

What does one say at a time like this? ... Thanks doc? Do I get to take my dead boob home so I can give it a proper burial, or will you be taking care of that for me? And does medical insurance cover that sort of thing? What about a shrink, so I can properly grieve said boob's death? ... Dammit, what happens next? I guess I must've said the last bit out loud, 'cause the good doc is now holding my hand and talking to me about chemotherapy. All I can hear is, frozen cell growth, blah, blah, blah, hair loss, blah, blah, blah, nausea, blah, blah, blah.

Tears sting my eyes. I don't know if I'm grateful to be alive, or if I just wanna die. And what's worse – losing a breast or a husband? But I don't have that choice to make, do I, since I've just lost both. Nothing could be more painful. *Damn!*

*   *   *

Me and my war wound are now undergoing some serious post-op therapy, the chemo being the worst of it. But I still don't want anyone to know, other than the girls of course, without whom I couldn't have survived any of this. My biggest fear around people finding out: they'll look at me mournfully, even though I'm still alive. Worse – ignore me, 'cause they don't know what to say. And then there's Jeremy – how much longer can I keep him at bay, pretending to be on some exciting work tour? Thank God for cell phones.

The girls are pushing me to come clean with Jeremy, especially since the kids will be returning soon, and he's bound to find out then anyway. But I can't face him. The shiny mane of hair that he loved running his fingers through is no more than peach fuzz; the breasts we called my "on buttons", now destroyed. I know the hair will grow back, but my breast never will – and the prognosis for my self-esteem still remains a mystery.

I go into mourning, first my breast, then my relationship. But after I cry enough tears, until there's no more fluid left in me – no energy to cry any more – I uncurl from my fetal position, and get ready to be born again. ... One final scream and I'm finally grateful to be alive; the goddess in me strong enough to teach me new things. The only question which remains: how can I possibly turn around this painful ordeal, so at least some good comes out of it? ... The documentary – that's it. I'll let Lynda film my journey. Better to support life than fight my existence!

For the first time in a very long time, I'm actually excited about something. I call Lynda and ask her to meet me.

Ding, dong – she's half an hour early, and I don't even have my head scarf on. But I'm too excited to be worried about that – it's not like she hasn't seen that before. Enthusiastically, I swing open the door. But it's not her standing in the rain. It's Jeremy, on bended knee, holding up a bouquet of my favorite lilies and roses, held high over his shaved head. I'm expecting him to freak out ... run away ... get upset ... but he stays put on bended knee, and asks me to marry him – his face neither shocked nor appalled.

"But we're already married, remember?" I say, trying to cover up my head.

"Apparently it doesn't count – aren't *you* the one who said you're a different girl now and we'll have to start fresh?"

I'm now crying, profusely, and can barely manage, "A very different girl, a very different time."

"Well I'm done dating – I want us to be married again."

I start to slam the door shut in his face, but he's not

budging. He's still soaking in the rain, on bended knee, holding the flowers up for me. I take the flowers and let him in. What's wrong with him, I wonder? He didn't love me enough to stay faithful when I was hot, why would he want me now ... or be able to stay faithful to me? ... Unless it was *never* about me. For now, I'll give him the benefit of the doubt. ... He's kinda cute with his brave new bald and beautiful look. And he seems to have traded in his curves for a firm chest and belly. Just as well – I couldn't imagine myself being involved with someone who has bigger hair or cup size than me.

We go into the kitchen, so I may put the flowers in a vase. I drop them in and let them fall as they may. Sometimes you just need to accept things as they unfold. Letting go of control isn't easy, but once you get used to it, it can be quite liberating – no more worrying about exhausting details and minutiae. Maybe I'll take the same approach with Jeremy.

I sit down at the kitchen table with Jeremy, pour us both some tea, and decide to let *him* unfold. "So, how did you find out?"

"Promise not to get mad?"

"That remains to be seen – but do tell."

"Randy told me. I pleaded with him to tell me why the sudden cold shoulder from you, after I could've sworn that we were making progress – you did e-mail me those new vows, leading me to believe that we were starting over."

"Never could keep his big mouth shut. ... He's such a girl."

We both giggle. On to the next question. "So tell me Jeremy, why would you want me now ... like this ...

when I couldn't keep you interested before?"

"I was *always* interested. But as we got busier with our separate lives and started to pull apart, I thought maybe *you'd* lost interest. You certainly seemed to have a lot more fun with your friends than me."

Furious, I say, "*I* lost interest? Don't pin this one on me." But just as the words leave my mouth, It occurs to me that we're both victims of projection. Cyn did say, whatever we accuse our partner of is generally something they could just as easily accuse *us* of. Hence, boredom rarely happens to individuals – it's a couple's disease. So if you're bored, chances are, so is your partner. Who knew? Glad she's finally managed to finish her book.

Jeremy looks at my distant expression and apologizes, "I'm so sorry, that came out wrong. I wasn't trying to pin anything on you. ... I just *assumed* that you weren't interested anymore. Who'd blame you anyway? I was always too busy ... and the odd time that we were together, I was too tired for anything earth-shattering. Wasted all my passion on that stupid research project, trying to prove myself."

I try to encourage Jeremy. "Hopefully, one day it will all be worthwhile."

"Fat chance – they pulled the funding right when Suzanne and I were close to wrapping up the study."

"I'm so sorry Honey – I had no idea. Why didn't you tell me?"

"I wanted to. But when I came home that night, you were busy getting ready for your *Spice of Life* announcement, so I simply couldn't do that to you."

"It happened back then?"

"Yup! That's why I was such an asshole that night

– that week – even though I should've been excited for you."

"Why didn't you tell me the next day, or any other day after that?"

"Because I made a stupid mistake on top of everything else. Instead of coming to you, I cried on Suzanne's shoulder. It was our baby – she was just as upset as me – so I turned to her, thinking you wouldn't understand anyway. And then, after a few drinks, I went on to confide in her how I'd been feeling really low all around ... especially since my career seemed to be unraveling while yours was soaring. Suzanne tried to cheer me up by filling my head with all the stuff I wanted to hear, and I stupidly fell for it."

I say, "So now it's *her* fault?" and search within myself for the part that I might've played. I wonder how she saw him and what she said to him – things I'd neglected to say myself. Memo to self: look at Jeremy through the eyes of a woman trying to have an affair with him.

Jeremy struggles for words and then nervously spits out, "Nope, didn't mean that either. The only culprits are me and my fragile ego – no redeeming excuse or exciting storyline."

"Let's not forget your fragile penis – I'm sure he too fits into the equation somehow," I hiss sarcastically.

"Actually, my penis couldn't really get into it. It was never about him."

"Don't wanna hear who or what your penis couldn't manage to get into."

"It was so bad that she accused me of having erectile dysfunction."

"So you're coming to me 'cause she couldn't get you up and running?"

"No, I'm coming to you because I don't want her, I want *you*. Told you it was over for quite a while."

"So why the trial separation?"

"I needed to find out how deep my feelings run for you – figured it will take quite a bit of commitment to fix this thing, so might as well make sure that I want it bad enough and am up for it."

"So exactly how badly *do* you want it?"

"You have nooo idea."

"Even though I'm lesser of a woman now?"

"You're more woman than anyone else could ever be."

"What about the others?"

"*What* others – where did you get an idea like that?"

"I ran into Suzanne at the supermarket. She was kind enough to console me with how you didn't deserve me, since you were making the rounds so to speak."

"Reliable witness, wouldn't you say?"

"Was sex with the witness any good?" Can't believe I'm asking this, but I need to know, not that Jeremy's going to be a reliable witness himself.

"Depends upon who you ask. I thought it was pretty lousy. She claims it was downright awful!"

"Ouch!"

"Fuck her – sorry, wrong choice of words – all that matters is what *you* think?"

"There's always room to grow."

Jeremy strokes my arm and chuckles, "I think I'm

starting to grow now." I can feel the hair on his arm gently brush up against the smooth skin of mine – making me tingle from the excitement of an unexpected touch, that first kiss of skin against skin. But then I remember ....

Disappointedly, I stroke my bald head and say, "You gotta be kidding."

He strokes his own bald head and teases, "I think bald is kinda sexy."

Tears spring up in my eyes, as I stroke the left side of my chest, barely mouthing, "What about ...?" For the record, I still haven't had the courage to look at it. I've run my hand across it in the shower, but with my eyes closed. Wonder if Sunny has a class at The Goddess Ranch where we can hold up mirrors to our mastectomy scars, and make peace with them like we did with our vaginas – maybe even name and describe them, so they no longer feel foreign to us.

Jeremy places his hand on mine and says, "It's what's directly underneath that matters to me." If he means my heart, the way it's pounding right now, I'm pretty sure it's got a lot of life still left in it.

"That's so sweet of you, but I'm not sure I can do this right now."

"Then we'll wait."

"What if I'm *never* ready?"

"Never is a long time. Let's just take it one step at a time, okay?"

"What if I were to go for one of those reconstructive surgeries, where they use abdominal tissue to rebuild a breast? I know it won't have the same sensations, but at least it will look better."

"It's called a tramflap procedure ... and I'd rather

you didn't. The last thing you need is more surgery. ... How about we leave it as is, to remind us of what we almost lost. I know it's a horrible price to pay for a change in perspective, but I'm glad we woke up before it was too late."

"My perspective had already changed before any of this happened – wouldn't dream of taking you back otherwise."

Jeremy mouths, "You're taking me back? Thank you," and holds me tight, tears streaming down his cheeks. Soap opera music is now filling my head, a dimmer switch creating soft focus within it. ... Lucky for me, I'm saved by the bell yet again, before I turn into a pile of mush.

It's gotta be Lynda. Maybe our project will help me find a way to relate to Jeremy, in my condition.

But there's still the issue of trust. I know that two-thirds of marriages rocked by infidelity can never get it back – then again, they would've probably broken up anyway, for the same reasons that someone needed to have an affair in the first place. ... From what Cyn's told me, the only way to survive an affair is, if *both* parties *really* want to and are willing to work hard at it, sans judgmental comments. ... The way Jeremy and I are feeling about each other right now, I think we'll make it. As for the judgmental part: one thing that I've learned is, the harder we are on ourselves, the harder we are on others. Once I was able to accept my own imperfections and limitations, I could do the same for Jeremy easily enough.

In as much as I'm dying to share all this with my husband, I guess that conversation will have to wait for another time, since Lynda is now on her way in and Jeremy is on his way out – to pick up my big surprise!

I greet Lynda at the door, full of anticipation. She looks less enthused than me. The first words out of her mouth, "I was meaning to call you myself, since I have a bit of bad news to share with you."

After all the bad news I've had to deal with as of late, I'm sure this one's just another drop in the bucket. I take a deep breath and say, "Why don't we talk in the living room?" and guide her in.

Always to the point, no sooner does she plunk down into the couch, she just spits it out. "It appears that your co-host is giving us a hard time around *Spice of Life* – though it isn't anything which can't be fixed contractually, if you've still got your heart set on it."

"What seems to be the problem?" I ask.

"When James found out what you've been going through, the *compassionate* man that he is, he couldn't get his head around how your appearances would affect the show. ... He's convinced that it will be impossible to reclaim the chemistry and witty repartee that have made the show so successful."

I guess that explains the lack of get-well panty roses. No matter, I'm too excited to let anything get me down now. I put on my best "pondering face", and say, "Is that so? ... Never saw it coming? ... But no worries, because what I have in mind is going to need all of my time anyway."

"Go on."

"At first, I just wanted to have my recovery process filmed for your documentary, to encourage other women. But since I'm already part way through, looking forward to rebuilding my life, how about doing a show along those lines, to fill the *Spice of Life* time slot?"

"What do you have in mind?"

Out of the blue, I find myself pitching *Second Chances* – a show about women receiving help with rebuilding their lives, after a traumatic event.

Watching Lynda's encouraging expression, I elaborate, "They could be cancer survivors, abuse victims, or anything else which paralyzes women. Each week will reveal a different woman's story. We could establish her primary goal at the outset, and then follow her journey as we help her achieve it. From getting physical, emotional, financial make-overs, to top notch legal advice, we can cover it all. Just think of all the women we could help out in our viewing audience!"

Lynda uncrosses her legs, grabs her chin in thought, and says, "I like it ... like it a lot. But we'll have to find the right experts to get it off the ground."

"If you'll consider me for hosting, I can bring an awesome team with me – the greatest make-over guy ever, a topnotch financial advisor, a to-the-point therapist, and a legal eagle who is really on the ball. ... What do you say?"

"I'll have to audition them first, to see if they have a screen presence, are telegenic enough, and all that stuff – you know the drill."

"No worries – just give them a chance and I *know* you'll be impressed."

Lynda stands up, shakes my hand, then switches over to a hug, and says, "Let's set this up ASAP, shall we? You talk to your friends and find out their availability, and I'll set things up at the studio."

Just as time was stuck when I was feeling down, this time it flew by quickly – I guess 'cause I was having fun – where did the two hours go?

I feel refreshed, purposeful, and excited about everything. I can't wait to share the good news about *Second Chances* with my nucleus – my dearest friends and family, who *are* the very core of my being.

The gang has always wanted to bring our skills together to work on something worthwhile – perhaps a specialized service for divorcing people – but this is way better!

Thank goodness *Spice of Life* is over – *Second Chances* is going to require all of my energy. And in case you're wondering, I'm not the least bit upset, just a little surprised by James.

Speaking of surprises, I can't wait for Jeremy to return with mine – have I got an even bigger one for him. I want him to be the first one to hear this.

I *know* he'll be happy for me! ... And here he is now, standing at the door, in triplicate – my surprise being Jack and Amber. I guess he won this round. I hug my children, with tear-filled eyes. "What are you doing back so early?"

Jack says, "When Dad called and told us everything, we *had* to come. We couldn't be anywhere else. ... We were dying to call you right away, but he made us promise that we wouldn't, 'cause he wanted to surprise you. So we made him promise us right back, that he too would stay away from you until today, so he doesn't blow it himself." I guess that explains why Jeremy didn't come around until earlier today, when he found out last week.

I smile at Jack, but he doesn't smile back. He looks quite upset in fact. I'm trying my best to read his face.

After what feels like an eternity, he clears his throat

and says, "Now what I'd like to know is, why didn't *you* call us? About any of it? We knew something wasn't quite right between you two, but didn't have a clue about the separation. ... And now this."

I choose not to say anything about the separation – they don't need to know, especially since it's a moot point now.

But since I have to say something, I stroke my bald head and blurt out, "I was sure that seeing me like this could've waited."

Amber takes off her hat, revealing a buzz cut, and says, "What's wrong with this?"

I practically scream, "What did you do to your gorgeous hair?" convinced that she's milking the opportunity to show off her rebellious haircut.

She says, "Relax Mom, we still have it," and hands me a hat box.

Tucked inside is a wig made out of her hair, for me. She'd been working part-time with a costume designer in Paris to make a few extra bucks, when she got the news.

In as much as he hated the very thought of Amber chopping off her gorgeous mane, he agreed to have it made into a wig urgently, so she could fly back with it – there was no talking her out of it apparently.

I'm truly touched. I did not expect that from Amber – maybe the pink ribbon tattoo that's on Jack's arm, but nothing like that from Amber...

Then again, it's not the first time that I'm guilty of expecting the wrong thing out of the right person. Jeremy always did say that I was my worst enemy. But that was before I loved and appreciated myself.

Chapter 17 - *Second Chances*

It seems like old times, only better. We're all gathered around my kitchen table, brainstorming for ideas to make *Second Chances* a huge success.

Lynda just loved the team, as I knew she would. But what surprised me was how Jack and Amber wanted to get involved as well. While away, Jack met a videographer who revived his interest in filming. Music video it ain't – and he's not exactly behind the camera, yet – but it's a good experience for him to be involved as an assistant.

And Amber has taken a liking to Randy's work and feels she has lots to contribute, convinced that during her little brush with a certain special costume designer, a lot of great ideas rubbed off on her. All she's gotta learn now is, Randy *always* needs to feel in charge, or it will make for a rough working relationship for the two of them. Then again, it's her lesson to learn and I just have to trust her to do it for herself. Doesn't matter if she can't get it right the first time.

After completing the minute-by-minute, segment-by-segment layout, we're now looking through video clips of women who want our help. We have a wide range from desperate to comical, clueless to know-it-all. The first rough cut – no know-it-alls allowed in round two.

From there, Lynda tells us that in as much as we want to help out the desperate ones, it's still entertainment, so we must limit ourselves to only a couple of "train wrecks", while giving a strong preference to the dramatic ones.

With that in mind, we pop in another video. This one's a mid-thirties, slightly overweight woman, being taken to court for not giving hubby his "conjugals". She says that if we help her reconstruct her face and body, she'll have no problem. *Sorry Hun, wrong show!* Due to his weight, hubby insists that she be on top – a position she's not willing to take, insisting that the person on top always looks funny, thanks to gravity pulling on everything in unflattering ways.

I grab my compact mirror and look down into it. "Ohmigosh, it does look really funny." Next thing you know, everyone's grabbing the mirror from me, to have a look for themselves. Amber starts, but then pulls away – doesn't want to give Mom the wrong impression, I'm sure.

Cyn laughs, "Funny or not, I'd still be more worried about looking down at *him*." Needless to say, the video doesn't make the cut.

Watching us go all goofy, Jack and Amber take off, just as Lynda gets up. "I think I'll let you guys take it from here. Let's touch base tomorrow."

The next one we look at is a woman who desperately wants to get out of an abusive marriage but can't, due to financial reasons. Hearing a story that many women could identify with, Alison says, "Now *there's* someone I could work with."

"Are you planning on donating money from your not-so-little cache?" I ask.

"Nope – I'd like to help her build her own."

Cynical Cyn asks, "How? By hiring her for your soon-to-be-mine lucrative business?"

"Nope again – by getting her placed in a facility which pays you while you train. Hubby won't be expecting her to bring in any dough through that period, so she can easily stash it away until she has enough to plan her exit."

"And how is she supposed to do that – hide it under her mattress? What about the paper trail?" I inquire.

"All she needs to do is, get a post-office box for her bank statements. I know it sounds sneaky, but it's not like she's stealing anything from him."

We're all really impressed. Like Melanie Griffith in *Working Girl*, Alison's got a mind made for business and a bod made for sinning – now if we could only get Clive to do something about it, soon. At the outside, she'll get some by the end of the summer, on their honeymoon. When Clive told her that he didn't believe in pre-marital sex, she got all sassy, and said, "Pre-marital only applies if you plan on getting married." Next thing you know, she's got a rock on her finger.

Speaking of smart and sassy, Darla looks like her mind is still working overtime, even as I wander off into my own little world – some habits die hard. She suggests, "I can certainly take care of any legalities for the poor soul ... and advise her on *her* rights and *his* responsibilities."

Cyn's also looking really serious – dare I say even contemplative. "If I only knew back then what I know now." We're all looking at her in puzzlement. She elaborates, "When I was married to Justin, I became so dependent upon his cash that I couldn't see a way out, even though I knew he was fooling around. Then one day he hit me ... and I *had* to end it – one strike and you're out in my books. The irony: I came out on top, with the divorce settlement. See, being on top isn't always a bad thing," she chuckles. "Just hope that one day Jonathan and Michael will stop giving me a hard time over dismissing their dad's requests for a second chance – if they *only* knew. They've tried everything to get us back together – even went as far as trying to set up Rajiv, hoping to break us up. Didn't work, even though Jonathan's gal pal did her best to pull a Lolita on him."

I give Cyn a big hug. "I never knew that he had a violent streak in him."

"Neither did I, until that day. But the rest was kinda my own fault. I knew going in that his dick had a serious allergy to monogamy – almost like a shellfish deal, where you can't breathe – but I married him anyway. I think I was more attached to his money and lifestyle than him."

Alison interrupts, "That's why I believe in women making their *own* money – thank you very much!"

Cyn snaps, "Point taken. Now are you gonna sell me your business or what?"

"Actually, I've decided to keep it. If Clive has a problem with it, we'll deal with it then. I'm not *totally* inflexible, you know."

I laugh, "Well it's been a while since *I've* felt terribly flexible. The way my back has been acting up, I think I'll have to give up any hope of ever becoming a gymnast."

Darla says, "You and me both. Think I had my first hot flash last night. It was the strangest feeling, the way it rose into my head and left my back soaking wet – could've sworn I was having a panic attack."

Cyn shares, "You're way too young for that. It's more than likely just peri-menopause. ... You wanna know something funny? When I first overheard my mom tell my dad about having a hot flash, I imagined something r-e-e-e-ally dirty, possibly involving a raincoat." We all break into hysterics.

Alison teases Darla, "If you were to ask my mom about it, I'm sure she'll tell you that it's the fires of hell descending upon you, admonishing you to mend your ways. She's the only woman I know of who failed to tell her daughter about periods, and actually managed to turn them into a punishment for becoming a woman."

Darla chuckles, "Honey, I'm too bent to mend anything. My parents tried already and failed miserably."

I ask her, "So what's up with you anyway?"

"Rita's coming over for an extended vacation, so we can take a go at it ... and the 'rents are willing to acknowledge my existence, provided we *never* talk about my 'problem'."

"You think you can pick up right where you left off?"

"With the 'rents, doubt it! With Rita, don't know – but at least the sex promises to be sensational."

My mind wanders off to thinking how lovely it would be to nail a bed tremor or two myself. I may not be ready to expose my scars just yet, but at least I'm *thinking* about giving it a shot. Now that the chemo is over, Jeremy's suggesting that we drop everything and go to the Big Apple for our long-overdue sexcapade weekend. The old me would have nipped it in the bud – too much to do, plus not making it *that* easy for him. The new me is seriously considering it – what do I have to lose?

My revere is interrupted by Randy walking into the kitchen and handing me a garment bag. "Where the hell have you been?" I ask, wondering what's in the bag.

"Just open the damn bag, will you?" he says, laying it across my lap.

It's loaded with prototypes for his latest line, *Jillian*. One by one I pull out lingerie items designed to make me look lovely. My favorite is a baby doll with built-in pockets for falsies.

Watch out Jeremy, the trip is definitely on! Though knowing him, the lingerie will last on my bod for all of two seconds – not bad, considering he may not last much longer himself, after all this time.

I'm grinning from ear to ear, imagining Jeremy's hands touching my body – no music, no distracting dialogue, no one else ... just the two of us. And just when I think it can't get any better, Randy whips out the prints from my boudoir photography session – I'd forgotten all about them. "Which one can I use for my poster?" he asks.

I pick the subtlest one. "Launching a new line is expensive. Who's footing the bill for this one?"

"Believe it or not, Steven – he *did* promise me once."

"Steven?" we all say, practically in unison.

"Yup, Steven. And his two partners. ... He's shacked up with them somewhere in California."

"Let me get this straight – Steven is living with two guys and they're all supporting you?" I ask in disbelief.

"Relax, he's living with two lesbians, and *they're* supporting my *venture* ... along with him of course."

"Oh that makes so much more sense ... not! So exactly *why* is he living with two lesbians?"

"Duh! To be close to his baby – he's the one who donated his swimmers."

"How do you feel about that?" I ask.

"Pretty ironic, ain't it? But it's not like Randy has any time for that," he says, "Now that Randy is doing what he was always meant to do." Talking about himself in third person is a good sign – only happens the odd time when he sees himself not as a person, more like an uber-talented entity.

Darla asks, "The lesbians – are they cute?"

"Gawd, Darla, you're such a man!"

I'd been saving a bottle of Dom to celebrate the day when I accept my wounds. With all that's been happening around me, I guess this is as good a time as any to put the past where it belongs and move forward. I go to the refrigerator and bring out the champagne.

As I begin to pour, Cyn reaches into her bag and plops a completed manuscript on my kitchen table, titled, "Embracing Our Bodies – A Seasoned Woman's Guide to Sensuality," by Cynthia Kennedy.

I realize that I'm truly ready to embrace my *own* body, even though all the scars haven't healed up just yet. I raise my glass to her with the most heartfelt sincerity, since I've experienced what's in her book firsthand, as she stood by me. "You did it, Honey!" I say, with the same emotion that's felt by someone who's just witnessed childbirth.

Randy joins in, "Here, here! Hope there's lots of instruction on pleasuring your man."

Darla chimes in, "And a section on girly love."

Alison smiles, "May I have the first copy please, since I'm going to have to upgrade my old certification?"

Cyn clinks her glass with Alison's and says, "You

got it Honey! And if either you or Clive need any coaching, it's on the house."

I say, "This calls for a celebration. How about we meet back here in a few of hours?"

"Thanks, but I already have a date tonight."

"Anyone I know?" I ask.

She whispers into my ear, "Do you ever ... he gets around – are you okay with that?"

"Who could resist dark chocolate?" is all I say before she winks and takes off.

It is said that we all enter and leave the world in the exact same way – hence, it's all about the journey. Some see detours, others roadblocks, still others don't see at all. Like me, they fail to realize that life is what we make it ... even when it throws us a curve-ball and changes us forever – hopefully for the better, like it did me.

I've learned that life is so much better when you: appreciate what you have instead of complaining about what you don't, make an active decision to be happy instead of right, and then give it your best shot and let the chips fall where they may.

You'll be amazed at where life will take you, when you're not trying to coerce it to fit your agendas!

"The past is history, the future a mystery, today is the present." – Unknown

About the Author

Rebecca Rosenblat is a Registered Psychotherapist, Certified Sex Addiction Therapist, and Couple's Counselor, who's specialized in trauma and betrayal work. She's hosted various TV and Radio shows, where she's given over a thousand hours of guidance to millions of people worldwide.

Beyond all this, Rebecca is the author of eight books – *An Eastern Seduction; Smooth as Silk; Broken Promises; How to Drive Your Lover Wild with Pleasure; Seducing your Man – the honeymoon was just the beginning; Sexual Power, Overcoming betrayal;* and now, *Mid Rift.* Rebecca lives in Toronto with her family, where she runs her private practice, is an associate at a clinic, and does various forms of teaching, transforming thousands of lives. Her passion is to help people become the best they can be; and have the best relationships possible!

"It's your life; make it exceptional!" ~ Rebecca

To reach Rebecca, book an appointment, register for an intensive, or access free articles, video clips, and my social media posts, please visit: www.RelationshipAndSexuality.com.

Manor House / 905-648-4797

www.manor-house-publishing.com